THE WITCH and JET SPLINTERS

PART 1

"A Bustle In The Hedgerow"

ELIJAH BARNS

ISBN: 978-1-9998765-0-0

DEDICATION

Dedicated to the beloved memory of Louise 'Daemonia' Ridley

THE WITCH AND JET SPLINTERS

Part 1: A Bustle In The Hedgerow

SECOND EDITION

All characters and events in this publication, other than those clearly in the public domain, are fictitious and any resemblance to real persons, living or dead, is purely coincidental.

GREEN CAT BOOKS

www.green-cat.co/books

ELIJAH BARNS

CONTENTS

ACKNOWLEDGMENTS

Thank you to Hilary, mother Anita, Margaret, Vinnie & my sons Richard, Jozef & Sebastian.

To Bernie Torme, Dan Reed, Ricky Warwick, Mike Tramp, Cherie Currie, Lemmy, Skinny Molly, Space Elevator, Danny Peyronel, Risa Hall, Rosie Greenwood, Sam Robinson & Steve Haworth.

The area of Pendle, Lancs & the majesty of Scotland, still & forever casting a fascinating spell over me.
To for the modelling and music: Rosalie Cunningham

Oh & Jet, Spike, Monty & Stripes - pets extraordinaire.
And everyone I ever loved.

PARCHMENT 1

Down To The Crossroads

If a beautiful, black cat wandered into your house one day, would you feed it bat kidneys, boot it out or put an ad in the local newsagent's window? Or none of those?

Or if two Witches turned up and said they were staying for the week would you welcome them with open arms, make a brew and get the ciggies out or shoo them away with a shout of "On yer broomsticks!"? What if a Faerie dropped through your letterbox for a chat? Would you give it a glass of blackcurrant cordial or book an appointment with a psychiatrist?

And if someone could prove to you that Santa Claus really existed would you feel less cheated at Christmas?

Don't ask me, not yet anyway, I've simply been asked to pass this tale on ... a tale of such jiggery pokery as to make your ears curl.

Now bear with me because it's going to take a while.

What happened, if you can suspend your disbelief, was something like this...

'Twas a cold, sleety winter's night up in the hills of a small, northern English village known as Windlestraws.

Yes, you would be correct in thinking it was the same area from whence the infamous Pendle Witches hailed from, way back in the seventeenth century.

But the names have been changed to protect the innocent, of which there weren't many!

Anyway, bang in the middle of the crossroads sat a very splendid black cat weighing in at just over twelve months old and known, to those that knew him, by the name of Jet Jupiter Splinters.

THE WITCH AND JET SPLINTERS

Part 1: A Bustle In The Hedgerow

He was early and had been sitting in this strange location for over half an hour.
He wasn't keen on the cold but he persevered. Cats are like that when they're on a mission.
Luckily for him there wasn't any traffic about because he wasn't for moving. Not yet.
He had coddiwompled (Look it up in a medieval dictionary) about nine miles on this most inclement evening, all the way from the urban sprawl of a town named Barnley and his journey had given him plenty of time to think. Think about what? I hear you say … well that would be telling and it *will* be told.

Had he waited but another five minutes the whole course of this yarn would be completely altered and it would, therefore, not be the same tale to tell.
But Jet Splinters had made his mind up and was going to wait not a minute longer.
Instead, he wandered blithely into the inviting glow of the living room of a cosy, low beamed, open fired cottage.
The door was ajar as the owner, local Witch Jinny Lane, had nipped outside for logs to revive her dying fire.
Jet was an opportunist, make no mistake, but who would mind him being there? Really. He was the most regal, handsome, shiny cat you ever laid eyes on and he knew it.
Don't ask how he knew because cats aren't known for preening themselves in front of mirrors, but take it from me, he did.
Jet wasn't some kind of snoot, by the way. He was quite bohemian and for all his shininess he was a tad dishevelled.
But he looked 'good'. The way Keith Richards once looked 'good'.

"BOO!" shouted Jinny from the doorway.
Jet was spaced out in front of the fading embers of the cosy fireplace and didn't flinch.
"Oi! I said … BOO!"
No reaction. Just a slow motion blink of the eyes.
"You're a cheeky little sod and no mistake," she said. "You do know I could turn you into a grotty, black lump of coal and throw you on to the fire, if I so wished?"
Jet turned his head around nonchalantly and with his big, green eyes darted her a look that could only be described as casual. Then he yawned.
"My stars! In all my years (which weren't many - Jinny was only about thirty-five years old) I don't think I've ever come across such abject flippancy from a young animal. You do know I'm a Witch? Do you? You do know what a Witch is? Hellooo!"
"Hellooo!" Jet deigned to reply. "Yes, I know what you are because I can only speak to Witches. Well, Witches and other cats. Oh, and faerie folk and most animals of course. You're not a faerie or a cat, so…."
"And you're not even the slightest bit daunted?" said Jinny, flusteredly dropping the armful of logs on to the hearth.
"No, not really. Well, I mean you're very pretty, aren't you? Too pretty for a Witch. You have lovely sparkling eyes and your indigo hair is quite something to behold. Why would I be daunted by one so beautiful?" whispered Jet.
Jinny was indeed a darkly attractive Witch. Slim, tall, well dressed, in a Gothy way, you could easily find yourself bewitched by her.
"A Charmer to boot!" half smiled Jinny, lighting a cigarette "So what brings you to my house, of all places in this blessed land? And how does a young cat come to know what indigo is?"

THE WITCH AND JET SPLINTERS

Part 1: A Bustle In The Hedgerow

"I imagine you've never experienced life in an urban back street? Old, smelly mattresses, broken bottles, discarded tins, factory fumes, overflowing dustbins and violent Tomcats.

Add to that an 'orrible master and you can see why I'm not in a rush to return.

I haven't much idea where I am and not a clue how to get back, but wherever I am it's a step up from where I came from.

As for how I ended up here … it's something I'd rather not talk about just yet but I promise I will tell you, one day, when the time is right. Hey! Perhaps you brought me here with one of your spells?" teased Jet.

"I most certainly did not, you little swit!" Jinny then paused in afterthought, flicking her cigarette ash into the hearth. "Or did I? Only yesterday I had the fleeting notion that a feline companion might be in order. I mean, a Witch without a cat is a rather rubbish Witch, wouldn't you say?"

"A Witch without a cat is positively tragic and not very magic." Jet daftly replied.

"Amateur poet too eh? You're a proper little one-off aren't you? Anyway, if you're so bright, why were you sat in the middle of the road, on such a vile night, for over half an hour? I'm quite observant, you know?"

"I had a reason … but as I said, that'll keep. The weather doesn't bother me that much, I'm a cat. What's your name anyway?"

"Jinny, Jinny Lane. You can call me 'Your Wonderfulness'."

"Can I? Thank you very much. I'm Jet Splinters. The few friends I had called me Jetty."

"I'll call you Switty Scrub then," laughed Jinny. "That's if you mean to stay. Is that your intention?"

Jet let out another yawn and said, "If you let me play outside when I want to play outside and feed me and let me lie by the fire, I can't see why not."
"Don't want much, do you? How about adventures? Are you up for a few shenanigans? I need an ally, a familiar. Know what one of those is, do you?"
"Could you please ask me tomorrow Your Wonderfulness? I've had a very long walk and I feel a snooze coming on." And with that, Jet stretched that long stretch that cats do and fell asleep, almost immediately. With one eye slightly open.
'Ha Ha. What a fabulous feline,' thought Jinny as she settled down to watch an old episode of Bewitched on the unimposing TV over in the corner, nodding off herself within seconds.

"Your wonderfulness … I'm cold." purred Jet as he nuzzled his head into the back of Jinny's dark hair.
Jinny awoke abruptly. She didn't like to be roused, rudely or otherwise. She then realised that she had fallen asleep in the chair without putting the logs on the fire and the room was indeed, well, freezing.
"I thought the elements didn't bother you Mr Splinters?" said Jinny in a groggy, shivery way.
"That's when I'm outside. Outside I'm fine. Indoors, it's pathetic, I know, but I'm a bit of a pussycat."
"Oh, well, nice to have the choice. I really should get to bed now, I've got a day and a half on tomorrow," said Jinny "You can sleep on my feet if you like?"
"Are they clean?" Jet impudently asked.
"They're cold is what they are and your task tonight is to warm them!" said Jinny in a mock annoyed manner. "Or you can sod off back to where you came from!"

Part 1: A Bustle In The Hedgerow

"I would have thought you would have some kind of spell to ward off the cold or at least some thick socks." Jet thought out loud.

"What do you know of spells young scrub? Tonight, you keep my feet warm, tomorrow I'll have a bash at trying to teach you a thing or two, if you can keep both eyes and ears open! Now, quick sticks and up the jolly dancers to bed!"

Jet tutted a very small tut and followed Jinny up the spiral staircase to the land of what elderly folk used to call 'Nod'.

PARCHMENT 2

Born To Be Mild

Jinny had set her alarm for the usual 6.30am but ignored it, due to extreme snugness, and eventually arose at 9.43am-ish.

At this point it would be delightful to report that Jet had risen when the alarm went off, gone downstairs and made Jinny a huge cup of tea in her favourite Pentagram cup, cooked her a lovely sausage and egg breakfast and delivered the whole lot, along with her favourite menthol ciggies, to her bedside.

Unfortunately, he was still fast asleep on Jinny's feet because, when all is said and done, he's a cat and cats can't even make their own breakfast. But they do prefer a nice, cosy kip.

"My stars! What time is it?" shouted Jinny.

"I don't know much about time, or astronomy. I'm a cat."

"You are possibly the most impudent creature I've ever come across … can you cook?" groaned Jinny stupidly, still half asleep and very dozy.

Jet shrugged and begrudgingly sauntered over to the window sill.

"It's been snowing, otherwise I could have caught you a nice vole. Yum!

But cooking? No, I'm not really designed for it"

"Up! Up! Up!" screamed Jinny abruptly. "There's a lot to do today and I have the added burden of having to teach you a thing or two, good
manners being one of them. What are you
doing now?!"

"I'm spraying. Marking my territory" said Jet indignantly.
"Who said it was your territory to mark? That stinks! And they're my best boots! Impetuous, that's what you are! I've a good mind to feed you to the Hobgoblins, matey!" said Jinny, only a bit seriously.
"They'd have to catch me first." said Jet.
"I'll serve you to them personally, in a stew, ya little divil!" Jinny scolded.

And so the light hearted bickering continued until Jinny jumped up, donned her favourite Star Wars Chewbacca dressing gown and her zebra skin slippers and scurried downstairs.
"Double bloody double, toil and trouble," she mumbled. "Where's the kettle disappeared to?"
Jet was feeling marginally acerbic. "Is that it, over the fire, with all the steam coming out of it?"
"Awww, bless, the faeries must have known I'd overslept and they've come and lit me a fire and put a brew on. They're lovely things, you know? I don't know where I'd be without them half the time, really I don't." Jinny said with a warm smile.
"Very thoughtful of them, I'm sure, but I've been here for nearly a whole day now and I haven't seen you do one bit of magic. Are you positive you're a Witch?"
"You know full well I am or you wouldn't be speaking to me and I'm not very even-tempered when I've just woken up. Does it show?" she growled. "Not many cats would get away with your cheek, let me tell you that for nowt. Some have been walled up for less! Do you know, they found a cat skeleton over by Lower Black Moss, in the wall of an unearthed seventeenth century Witch's cottage it was. It was in the newspaper. Not the cat - the story. Anyhow, don't provoke me because it's all very

doable, cat walling, trust me." Then she let out a loud laugh, jollier than the usual laughs you hear from Witches and suchlike in films.
Jinny beckoned Jet over to the fire hearth.
"Come on you little rascal," she said. "Get warm and I'll see what I've got in the cupboard to feed you with. Are you partial to bat kidneys?" And with another laugh she shuffled off into the kitchen, as that's what zebra skin slippers make you do. Shuffle.

Jinny found an old tin of sardines in the pantry (there's always an old tin of sardines in the food cupboard. Go and look!). Luckily, they were in sunflower oil, because cats aren't usually keen on the ones done in tomato sauce, so Jet feasted on them heartily.
He was also served a fresh saucer of water, drawn from the nearby wellspring which hadn't, miraculously, frozen over.
Anyway, even if it had frozen over Jinny could have worked a spell to thaw it, couldn't she?

Jet looked contentedly around the cottage living room. This was a beautiful place to live.
It wasn't too big, very cosy. Old oak beams on the ceiling and on the walls, an old weathered ox blood Chesterfield couch and armchair to match, a deep red Indian rug and red tartan curtains.
An ornate old broomstick nestled to the left of the fireplace, a fireplace that was made from local stone and was probably about two hundred years old, as was the house itself, naturally.
A wooden 'chandelier', for want of a better word, held four candle bulbs and sported a rare, stuffed black eagle perched in the middle. What an odd ornament, he thought.

Part 1: A Bustle In The Hedgerow

There were three witch dolls on broomsticks hanging from all but one corner of the ceiling (you know you can only have three to a room, don't you?).
These, it turns out, were bought from the quaint little gift shop in the nearby village, probably the only place around to acknowledge the area's long history of witchcraft.
But that eagle … Jet stared up at the ceiling again. There was something about it …

"Are you alright there Switty, sorry, Jetty?" asked Jinny. "You look like you've gone into one of your trances again."
"I was just thinking what a lovely house you have."
It was indeed a far cry from the dank, wet, miserable back streets he had come from.
"It's not what you'd expect from a witch. I would have imagined a smelly, run down, wooden hut with cobwebs and rats everywhere. And little children hanging over the fire. Ha Ha."
"Oh, there's plenty of cobwebs, trust me, but I'm not the kind of witch that would harm anyone, not unless they thoroughly deserved it. The sad thing is, people 'round here have the idea that that's what I'm all about - rats and eating children. And poisoning princesses with apples and suchlike. But tish tosh, what do I care? I am what I am and I don't give an owl's hoot what they think. Though it would be nice if someone, anyone, said 'good morning' to me once in a while." said Jinny with a tinge of sadness.
"It's their loss Your Wondrousness."
"Aye. And that's 'Wonderfulness' actually mister!"

The snow started to fall again and Jinny realised that what she had planned for today wasn't going to happen.

It was intended to involve a trip to visit the faeries but they would be holed up underground now. They aren't keen on snow, or rain for that matter, and four inches of snow is very deep to a faerie, so, safer to stay indoors.
Anyway, sometimes the snow is best viewed through the window of a cosy, warm room with a glass of mulled wine and some hot cheese on toast. With a good friend.
And Jetty Splinters was turning out to be very good company for one so young, thought Jinny.
On the one hand, he was quite erudite, on the other he could be infuriatingly inane, but then that could describe most creatures of his age. Nevertheless, the pair had spent several hours by the fireside and it had passed, like, fifteen minutes.
Jinny was doing her best to patiently explain what the world of a witch involved and Jet listened intently to her every word, despite the fact that, unbeknownst to her, he had previous experience of such things. Any way round, he was under her spell ... and she hadn't even cast one!

It had gone quite dark for 4.00pm. Jinny suddenly jumped up and remembered that Jet hadn't been allowed out today.
"Blimey," she said. "I suppose you'll be wanting to get outdoors and do a bit of carousing won't you?"
"Not in this weather, thank you your magnificence." said Jet.
"Wonderfulness," corrected Jinny, "And what happened to the wild, invincible cat that has no fear of the elements?"
"I never said I was invincible! Anyway, this cat doesn't feel the need to stray today, or any other day, methinks."
Jinny smiled at him lovingly and Jet jumped into her arms, nuzzling and snuggling up to the one person who

right now, for no explicable reason, seemed to mean the whole world to him.

But he wasn't going to let her know that. Not in words. He's a cat, and cats revel in unpredictability.

PARCHMENT 3

Don't Eat the Yellow Snow

Early next morning, just as the sun was yawning, after what had been a wasted day with regards to achieving anything, Jinny and Jet woke up, still by the fireside, Jet still in Jinny's arms.

It was a glorious day, though the snow still lay fairly thick on the ground. Jinny had an appointment with the faeries which should have been kept yesterday but for obvious reasons it wasn't.

Jet wasn't entirely sure that he was any the wiser when it came to Jinny's interpretations of witchcraft but what the heck, there was plenty of time for all that stuff and at this point in time his main concern was snugglement.

It was still early, so time was in abundance.

A quick brekkie of cheesy poached eggs for them both and they were ready for the off.

"Now then young Splinters, we're going to have to do a bit of snow shifting if we're to get any faeries to bite today, are your little paws up to it?"

"Oh no! They don't bite, do they? I'm not keen on being bitten. I dig best when I've had a poo by the way." Jet added, after a short pause.

"How quaint! We'd better make haste then … potty mouth." sighed Jinny, semi exasperatedly.

And off they trundled. Jinny wrapped herself up in her best Queen of Narnia style furs, with curly toed wellies and the obligatory pointed hat, with a bend in it, her trusty besom, Batilda, in her hand. Jet was, of course, in his very best (and only) black fur coat.

Part 1: A Bustle In The Hedgerow

Up the hillock, down the dale and onward through the dark forest, whose spooky trees still stood strong from medieval times.

The pair eventually came upon a very small clearing, next to a hedgerow, although everything had blended into one with the snow.

"I think this is it," called Jinny. "It's a bit tricky to tell. Tell you what, let's start scraping away near that hole in the hedge and hope for the best."

"Or you could just magic it away and save us both a job." said Jet, glibly. "You are showing yourself to be a right little lazy beggar, mister! A slothful creature!" shouted Jinny. "Get them paws out and get scraping!"

"I'll just nip over there for a minute first." Jet blushed, as much as a cat can blush.

Jinny's black eyebrows raised up to beneath her hat as she muttered something about 'not another one', something about lavatories and something about someone called La Croix.

Jinny had done a good two minute's worth of clearing the snow away from what, she presumed, was the faerie hole when Jet reappeared from behind a small drift where he had done the necessary 'number twos'.

"Right, watch this." said he, as he dived head first into four inches of snow and proceeded to shift mountains of the stuff in seconds.

The full extent of the faerie hole was now revealed and with it a pathway, exposing an area of short, damp grass, where the remnants of some kind of circle lay.

"Thank you and blessed be," The words came steamily from Jinny's mouth.

"Now, let's see if we can stir the little creatures."

She closed her eyes, outstretched her arms and imagined an intense green glow.

She appeared to be meditating. Jet kept very quiet and still. He could speak to faeries (cats just instinctively know) but he'd never actually met one to speak to.

In a hushed voice Jinny spacily chanted, "Slinky, Slinky, come to my side.

'tis Jinny Lane, friend of thine."

Jet shook his head. "You've just made that up on the spot!"

Yet, in a thousandth of a trice, a figure of about five inches in height, shimmering with a yellow aura, fabulous pointy ears and the finest translucent wings, suddenly made herself visible to Jet and Jinny. Oh, and that little Robin which was perched on the hedge.

"Greetings fair Jinny," spoke the faerie, without actually speaking. "What news have you? Good or not very good at all?"

"Merry meet to you Slinky. The not very good news is that that scoundrel

Crook, and never a human so rightly named, has indeed applied to the Council for planning permission. The good news is … we're going to ruin his plans. Oh yes!"

"Is this young creature your new familiar then?" Slinky somewhat telepathically said. "Will he be assisting you in your quest?"

"Aye, this is Jetty Splinters. Say 'Hello' Jet and mind your manners, for Herne's sake." Jinny whispered.

"Salutations Miss Slinky. A pleasure to make your acquaintance," bowed Jet. "I am unsure of what the quest is as yet but I'll do all in my paws to assist."

"Alright, alright, don't overdo it yer little switgobbler, there's such a thing as over polite y'know?" Jinny grimaced.

"Gracious, what a charming feline," chirped Slinky. "Is he, is he … fully initiated then?"

"Good grief no! Not yet. He's got a lot to learn and a short time to learn it in but hey ho! Now then, let's not forget we have Raphael on our side. Never underestimate the power of Raph. Hopefully your little lot will be lending a helping hand too?"

"Who's this Raphael then?" Jet bluntly piped up, seeming almost agitated. "You've seen him, he's perched on my chandelier."

"What? The stuffed eagle? How, in the name of Simon's Cat, is he going to help?"

"Well, you've got an abundance of surprises to come Jet Splinters, and Raph is one of them." Jinny winked.

"It is very cold. Jack Frost has been a busy bee, has he not? I wish I had my woolie with me," shivered Slinky, poshly. "I must be getting back inside now but please remember, we only have until the end of April to achieve this task, or not. We will come over and visit you when the snow clears. In the meantime, I will leave it to you to make the necessary preparations.

Good luck to you Mr Splinters and lovely to meet you!"

"Lovely to mee… oh."

And with that, Slinky vanished through the hole in the hedge and down into the realm of the faeries.

"Well, she was very pleasant, wasn't she?" said Jet.

"Not when she's riled she isn't." Jinny said under her steamy breath. "You wouldn't want to be riling a faerie, trust me."

"I wasn't thinking of doing …"

They coddiwompled off back through the clearing and on into the spooky wood. It felt a tad warmer now and it looked as if the snow was thawing slightly.

Jinny swished a kind of makeshift path in front of her with her broom, which helped Jet enormously as he was struggling a wee bit.
"You coping down there Jet?"
"Aye, just about, Your Wonderfulness." he replied. "Did you notice we're being followed by a robin?"
"Ooh yes," said Jinny. "That's a sign of good luck you know."
"Is it? Well, I never knew that. I'm learning things all the time."
"Apparently it signifies stimulation of new growth and renewal, I read it on the internet."
"Then it must be true!" said Jet sarcastically.
"You're very cynical for one so young, are you not, little dark one? We'll soon have you learning new ways of thinking … and acting. Now quick sticks and onwards - I'm starving!" Jinny starvingly announced.
"I was just thinking, why don't you use your broom to fly us home and save us a lot of bother?"
"I am NOT flying through the air in broad daylight. The locals already have a grim view of me and I don't want to foster their warped ideas more than is necessary. Broom flights are for emergencies only."

As it turned out, it didn't take too long to reach the homely cottage. Jinny swiped her hand through the air and the old front door creaked open.
"Better than a key, eh?" she laughed.
"Brilliant." smiled Jet. "Maybe you should install a cat flap for me. I can't do stuff like that."
"You won't need a cat flap mister. We'll have you magically in and out of that door before you know it."
Jet didn't reply as he had slipped off the icy window sill and landed in a small conifer. He looked like a cat that attacks the Christmas tree (you know the sort) and

peered through the branches with snow covering his ears, nose and whiskers, letting out a tiny sneeze.

"Hobbledehoy! That's what you are!" Jinny giggled and scooped him up in her arms. "But I love you … I think."

PARCHMENT 4

Can You Do the Fandango?

The robin had gone unnoticed since they had first set off but now here he was, perched on the same slippy window sill. Shivering.

Inside, Jinny had magicked up a roaring fire. It was, by now, late afternoon and outside the light was fading and the temperature dropping.

"Your Wonderfulness!" shouted Jet.

"Please, can we dispense with the sarcasm now and just call me by my name?" pleaded Jinny. "What's to do?"

"You told me to call you that!" Jet said defensively.

"I was being, erm, flippant." admitted Jinny.

"Oh. Right. Anyway, that robin is sat on the window sill and he looks perished. Can we let him in?" Jet said with a hint of concern.

"You don't want to eat him, do you?"

"Do I 'eckerslike! I'm worried about him." said Jet.

Jinny glided or perhaps glid over to the door in a way that Morticia from The Addams Family might and undid the thumb latch.

"Come in Mr Robin, you're going to catch your death out there." she said softly.

The robin flew on to Jinny's shoulder and she walked back into the warm, now candlelit room.

"I'll see if I've got any dried grubs in my potion jars. Have a perch by the fire." And with that Jinny went off into the kitchen in search of anything a bird might find palatable.

"So, what brings you here on such a nippy day?" asked Jet of the now thawing robin.

"I've got some information that might be of use to you," the bird proclaimed, "I overheard you talking to the faerie and couldn't help but hear the name 'Crook' mentioned. Now, if I'm correct, this would be the same Crook as lives not six minutes away from the faerie clearing. A cantankerous, horrid man he is. Do you know, he threw a stone at me?! Anyway, what I'm trying to say is, I know where he lives and I can show you the way. The rest is up to you lot."

Up until now, Jet had no idea what all the fuss with Mr Crook and the faeries was all about so he just mewed "interesting" and awaited the return of Jinny from the kitchen.

Jinny emerged with an armful of Avian delights

"I've found these mealworms Mr Robin. I was going to use them the next time I went fishing but I, well, I've mistimed it a bit. I mean who would go fishing in this weather? Ha Ha! Oh and there's an apple slice and some water to be going on with. Bon appetit!"

Jet looked up at her admiringly. He liked French words for some reason.

"Why thank you very much indeed. What a kind lady." chirped the robin. "I'm only kind to those that deserve it and that's usually anyone that isn't human ... and wasps."

"Very much appreciated, I'm sure." said the Robin as he gulped down the splendid feast.

"So … what brings you to my humble abode on such a nippy day Mr

Robin?" said Jinny.

"I just asked that." said Jet.

"Well I'm asking it now." corrected Jinny.

"I was just telling the cat here about Mr Crook and that I overheard you talking to the faerie and I know where he lives, Mr Crook that is, and I can show you where it is, if it helps you at all?"

"That would be very helpful indeed," said Jinny. "Can you get back here when the snow has cleared? I would think in about two day's time. You live near the faeries, don't you? When you see them making their way towards the woods would you be good enough to follow them back here please?"
"It would be my pleasure." the Robin replied.
"Top notch! In the meantime, do you want to stay here until morning? We can't be sending you out in this cold."
"You're very kind, I would love to, thank you very much."
"I'll make you a little bird house if you like, for future use. Stuff it with straw and things. Then you can come over whenever you like."
"How very thoughtful you are. As long as it's not a problem. Thank you again." said the robin with a watery eye. "Do you know, I don't even know your names …"
"I'm Jinny Lane and this little Scaramouche is Jet Splinters. Oh, and there's Raphael up there on the chandelier."
"Aareeeaaah!" screamed Raph.
"Blimey! It lives!" exclaimed Jet.
"Don't be lippy Jet," said Jinny, as she flicked the TV on with the remote.
"He moves, talks and eats when it suits him, that's his way. Anyone for an episode of Bewitched?"
"Der der - der der - der der der der der – der." sang Jinny as the programme started.
The creatures looked at her as if she was quite insane, shrugged and settled down in front of the fire for a long, lazy evening.

Part 1: A Bustle In The Hedgerow

Two days had passed, and in that time Jinny had done two days of tutoring with the little black cat affectionately known as Jetty.

She had taught him how to walk through a solid door (without opening it, obviously), and how to tune his ears in to distant sounds. Only a couple of things but not bad for two days work.

The latest game was for Jinny to go upstairs to the bedroom and whisper something under the duvet cover, then run back down and test Jet on what he had heard.

Eighty per cent success! What a clever chap he was.

The snow was clearing - not much on the hills but it was clear enough, thought Jinny, for the faeries to make an appearance, which they did, within the hour.

Suddenly the letterbox flapped open and there stood Slinky and her chaperone, a young, male pixie by the name of Spudsley Sparrowhawk.

“Greetings!” announced Slinky.

“Merry meet.” Jinny replied.

“Helloooo!” sang Jet.

Spudsley just nodded as he was feeling a bit awkward, what with not knowing any of them. You know what youngsters are like. Oh, and his hearing wasn’t very good.

“Have there been any developments?” asked Slinky.

“Well, we had a robin red breast ‘round the other night, where *is* he by the way? And he reckons he can show us where Mr Crook’s house is. Apparently it’s not too far from where you live. If we can get in there we can cause some serious mischief and no mistake. If it were down to me I’d scare him so much he’d move to another county.” Jinny said in a wicked witchy kind of way.

“I understand you feeling that way but we have to be fairly subtle with this Jinny, we do not want anything that might arouse suspicion, or even superstition, do we?"

"I can't say I'm fussed personally," said Jinny blankly, "but I understand that it's your home, and has been for many a year, so we'll try to be as inconspicuous as possible. Within reason anyway…"

"Can you even imagine it though? A golf course on our hallowed ground? Can you? … Jinny … what *is* a golf course?" Slinky innocently asked.

"Stars above Slinky, well, according to the eminent author Mark Twain, the game of golf is, I quote, 'a good walk spoiled'. Lots of silly human beings, ambling around a large field with a bag full of iron sticks, which they use to hit little balls into little holes, over and over again! Then there's the 'club' part of it where they all meet up for drinkie poos after pointlessly tiring themselves out all day. And the balls are really hard. You wouldn't want to be hit by one while you're having one of your faerie circle dances."

"Oh dear, no. That sounds positively frightful." cried Slinky "I had not realised the full horrific implications of it all."

"Alice Cooper plays golf you know? You'd think that'd be one person who would know better," said Jinny, haughtily. "Who is Alice Cooper, Jinny? Is she a local witch?"

"No, he's … oh, never mind about all that Slinky, I'll explain another time. Look, I'm expecting a visit from my two partners in devilry tomorrow: Miss Riz and Miss Lou. What a delightful coven we make!

We'll hatch a plot and let you know our intentions. You don't have to do a thing Slinky, leave it all to us."

"And me!" piped up Jet, who had been listening attentively.

"Of course, and you, my little Chat Noir." purred Jinny.

“Is that French? I like it when you speak French.” said Jet.

“Gomez!” laughed Jinny.

And with a “Merry meet, merry part and merry meet again” from Jinny and a “Toodlepip” from Slinky the company parted and still not a word from Mr Sparrowhawk, Slink’s ‘minder’, for want of a better title. But … where *was* that robin?

PARCHMENT 5

Silly Sisters

The next day brought some fine drizzle, you know, the kind that drenches you without you noticing and makes your hair shrink and go frizzy? Not that that has any bearing on anything, just that the weather was a trifle grim.

It's days like this when you really can't be bothered to leave the house, or even a faerie realm for that matter.

But Jinny had agreed to go into the village to meet up with Misses Riz and Lou, who were due to arrive within the next couple of hours, around 11.00am, supposedly.

"Bugger. I hope it clears up in a bit," moaned Jinny, "I hate being damp."

"Hey! Your Wonderf … Jinny! Watch this!" And with that, Jet pounced through the front door as if it wasn't there. Then back into the room again.

"Show off," snorted Jinny. "I couldn't do that at your age."

"I'm twelve and a half in human years you know." said Jet cheerily.

"So? I couldn't do it when I was twelve and a half either!"

"How old were you when you became a witch then?" Jet asked, nosily.

"I think I've always been a witch but it takes a while to realise what your capabilities are. Sometimes, when you're young, you don't quite know exactly what it is that's happening to you or how you should be controlling it. Then one day it all becomes kind of vividly clear to you, if you know what I mean, which you probably don't because you're a one-year old cat!"

"Do some magic. Wave your wand! Where is your wand? I've never seen it. Show me it!"

"Querulous Tom child!" she softly muttered, "I'll tell you where it is because one day you might have to get it for me. You'll be the only one who knows where it's kept so keep it hushed, eh? Follow me, quick sticks."

They trundled up to Jinny's bedroom where she got a stool from the corner and propped it next to her wardrobe.

On top of the wardrobe was a smaller version of the witch dolls she had downstairs, a toy lion and a roll of old posters tied up with string: Black Sabbath, The Beatles, Led Zeppelin, Purson and the like.

There, between the folds of Purson's 'The Circle and the Blue Door' album poster nestled her wand. The perfect place!

"Here we are then. This is Rosie. My treasured sprig. What would you like me to do with her?"

"Some magic please." purred Jet.

"Anything in particular or just any old stuff?"

"I don't mind, really. How about turning your bed into a Crocodile?" "Whaaat?! How dangerous is that?! How about if I turn it into, ermm, a giant sachet of cat food?"

"Boring!" scoffed Jet.

"Not if you were hungry it wouldn't be. Alright, how about … a huge, Siberian tiger, only for a few seconds, mind you."

"Hmmm, I've heard they can be quite dangerous too … let's have … I know! It's a bit of a cliché but … a unicorn!"

“Done, done and thrice done.” and she twirled her wand like a gunslinger and
Ker-ting!
A beautiful, white unicorn stood mesmerised in the bedroom.
“Get it some hay Jet.” said Jinny.
“Uh, where from?”
“Sod it. I’ll wand some up.” and Jinny twirled Rosie, just like a flash drummer would with his sticks, and there was a bale of hay. Jinny grabbed a handful and made her way over to the unicorn.
“Only a virgin can truly embrace a unicorn you know?” said Jinny as she held the hay up to its mouth. “Are you one Jinny?” enquired Jet.
“Not yet, no, but I bet you are”
“I am not!” shouted Jet indignantly “Anyway, what is one?”
“Oh please, let’s not get into all that business now. Give the unicorn a nice stroke and let’s get him back to being a bed.”
So Jet stood on his hind legs and raised his front paw as high as he could. The Unicorn shook its mane and muzzled up to Jet’s tiny scarred nose then gave him a gentle lick on the top of the head.
“Virgin!” squealed Jinny “I knew it!” and twirled her wand once more, turning the mythical creature back into a run-of-the-mill double bed.
“Awww, he was lovely. Can we get him back again another time?” Jet simpered.
“Another time, yes, but not in the bedroom. He’s done a fair old dollop on the floor here. It’s a good job it isn’t carpeted.”
And with that Jinny scuttled downstairs to get a dustpan, brush, mop and bin liner.

Part 1: A Bustle In The Hedgerow

Time was getting on and Jinny had totally forgotten about her liaison (that's French you know), with the Misses Riz and Lou.

"Oh my stars! Look at the flippin' time!" she cried, eyeing the antique grandmother clock, over in the corner, with its enchanting moon phases. "I've got nine minutes to get to the village! Well Jetty, this is going to have to be one of those broomergencies. Do you want to come along? I'll be flying low down the back lanes."

"That'd be brilliant! I'd love to!" squeaked Jet.

"Quick sticks then, come on, through the back way and hop on Batilda." "What's Batilda?" asked Jet.

"My broom, of course! Jump on behind me. We'll do it just like you see it in pictures."

Jinny chanted a short spell:

"Forces of nature I call upon thee, lift me up and let me fly through the sky, let me be free, keep me safe, so mote it be! Oh and please save this chant so I don't have to keep repeating it." and the pair were scooped into the air and off down the rustic back lanes where hardly anyone walked, not in winter anyway.

Jinny and Jet reached their destination in six minutes, giving them a good couple of minutes to compose themselves.

"That was the most exhilarating feeling Jinny." laughed Jet, brimming with happiness and excitement.

"Not a bad way to travel, is it?" said Jinny matter of factly. "Now where are those two Harpies I wonder? I told them to meet me outside the pasty shop. Fancy a pasty, Jet?"

Without waiting for an answer, she sauntered off through the low opening of the shop door.

"Merry meet! Could I please have a salmon pasty and, I think, errmmm, a cheese and onion - not flaky ones - them flakes get everywhere."
"Certainly madam," grunted the snooty looking woman behind the counter.
"That'll be three pounds please. Are you paying cash?"
"I certainly am! You don't think I'm going to use a credit card for three pounds, do you?"
"Some do." replied the snooty woman as she handed the delicacies over.
"Fur coats and no knickers some people." humphed Jinny and off she shot. Jet was waiting outside because, as you know, animals aren't allowed in food shops. They'd probably just go food-struck with the aroma and wreck the place.

"Ahoy! Captain Jinny! Over here!" came a loud, couldn't-care-less-what-people-thought voice.
It was Miss Lou, a tall, slim, highly attractive woman with vivid red hair and even vivider red lipstick. "Hey up Lou, how are ya?" Jinny smiled "Where's Riz?" she said as she passed the salmon pasty to Jet.
"Guess."
"Toilet?"
"Yup!"
"Where does it all come from do you think?" Jinny wondered aloud. "I think it's the wine. It must store itself up in her system with a slow release process. She's a wine camel! Haaa Ha Ha!"
"You on about me?" said a beautiful, even taller, blonde woman with silver rings on every finger (and thumbs) "Going on with yourself just because I needed a wee. You're just as bad Miss Lou only it's Bacardi to blame with you, isn't it?"

"There isn't the same volume involved in a Bacardi though," quipped Lou. Riz and Jinny laughed then Lou and Riz broke into an old ABBA song, badly out of tune. Their dancing was exceptional though.

"Blimey O'Riley." thought Jet. "What in the name of pedigree cat treats have we here?"

"Is this little feller yours Jinny?" Lou enquired. "He's a bonny little thing, isn't he?" she said as she planted a huge Miss Lou kiss on the top of his head.

"Oh Lou, you've redded his head now." laughed Riz. "That'll take days to come off."

"Fear not," said Lou. "It's pet friendly lippy, that is. Untested on animals." "Well, maybe it should have been, eh?" howled Miss Riz and they all cracked up laughing, even Jet, with Jinny spitting pastry crumbs all over the place.

"It's a treat to see you both, it really is," said Jinny smiling. "I've missed you sooo much."

"Awww, we've missed you too." said Lou in a squeaky, little girl voice.

"Yes, we have luv." added Riz in an equally squeaky voice.

They did this all the time, Miss Riz and Miss Lou. They were like Chloe and Radcliffe from The League of Gentleman, or even Edina and Patsy, times ten, but taller and prettier. And funnier, some thought.

PARCHMENT 6

Beer Drinkers and Hellraisers

The four of them made their way to a quaint, thatched, seventeenth century, pet friendly pub nestled off the village square. 'Old Demdike's Neck' it was called, or 'Demmy's' for short.

"I'm going over to the pet shop to get you a suitable collar afterwards, Jet," announced Jinny. "We can't have you going 'round looking all unwanted, can we?"

"Indeed we can't Miss Jinny. Thank you." said Jet.

"You're welcome, now what do you want to drink? That'll be water, won't it? They've got their own well spring here you know? None of that

chemical rubbish. Miss Riz! Sauvignon Blanc is it?"

"Yes please Jinny. Large." said Riz quietly.

"Lou - Bacardi and Coke?"

"Double please Jin, and only two lumps of ice. We don't want it watering down, do we?"

"No, you don't dear." chortled Jinny as she jostled her way to the bar.

"Fee Fie Foe Fum, I smell the smell of a big, white rum." sang Lou, to herself, whilst gazing nonchalantly around the pub.

"Let's sit over here by the fire." she decided and off the three of them went, obediently.

"I love this place," beamed Miss Riz with her fabulous smile. "It reminds me of my childhood, four hundred and odd years ago! Tee hee. Just kidding."

"It reminds me of a time when they used to hang witches," Miss Lou said darkly. "Just look at that painting over there - a hanging witch! How un PC. How insensitive. How … unsavoury."

"Ooh that's terrible," said Jet sadly "Did they really used to do things like that to witches?"

"They did indeed Jetty, on a regular basis. It stopped in 1727. That was when the last witch was 'officially' hanged in Britain, or so they say anyway. I'm not sure I believe it myself." Lou said with a hint of bitterness.

"But why would people do that? I mean, I've only met one witch, up until meeting you two, and she's the most caring, wonderful, loving person I've ever come across. Why would anyone want to do away with someone like her?"

Jinny returned with a tray of drinks, placing Jet's saucer of water on the hearth by the fire.

"Here you are girls: one *double* Bacardi, two ices, and one *large* Sauv.

Good health to you. Merry be!"

Riz joined in with a, "Bacchus, God of joys divine, be thy pleasures ever mine."

And Miss Lou simply roared, "Up yours! Ha, ha and thrice ha!"

Jet just lapped at his water and glanced at them all, bewilderedly, as Lou casually looked over her shoulder, waved her hand and turned the hanging witch picture to face the wall. Job done.

Jinny cleared her throat and remarked, "Now then, on a serious note, as you're both here anyway and hopefully staying the week, I'd like you to do me a very big favour. How would you like to help to save a flutter of faeries from being made homeless?"

"Oooh, I love faeries me." slurred Miss Lou.

"Yes, me too, couldn't live without 'em." sipped Miss Riz.

“So, that’s ‘ayes’ all round then ladies?” and then, as if on cue, a tapping was heard at one of the old leaded windows. It was the robin.
“I’ll be back in a minute, girls, I need a quick chat with this little feller.” said Jinny as she rose from the comfortable armchair she had only just settled into.
“I’ll go if you like,” said Jet, “I know what’s going on now”. he winked.
“Awww bless you Jetty, how considerate of you,” Jinny smiled. “Off you go then, quick sticks.”

Jet elegantly paddy pawed his way to the entrance of the pub, looked around to see if anyone was watching, nobody was, so he silently walked straight through the heavy door and out into the cobbled street, as if by magic, which it was actually!
“Merry meet Mr Robin” Jet said politely (he was getting the hang of these
witch phrases now). “Where have you been? We expected you a few days ago.”
“Oh, you won’t believe it. I had that much to eat at your house the other afternoon that I must have gone into some kind of hibernation mode.
Turned into a common Poorwill I did! I’m dreadfully sorry. I do hope I haven’t fouled things up for you.”
“No, not at all, we’re still in the planning stages, so, whenever you’re ready to steer us in the right direction, we’ll be there. I’m getting a new collar today you know.” Jet said proudly.
“That’s nice. Make sure it hasn’t got a bell on it, that could cause all manner of problems.”
“How so?” said Jet raising an eyebrow. “Well, they’re noisy, aren’t they? You need to be more like a Ninja cat. Unseen and unheard.”

“Hmmm I suppose you’re right there Mr R. I’ll try to make sure her wonderfulness doesn’t make that mistake.”

“Have you cut yourself Jet? What’s all that red on your head? You’re not trying to turn into a cat red head are you?”

“You mean, as opposed to a robin red breast?” laughed Jet “No, it’s one of Jinny’s pals, Miss Lou, she kissed me with her luminous lipstick.”

“Oh dear, I do hope it comes off, that could cause all manner of problems.” “I’ll give it a wipe later, I’m sure it’ll be fine.” Jet said, unworried. “We’ll be back at the cottage within the hour I should imagine, so we’ll meet you back there, eh?”

“Yes, not a problem,” said Mr R. “I’ll see if I can unearth a few worms in the meantime. Bye!” and off he flew.

Jet decided to try his paw at getting through a window without opening it but he just ended up stubbing his nose, so went for the surer option of the door.

As he strolled back over to the fireside he couldn’t help but notice a rather rotund and greasy looking gentleman eyeing him and the, for want of a

better word, ‘coven’ that was gathered around the table.

He was bald, apart from whispy, black hair at the sides, sported a completely out of date grey moustache, a spongy nose and had his trousers tucked into a pair of tartan diamond socks, or so it appeared. He was altogether a rather archaic and smarmy looking individual.

“Who does he think he’s looking at?” muttered Jet and carried on regardless.

"Who does he think he's looking at?" exclaimed Jet as he reached the table. The three ladies all turned around and it was Jinny who, naturally, recognised the starer.

"Well, well. It's old Crooky, as I live and breathe. He's the one I've been telling you about girls."

"Is he *really*?" said Riz. "Go and give him a piece of your mind Miss Lou."

"Nay lasses. Not here. Not anywhere actually, we need to be invisible."

"What's about to happen has nowt to do with us, savvy?" Jinny whispered. "Oh yes, yes, you're right there Jin," whispered Lou. "How about I go and accidentally spill a drink on him? Something with blackcurrant in it …"

"No, ignore him, the man's an arse, not worth the effort. Not yet anyways."

"Fair enough captain." said Lou as she saluted Jinny.

The magical group finished their drinks, donned their coats and made their way to the door, but were stopped in their tracks by the fat fellow who had been leaning on the bar, watching them.

THE WITCH AND JET SPLINTERS

Part 1: A Bustle In The Hedgerow

PARCHMENT 7

Lipstick On Your Collar

"Oh, excuse me darling," said the man identified as Mr Crook, loquaciously. "Aren't you one of my neighbours?" he enquired of Jinny.

"I haven't the foggiest idea - am I?" Jinny said aloofly.

"Yes, yes, you live in the little house near the crossroads, don't you? What's it called … Ammonia Cottage or something?"

"Demonia Cottage, 2, actually." retorted Jinny in her Sunday best snooty voice.

"Yes, that's the one darling. You're only about twenty minutes away from my house you know?"

"Hardly '*neighbours*' then eh?" Jinny said sharply.

"Well, no, not strictly speaking but in a remote village like this it's near enough." Mr Crook replied, as a bead of sweat ran down his forehead.

"And your point is?"

"Ooh, there wasn't really a point as such darling, I - I was just introducing myself and being, well, neighbourly, if you like." Mr Crook stammered. Jinny really was a stunning looking woman, and you can only imagine the amount of courage it had taken Crook to sidle over and actually speak to her.

About four double whiskies worth in truth!

"I know your name, Mr Crook," snapped Jinny with her dark eyes blazing.

"No introduction necessary."

The party then continued their way to the door, Lou turning around and pulling her tongue out at the crestfallen man, Riz showed her bottom and last in line, Jet, sprayed on his leg.

"You'll want to know me one day darling!" shouted Crook across the room. "Mark my words!"

"Three!" Jinny shouted back.

The quaint quartet sallied forth across the road and on towards the pet shop.

"Collar time!" rapped Jinny

"Excellent news." said Jet.

The pet shop had been on this spot for nigh on a hundred and twenty years and its owner, Tom Entwistle, looked as if he was there at the opening. "Can I be of some assistance, modom?" He whistled the 'S's in faux posh tones, even though he was Lancastrian through and through, for goodness' sake!

Jinny thought she'd have a bit of fun, so affected her own tones accordingly

"Yeees my good man. I am looking for a collar for my esteemed feline friend here. Maybe something in velvet? Green maybe?"

"We have an excellent selection available modom. Follow me if you please." said Tom as they made their way to a corner of the little shop.

"You won't find a better quality cat collar anywhere in the region," he bragged. "I say, has your cat cut its head?"

Jinny scanned the goods in a speed reading stylee and spotted the perfect collar. It was sort of velvety and green with hieroglyphics and stars emblazoned upon it.

"No sir, he hasn't cut his head, thank you. I'll take this one." and handed the collar to the shopkeeper.

"That's very swish," purred Jet "I likes that a lot."

"Great minds eh?" smiled Jinny. "How much is that please sir?"

"That's twenty pounds, modom."

"I only want one!" she exclaimed loudly. "Not the whole range!"

"Yes, that's twenty pounds for the one modom." said Tom, keeping his composure. He would have made a good butler for someone.

"Blood and sand man! What a dear do!" Jinny spluttered.

"You just so happened to have picked the Rolls Royce of cat collars, modom. Made by hand by skilled Artisans they are."

Jinny steadied herself then said "Yes, I can see that now. A very high end finish, aren't they? The sort of product I'm accustomed to. Do you do student discount?"

"We don't modom, students can't afford to keep themselves let alone a pet."

"Oh, right, I was just asking for my nephew, who isn't here, obviously." said Jinny as she handed a crumpled twenty pound note over to the man. Mr Birtwhistle turned his back to the ladies and started to key into his till. Jinny, in a trice, wafted her hand and brought another green collar floating toward her, then pocketed it.

"I'll wear that around my wrist," she thought. "We'll be like twins."

"Tut tut," whispered Riz. "Nicking from an old man …"

"Oh bugger Riz. I know. Sorry. Couldn't contain meself," and just as she was about to put the collar back Tom turned 'round and stated "Good Lord, I forgot, it's two-for-one Wednesday, isn't it? You can choose another if you like?"

Part 1: A Bustle In The Hedgerow

"But it's not Wednesday, is it?" said Lou between her teeth.
"I've no idea what day it is," laughed Jinny, "but I'm going for it."
"How fortuitous," said Jinny with her newly adopted posh demeanour. "I'll take this one. Thank you my good man, muchly."
And off they went, back into the main street, smiling, chattering and dancing.

"See that girl, watch that stream, dig up the dancing queen." sang Jinny breezily. "I'm pretty certain that's not how it goes Jin." corrected Riz, only to be ignored.
"… feel the heat of the tangerines…"

Jinny had cable tied her broom to some railings outside the public conveniences, where a small crowd had now gathered.
"Hey up. What's occurring here?" she said worriedly.
A young whippersnapper of a lad piped up "This brush - it's, it's trembling."
"Oh, it must be the wind luv … and it's a *Broom.*" said Jinny, correcting him in a condescending manner.
"But it ain't windy mrs," and with that the lad licked his finger and stuck it into the air. "Nowt! See?"
"I'll take it home and put it by the fire, it's probably cold." said Jinny who was actually lost for a proper explanation.
"A cold brush? How does that happen then?"
"Silence child!" snapped Jinny, taking out her Swiss army knife and cutting the cable tie "Let me tell you - *a new broom sweeps clean but the old one knows the corners.*" she said bafflingly, walking away as if there

weren't about fifteen people staring at her. Devil-may-care … La de da …

"Ahoy Miss Jin! Get a wriggle on." shouted Miss Lou.
"I'm here!" she shouted back. "Come on Jetty, quick sticks!"
Miss Lou and Miss Riz had arrived in the village in Riz's old silver Hyundai Coupe - it looked like a swanky sports car but in fact was a low budget, Korean four-seater with two doors. It had a sun roof though! And a sticker on the boot proclaiming, 'Powered by a Wendle Witch'.
Riz and Lou were leaning on the back having a ciggie, shivering.

Inside, were two mischievous but beautiful cats. The male was called Spike, who obviously had a touch of Bengal in him, and the female, Stripes, a slender Siamese.
Spike was sat at the steering wheel pretending to drive and Stripes was his passenger. They didn't even have their seat belts on!
Jinny put her precious Batilda into the boot and the four of them squeezed into the car, Riz turned on the ignition and put the heater on straight away.
"By the left!" she said. "It's bloody perishing. Anyone want a Jelly Baby?" Two "ME!"'s rang out, and Riz distributed a handful of Jelly Babies each to Jinny and Lou.
"Yumzah." sighed Jinny.
"Praise de Lard!" shouted Lou.
"Who's this then … the chap with the head wound?" sparked up Spike nodding at Jet.

Part 1: A Bustle In The Hedgerow

"Sorry, I forgot to introduce you Spike, and you Stripes - this is Jet Splinters, he's my new 'friend'." Jinny said lovingly.
"Fiend you mean?" said the cheeky Spike. Stripes didn't say anything, but then she didn't have a lot to say at the best of times.
"How do, Spike," said Jet, "and you Stripes."
They both bleated "Merry meet Jet," and snuggled up to their respective owners - tricky for Riz because she was driving and Spike had a habit of nuzzling into her throat and licking it for minutes on end. Had done since he was three months old.
"Let's try your collar on for size Jet." said Jinny.
"Oooh, that's very swish," said Spike.
"I said that" grinned Jet.
"Great minds" said Spike.
"Keep still then Jetty, let's make sure it fits properly," Jinny put the collar around Jet's neck, fastened it, then checked if you could get two fingers behind it. "There. How does that feel? It looks very elegant."
"It looks good from here," said Jet. "Aren't you putting yours on?" Then Jet noticed that both of the other cats had red smudges on their heads. He laughed quietly to himself. They had no idea.
"I just remembered," Jet started suddenly, "I said we'd meet Mr Robin back

at the cottage in an hour and it's nearly that now!"
"Get yer skates on Riz, there's business afoot." Jinny said impatiently.

Meanwhile, back at the pub, Mr Crook had downed another four or five double whiskies and was becoming argumentative at the bar.

"You don't know who I am, do you?" he shouted nastily to any of the three blokes perched on their barstools.

"A pain in the arse?" one of them shouted back.

"Mr Gobby?" shouted another.

"Russell Crook. Crook by name, crook by nature," said the third fellow rising from his seat. "Anything else we should be knowing?"

"There is atcherlly," slurred Crook, "that one day, shoon, I will be the mosht important person in this village and you lot, eshpecially you pal, will be barred from this pub becaush I will *own* it! And every other businesh worth having in thish godforsaken hole," then let out a horrible, loud burp "Beeeeelch!"

"Well, you've certainly got your fingers in all the right pies, haven't you?" said the third man. "Bungs for the council, bungs for local government, you've even managed to bribe the church!"

"What do you know of anything?" barked Crook. "Shpeculation that is and which one is it? I get 'em mixed up, oh yesh, shlander! No, libel. Yesh, shlander!"

"It's fact and well-known fact at that." crowed the second man.

At this point, the landlord of the pub interjected "Right Mr Crook, would you be kind enough to finish your drink and vacate the premises please? I think you've had enough."

"I'll go when *I* think I've had enough!" Crook dribbled and just as the words left his mouth the three men got up, hoisted the obnoxious man off his feet and carted him off to the back exit.

"You're going NOW!" said the third man menacingly, "and if I see you in here again I'll brain you. Understood?"

"I've got friends you know," said Crook pitifully. "I'll be back whenever it suits me. Mark my words."

"One and a half," said the first man and with that gave him a swift kick to the seat of his pants "Bye!"

PARCHMENT 8

Fox On the Run

Jinny, Riz, Lou, Jet, Spike and Stripes were, in the meantime, weaving their way to Demonia Cottage 2 in Riz's glam Coupe.

A small witch doll on a broomstick was hanging from the mirror, twizzing round at a great rate whenever Riz turned a corner or accelerated.

"Nearly there, girls," said Riz, staring intently ahead. It was a very narrow, winding lane and if a car should come the other way there would only be room for one of them. A split second with her eyes off the road would mean a head-on collision and they didn't want that. No.

Within five minutes, Riz pulled up beside Jinny's pretty, old cottage and indicated right, turning up a very tiny side path, just wide enough to fit the car.

Privets and branches were scraping along the bodywork and windows, making it sound as if the car was going to look like a proper wreck by the time Riz had parked up.

But it wasn't, so that's good, isn't it?

"Everybody out," said Riz and the crazy sextet struggled their way out of the low set vehicle.

"Can you open the boot please, Riz?" asked Jinny. "Mustn't forget Batilda."

"Done." she said. "Come on, let's get in - it's flippin' freezing!"

The ladies walked in through the back door with their faithful felines following.

"Can you walk straight through doors, Spike?" asked Jet.

"Course I can, all witches' cats can." replied Spike

"Oh, right, I didn't know. Nobody tells me anything round here …"

Jinny spotted the robin chattering on the front window sill
"I hope we're not late Mr R. Come in for a minute, we're just going to have a brew and a ciggie then we'll follow you to that excuse for a human being's place, eh?"
"Thanking you indeed," he said. "Are there any of those mealworms left? If you don't mind me asking?"
"I think so, hang on and I'll check, you cheeky chap."
Thankfully there were some mealworms left and Jinny arranged them on a saucer in the shape of a funny face.
The robin smiled (with his eyes of course), and weighed delightedly into the scrumptious cuisine.
"Now then - Miss Riz, Miss Lou - you both know where we're going after this brew, don't you?"
"I haven't the haziest notion." said Lou wickedly
"Are we going back to the pub?" said Riz mischievously
"We're following Mr Robin here and he's going to show us where the Crookster's dwelling is. We can maybe slip a spell or two in for good measure while we're there." corrected Jinny.
"Sounds good Jin. Count me in. I'll just go for a wee first." said Riz, stubbing her cigarette out.
"No real rush!" shouted Jinny, behind her, sarcastically.

Within ten minutes or so, everyone had done what they had to do - supped their brews, smoked their cigs, been to the loo, eaten their mealworms etc. The cats had had a special treat of a confection known as 'Breamies', a fish based kind of kibble thing (they could only have a maximum of eleven Breamies in any given day) and were so content their purring sounded like drilling behind the couch.

"Do you want to fly Mr R or are you coming in the car with us?" asked Jinny

"We can't go in the car Jin!" said Riz. "It's a hill, dale and forest jobby, isn't it?"

"Of course it is, sorry. I've got that used to travelling by car now it's like second nature." Jinny replied.

"That *used?* Second nature? We've only been here a few hours!" giggled Lou.

"I've got an addictive personality Lou, as well you know!" said Jinny, seriously (ish). "Anyway, let's get off before the dark kicks in. Everyone got enough clothing on? Good"

And off they set. Three cats, one bird and three ever so slightly unhinged young women.

Was Raphael joining them? No, not yet. Maybe later.

The magnificent seven had been trudging through what was left of the snow for a good fifteen minutes, when Riz spotted something orangey coloured up ahead, seemingly struggling.

"Awww look, that dear fox is caught up in something," she said and upon further investigation, sure enough, the poor fox had become entwined in some discarded barbed wire. His back legs were bound together with the stuff and he was in tremendous pain.

The group gathered around the helpless vulpine and Jinny whispered,

"Oh, monsieur Renard (that's French Jinny!)," said Jet excitedly.

"Gomez!" smiled Jinny. "Close your eyes and I will free you of these

Fetters."
The fox obeyed and Jinny, her trusty wand, Rosie, in hand, pointed it at the rusty wire around his legs.
"Binds that tie, binds that harm, disappear and bring him calm."
A wiggly blue light shot from the wand and the barbed wire was no more.
"That's a nifty spell Jin," said Lou. "Never heard that one before."
"I just made it up off the top of my magic little head." Jinny laughed.
"Sooo gifted." Riz beamed.
"You spoke French." said Jet dreamily.
"I shall not forget this day, fair lady," said the relieved fox. "If ever you are in need of help, please don't hesitate to shout me. My name is Zorro. I will hear you, wherever you are."
"Zorro? As in the masked swashbuckler?" enquired Jinny.
"As in the Spanish, for fox!" winked Zorro.
"Well! You learn something every day in this game. Take care Mr Zorro and erm, adios amigo!"
"Thank you a thousand-fold Bella Dama," and off he sped into the bushes.
"I'm not usually over keen on foxes," Spike announced, "but he seemed a very civil fellow."
"Onwards!" shouted Jinny. "Let's find this flippin' house then get home for a warm."

All this time, the robin had been flying ahead of the group. They were just about to pass the faerie hedgerow which meant that it was now only a short trip to the notorious Crook's house.

"Turn right here!" he cheeped, "and it's about five minute's walk" "We could've used our brooms you know," said Lou. "There's no one about."

"Next time Miss Lou, next time." Jinny said gravely.

They eventually came upon a large, detached bungalow. It was built in the nineteen eighties and was completely characterless.

All the doors and window frames were done in white UPVC and the windows hadn't been cleaned in months.

The house had about a quarter of an acre of land surrounding it and a few overgrown, mature flower beds near the entrance. "Ye Gods, what a bland dump!" Lou said, pulling her face.

"Aye," said Jinny. "Well, we know where to come in future, that's the main thing. Let's leave a little calling card in the meantime, shall we?" She pointed Rosie at the door casing and a wiggly red light shot out, welding the frame and the door together.

Next were the windows. Another sharp red beam and they were sealed tight. "There'll be no opening them without a good crowbar or maybe even the fire brigade." laughed Jinny as she shifted round the back of the property and proceeded to do the same routine.

For good measure, she also sealed the keyholes, just for the hell of it and because she could.

Before they departed, Riz used her finger to write the words "BOO!" in big letters in the grime on the front window.

"What a wizard wheeze!" howled Lou. "Come on, let's go and have a celebratory snifter. Thank you for showing us the way Mr R!"

"Not a problem," said Mr R and fluttered back to his nest as the strange little band made their way back towards Demonia Cottage 2.

Part 1: A Bustle In The Hedgerow

Darkness was approaching, even though it was only mid-afternoon and Mr Crook had been making his unsteady way, by foot, along the winding lanes in an effort to find his drunken way home.

There were no taxis or anything like that and who on earth would ever give him a lift?

As he approached Jinny's house, he knew he had another twenty minutes or so (maybe seventy minutes in his condition) to go and he was already flagging.

"I'll nip in here and see if I can scrounge a coffee or something." he thought, stupidly.

Up to the front door he staggered, knocked a loud knock in the manner of, say, a bailiff and waited a minute. No answer. Well, they weren't back yet. Another loud knock ensued. Still no answer.

He kicked the door but only succeeded in stubbing his big toe. He'd feel that in the morning!

"I'll try the back way," he mumbled to himself and made his way through the side gate to the back doorway. Somebody had forgotten to lock it, hadn't they? Oh lawdy dawdy!

In walked the inebriated fellow, tripping over the 'The witch is home' coconut hair door mat and landing in a heap under the kitchen table. "Shite!" he cried as he endeavoured to pick himself back up.

As he did so, he somehow managed to focus on the décor within Jinny's little palace.

A pentagram here, a stuffed owl there, a broomstick, witch dolls, pointy hats, pointier shoes and a framed picture of Lily Munster looking for everything like some wicked religious icon.

"What the hell kind of place is thish?" he muttered, when out of the blue (well, out of the lounge actually) came a loud swishing sound followed by a black shape heading swiftly towards him. It knocked him clean back off his feet and sent him hurtling out of the back door from whence he came, slamming and bolting the door behind him. Beware! Do not disturb a sleeping Raphael! Crook lay on his whisky sodden back, in a bed of damp soil, for a good couple of minutes before he could get any semblance of his senses back.

THE WITCH AND JET SPLINTERS

Part 1: A Bustle In The Hedgerow

PARCHMENT 9

Power Windows

"Oh my senses," groaned the pitiful Mr Crook, "where did they go?!" just as three delightful witches and their equally divine familiars marched down the side lane and in through the gate of the small but perfectly manicured back garden.

"What in the name of Edgar Allan Poe is that specimen doing sat in my Night Scented Stock?!" Shrieked Jinny "Oi! What are you doing on my premises please?"

"Shorry darling, I shtrayed off the road and shomehow ended up in a flower bed." cried Crook.

"So, you strayed off the road, through my gate, into my garden and fell? And DON'T call me 'darling'!!!"

"Aye, aye, summat like that darl... I've had one or two cocktails you see …"

"I would say you've had one or two eagle tails too," said Jinny, picking a couple of Raphael's smaller black feathers from Crook's waistcoat. "You've been snooping around my house, haven't you? You bloody blighter!"

"No, no I wouldn't do that mish … I jusht ended up here by haccident." wined the hapless rogue.

"Tosh! Get off my property NOW! If I see you here again you'll be spending the remainder of your wretched life in a wasps'nest! Now

SCRAM!" screamed Jinny furiously.

Then she remembered what Mr Crook had in store for him when he got home and a wry smile came upon her face.

Crook leapt up and scurried towards the gate "No chance of a coffee then shweetheart?"

Part 1: A Bustle In The Hedgerow

Lou helped him out further by aiming a sharp pointed boot at his very kicksome backside.
"Git!" said Riz, as Jet sprayed another spray on the back of his trousers as he hobbled up the side lane.
Stripes let out one of her evilest growls and Spike just stared ahead, looking handsome and Tigerish.

Jinny swished her hand, as she does, unlocked the back door and the seething sextet made their way into the kitchen.
It was a homely, welcoming kitchen but something had upset it's Chi. "We've had unwanted visitors, haven't we Raph?" half shouted Jinny, putting her head 'round the corner of the door into the front lounge. The large, solemn bird, who was sitting on the chair arm, looked at her with his best piercing eye and nodded.
"You got rid of him, didn't you?" Raph nodded. He couldn't speak English because he was from India, but he could understand every word Jinny said.
"Good lad," she smiled and planted a big kiss on his head "You're a star." Jet sidled into the lounge and said, "Hello Raph, I'm Jet. We haven't actually spoken yet …"
"He won't speak to anybody Jetty, he's not from these parts, but he does understand everything we say." Raph winked at Jet and Jet blinked back. He hadn't mastered the art of winking, not many cats do.
"Drinks all round me dears. Ahoy!" Lou said in a piratey kind of way, handing out the bevvies to the other two. The cats had a big bowl of water between them and Raph, well, Raph didn't ever seem to drink anything. Or eat!

Riz magicked a fire and all was snug. “Want some music on or would you rather watch some TV?” asked Jinny.

“Let’s empty our heads and watch some TV.” said Riz “Addams Family,

The Munsters Bewitched, Lovejoy or … Escape to the Country?” Jinny enquired.

“All of them!” laughed Lou. “”Der der, der der, der der der der der-der.” trilled Jinny and they cosed up on the couch, stretching their legs and wiggling their stripey socked toes with contentment as, on the TV, Samantha Stephens, their heroine, raced across the sky on her broomstick. Naturally, not one of them saw more than ten minutes of anything as the whole group nodded off in front of the roaring fire. It had been a long day and the days were going to get longer for them, just you see.

While all this was happening (All what? They weren’t doing a thing!), the man they called Crook was meandering through the cold, lonely lanes and on through the Spooky Woods, in an effort to somehow find his miserable hovel.

“Curse that bloody whishkey!” he whined, as he made his way slowly over the fields that would one day, he hoped, be his beloved golf course. Suddenly, he felt a hard tug at his coat tail. Hard enough to pull him to the ground and land him flat on his back.

“What the…?” he looked around in the half light and spotted six or seven small dark shapes jigging around him. “As God is my witness I shall never drink again!” he muttered “What the blazes is occurring?”

He then felt a sharp pinch to his left ear and another to his nose and another to his eyelashes then he felt his top lip being lifted as he received a good ol’ crack to his front teeth.

Part 1: A Bustle In The Hedgerow

He was speechless. And nearly toothless!
"Baddy Bumdrops." he heard a high-pitched voice exclaim, as if forcing the words directly into his mind.
"You shouldn't be making your way through these parts at this hour, or any hour for that matter. Not if you know what's good for you!" the voice squeaked. "Get yerself home! RUN! Run for your selfish life!"
Then suddenly he was alone, out of the clearing and outside his very own home.
"I. I don't… Whaat?!" he spoke under his breath. He pulled his mobile phone out, selected the memo pad and typed in 'Never drink that Green Antler whiskey again. Ever.'
The dishevelled Mr Crook then searched his pockets for his keys, got them out and shuffled to the front door of his house.
He could see a dull, red glow playing in the keyhole but blithely ignored it and pushed his key into the aperture. Only it wouldn't go in and the key bent back, on the verge of snapping.
"I do NOT believe this!" he bellowed. He tried another key and another until all of his door keys were bent.
It was getting darker by the minute and a panic came over the now shivering Mr Crook.
"I'll have to break a window," he thought. "No. That would be expensive.
I'll prise one open."
And off he went to his garden shed in search of something that would prise a UPVC window open, without causing too much damage, of course. Every penny counts.
Using the torch on his phone he found an old, long, flat head screwdriver and walked back round to the front of the building.

He noticed the big 'BOO!' etched on the window pane, but it didn't scare him, and self-obsessed that he was, he didn't bother to put two and two together to work out who might have been responsible for this trickery.

Twenty minutes passed and his fingers were getting numb with the cold.

He was getting nowhere with the window and was now feeling extremely hungry and extremely desperate.

The idea hit him to sleep in his shed and get the locks sorted in the morning, so he walked dejectedly back to the small wooden hut, cold and hung over with an aching head and a mind that was bordering on insanity. He lay down on the damp wooden floor and pulled his overcoat up to his chin, using a bale of hay in a plastic bag as a pillow. He remembered that he had once bought it for a hamster he had as a pet but the crafty little rodent ran away, never to return.

What had he done to deserve today, he pondered.

Some people just never learn …

THE WITCH AND JET SPLINTERS

Part 1: A Bustle In The Hedgerow

PARCHMENT 10

Through the Keyhole

A new, cold but sunny day dawned and Jinny and her companions rose reasonably early.
Riz and Lou were busy making a fry up in the kitchen, of all places, and the cats were having a mad minute in the back garden, fighting playfully. Apart from Stripes, who meant it!
Each one of the cats had newly red heads, a gift from the lips of Miss Lou. Bless her.
Jinny was in the bathroom in her beloved Star Wars Chewbacca dressing gown, brushing her fine, white teeth. None of your rotten, green, wooden molars for these witches, no.
Raph was still dozing on the wooden chandelier. Zzzzzzz.
The scene painted an idyllic picture of everyday witchcraft and serenity.

It was in complete contrast that Russell Crook's morning began with a severe hangover, a sneezing fit and a very sore back and big toe.
"Uuurggghh!" he moaned. "Where am I?"
"You're in a shed." said a voice in his head.
"Uuurrggghhh!" he replied to himself.
"Oh no! The door, the window, I've got to get in the house. Owww! Me toe!"
He reached for his phone, noticed it had hardly any charge left on it and rang 999.
"Emergency - which service do you require?" came a robotic voice at the other end.

Part 1: A Bustle In The Hedgerow

"Fire please and make it snappy!" said Crook rudely.

"I'll have to take some details from you first, where are you situated?"

"In a shed in my back garden, look, just put me through to Bill Kelly at Clitheroe fire station will you? My phone charge is running out!"

"I need to take some details from you first sir …"

"Sod it!" he said and turned the phone off.

No such thing as a hearty breakfast for Mr Crook as he resigned himself to the fact that he would have to walk all the way back into the village, down to Ye Olde Ironmonger's shop and hope that someone there could help him to get back into his house.

What. A. Life. he mused. And as his memory slowly drifted back into his consciousness he recalled that, yes! he had a car!

It was parked up in the lane opposite his house.

Crook got up and raced out of the shed, skidding down the short gravel driveway and out into the lane.

"Thank God the tyres aren't flat." he said taking the host of bent keys out of his pocket and praising the powers that be that he hadn't tried to open the front door of his house with the car key.

Unusually, because, let's face it, things weren't going too well for the fellow, the car started at the first attempt, and Crook was soon manoeuvring his old Range Rover down the twisty lanes of old Wendle, which is where all of this takes place, by the way.

Back at the faerie hedgerow, in the clearing, the fay (as faeries are often known) and a small troupe of pixies were frolicking in the sunlight. It was a beautiful day considering this was the North of England and Wintertime and the fay were taking full advantage of it.

A small fire was burning, away from the clearing and the hedgerow.

These fires are named eternal flames as they are never allowed to die.

Pixies must take turns to stand guard over them and keep them burning. Should one ever go out a magpie must be summoned to find a piece of

glass with which to reignite the fire via the sun's rays.

An older gnome by the name of Wilf was put in charge of cutting down some of the pesky bramble bushes to fuel the fire and to further prevent any of the faeries from snagging their wings on the thorns.

Slinky had, only recently, almost torn one of her wings on the troublesome things and had ordered that a clean-up be done forthwith.

The fay used the discarded thorns in much the same way as humans would use a knife. Anything that needed cutting, a bramble thorn did the job.

"I'm getting too old to be scratching and snagging myself like this" lamented Wilf.

Wilf was two hundred and forty-three years old after all.

"Miss Slinky, why don't you ask young Sparrowhawk to do these prickly tasks? He's a proper idler, that lad, and no mistake."

"I know Wilf," Slinky shimmeringly whispered "but when I say anything to him he does not seem to hear me. Or maybe he pretends he does not hear me, I am not sure. Watch … Spudsley! Spudsley Sparrowhawk! Would you mind trimming some of these brambles back please?"

"A rambling pack?" said the young pixie "Why would I want to go swimming with a rambling pack? I could drown! What *is* a rambling pack?"

Part 1: A Bustle In The Hedgerow

"Do you see what I mean Wilf? I think he has got a severe hearing problem, either that or he is simple."

"I'd go along with both of those Miss Slinky," said Wilf, shaking his head. Slinky tutted and gracefully flew over to Spudsley, tugged him by the ear and pointed to the brambles.

"I. Would. Like. You. To. Please. Trim. These. Brambles. Back." she said very slowly.

"I. Would. Very. Much. Like. To. Trim. Those. Brambles. Back. For.

You." came the answer. "When. Do. You. Want. Me. To. Start? Tomorrow?"

"I AM NOT DEAF SPUDSLEY!" shrieked Slinky, "YOU DO NOT HAVE TO TALK LIKE THAT TO ME!"

"But. You. Started. It" said Spudsley in a whimpering voice.

"Spudsley - forget it! Wilf, please ask some of those fellows over there, the ones lying about with corn stalks in their mouths, if they would help you. We do not want you getting a bad back." said Slinky impatiently.

"Too late for that Miss Slinky." gruffed Wilf, stooping.

Just then, Slinky noticed a prile of figures approaching in the distance, with a prile of smaller figures, closer to the ground. She hovered carefully until their features became visible.

"Miss Jinny!" she squealed "and Mr Splinters!"

"Merry meet Slinky, how's it with you?" said Jinny cheerily.

"Oh, do not ask Jinny, I am in the middle of a despair … but nothing too serious."

"Sorry to hear that, anyway, this is Miss Riz and Miss Lou and their two little scallywags Spike and Stripes. They don't have surnames I'm afraid."

"I am very pleased to make your acquaintances. Are you of the same persuasion as Miss Jinny?" asked Slinky.

"We are indeed captain!" trilled Lou, "and here to help"

"How lovely of you, would you care to partake in an acorn cup of honey wine?"

"Have you anything bigger than an acorn cup Miss Slinky please?" Riz asked as she lit up a cig. "I'm fair parched."

"Bigger than an acorn cup? My goodness, you must be very thirsty. Now, what do we have…?" said Slinky as she wracked her faerie mind for something that might be bigger than an acorn cup.

"… we have a selection of old conker cases, would they do?"

"Aye," said Riz grudgingly, "if that's as big as it goes then that's what we're stuck with, though I was thinking of summat along the lines of a coconut shell."

The group laughed heartily and Slinky summoned a nearby pixie to bring an armful of the larger conker shells.

"Careful with the spikes." said Slinky as she carefully poured the drinks into the conker shells.

Jinny related the tale of Mr Crook to Slinky and how they had bumped into him, or how he had bumped into them, in the pub, and how she had sealed his windows and doors and how they had found him sat in the middle of her back garden.

"I wonder how he went on last night." smirked Jinny.

Not very well was the answer.

Part 1: A Bustle In The Hedgerow

While all this was going on, Crook had driven into the village, parked up and strolled tiredly into Ye Olde Ironmonger's shop.

"Hey up!" he yawned cantankerously, "Is there anyone here that can help me get back into my house? I've been locked out."

"Was it a domestic sir?" enquired the professorial chap behind the counter, peering over his glasses.

"A domestic?!" growled Crook. "No it was not! I'm not married thank you very much, nor do I want to be!"

"Apologies. I had to ask so as to ascertain whether someone is actually residing within the dwelling at the moment." said the ironmonger professionally.

"There's no one residing in the dwelling, no, because no one can get into the bloody dwelling!" came Crook's sharp reply

"Please calm down sir. No need for profanities. I've got a business card here somewhere. Ah, here it is, Nancy Redfern, Locksmith. No job too small. Maybe you could give her a call?"

"A woman? Locksmith? What's the world coming to? Is that the best you can do?" said Crook ungratefully.

"I'm afraid she's the only locksmith in the village sir, that I know of." Crook mumbled a few curses under his breath and asked if he could charge his phone for a few minutes while he called over to the pub.

"I'll have to ask for a small fee sir, electricity doesn't come cheap."

"Here we go," exclaimed Crook. "How much?!"

"Five pounds will cover it sir."

"Hell's teeth man - that's extortion!" shouted back Crook.

"Well, I'm sure you would know more about that than I sir." said the ironmonger with a smile.

"Here, I want it charging for an hour for that kind of money," said Crook and handed the phone over to the chap. "I'll be back in a bit."

And off he went to Old Demdike's Neck for a spot of the old

'hair-of-the-dog', the fool.

THE WITCH AND JET SPLINTERS

Part 1: A Bustle In The Hedgerow

PARCHMENT 11

Some Kind of Devillry

It's all go, isn't it?

While Mr Crook was unsuccessfully attempting to get someone to help him to get back into his house, Jinny, Riz, Lou, Jet, Spike, Stripes, Slinky and various pixies and faeries were having a relaxing afternoon by the faerie hedgerow.

Apart from Wilf and his helpers who were still clearing the bramble bushes.

Thankfully, the honey wine wasn't available in anything larger than a conker case because this stuff was dynamite!

"My shtars!" shlurred Jinny, "I'll never make it back home if I have any more of this"

Luckily, the cats were drinking freshly filtered dewdrops or they'd have been in a right state.

"It's certainly got a *sting* to it, I'll give you that captain." howled Miss Lou. "It has indeed" said Slinky. "I will be dropping my 'H's if I partake of any more. 'ic!"

"I need a wee." said Riz, as if it was news to anyone.

An hour or so passed as they hatched their plans over what to do with Mr Crook and how best to execute them.

"Having said all that," spoke up Jinny "He's got to get himself back in the house before we can do another thing. Tell you what, I'll nip round there now and undo the spell on it. He'll think he's going doolally! Ha! Ha!" And off she scurried, Jet in fond pursuit of his beloved mistress.

Back at the pub, Crook was having a bacon butty and a pint of Moorhouse's best bitter.

Part 1: A Bustle In The Hedgerow

He'd had time to think about the strange goings on that had befallen him and came to the conclusion that he had been hexed! Good and proper. The area had an age-old reputation for witchcraft and now it seemed it was raising its black head again.

He finished his pint and butty and made for the door, heading back towards the ironmonger's.

"Back at 3.00pm." it said on a note on the door.

"Bugger and twice bugger!" snapped Crook as he returned, once again, to 'Demmy's'.

He only had three quarters of an hour to wait until the ironmonger's reopened so it wasn't that much of an inconvenience he supposed.

"Pint of Moorhouse's best!" he called over the bar.

"Please?" said the landlord.

"Yes, PLEASE!" he scowled.

"Thank you, manners cost nothing, do they?" said the portly innkeeper, slamming the pint on the bar so the froth flew all over the place.

"Cheers!"

Crook sipped at his pint as he had to make it last. He didn't want to be over the drink driving limit.

As the clock behind the bar struck three he gulped down the final drops and set off once more for the ironmonger's shop.

He was feeling quite agitated at this point and demanded the locksmith's business card and the return of his phone.

"A bit on edge are we today sir?" said the ironmonger.

"I AM *NOT* ON EDGE!" he roared.

"There's the card and here's your phone,
fully charged it is."

"I should think it is after all this time!" said Crook crossly.
"We have to eat sir." smiled the ironmonger.
"More's the pity." replied Crook and stamped out of the shop.

He entered Nancy Redfern's number into his phone then rang it.
"Hello, Redfern's, locksmiths to the stars." came the reply.
"Oh, hello, I was wondering…"
"I'm sorry but we cannot be bothered to answer the phone right now, please leave your name and number and we'll get back to you as soon as possible."
"AAAARRRRGGGHHH!" screamed Crook down the phone.
Frustrated beyond compare, he composed himself over a period of minutes, rang the number again and left his message, crossed the road to
his car then sat in wait for the all-important call … and fell fast asleep.

It was the theme tune from Top Gear that roused Crook from his slumber.
"Hello." he mumbled groggily
"Could I speak to Russell Crook please?"
"Yes, it's me, speaking."
"Oh, right, you left me a message. It's Nancy Redfern, locksmith to the stars here"
"Great! Thanks for ringing back." said Crook enthusiastically "I need to get into my house. For some reason I can't get any keys into any locks and the windows seem like they've been welded! I know it

sounds strange but I think there's been some kind of devillry going on."
"Hmmm. Devillry you say? Well, you're in the right location for that!"
Nancy laughed. "What's your address?"
Crook passed on the details and Nancy promised to meet him there within half an hour.

"Huzzah! All done!" said Jinny mischievously, "I'm actually starting to feel a bit sorry for our Mr Crook, poor thing." then laughed uproariously. She then proceeded to mutter a low spell that wasn't audible to any of her friends:
"Bats in hats, a dancing daisy, send Russell Crook slightly crazy."
"Good oh, captain!" said a celebratory Miss Lou, oblivious to the spell "Let's go and have a celebratory snifter!"
"You always say that Miss Lou." said Jet (remember him?) "What is a
'snifter'?"
"A drink, my good cat! A DRINK!"
"Can I try one?" Jet asked
"You most certainly cannot." said Lou, half-jokingly.
"Come on then, let's get back home, it's getting nippy," said Riz. "It's making me want to wee."
"Are you coming Slinky?" asked Jinny.
"Ooh no Miss Jinny, I have a few bits and bobs to finish off here, then I am going to have a nice lavender bath."
"Ask a few fireflies to sit round the bath. It'll look very luxurious." said Spike, earnestly.
"That is not a bad idea Mr Spike, what a cosmopolitan fellow you are," said Slinky. "I shall!"

"Quick sticks then, you lot." said Jinny in her best female drill Sergeant's tone, as Riz picked a snowdrop and planted it in her crooked, conical hat.

"Ta Ra Slinky."

"Farewell Louise."

And they were gone.

Nancy Redfern screeched up to the front of the Crook residence but there was no one in sight.

She got out of her van and opened the back doors.

"No lock-busting equipment left in this van overnight." proclaimed the sticker on one of the doors, not strictly truthfully.

Out came her trusty toolbox and she marched towards the front door. She checked the windows but there didn't seem to be anything untoward with them, apart from the muck on the panes.

She next tried her universal key in the front door and opened it without a problem.

Round the back she went and the story was the same.

"Have I been lured here under false pretences?" she thought as Crook's old Range Rover pulled up behind her van.

"Any luck?" shouted Crook over the wall.

"No luck necessary, there's absolutely nothing wrong with your windows or mechanisms. Is this the right house?"

"Yeah, course it is," said Crook, baffled "Let me see…"

He went around to every door and window, even the shed and everything was as it should be.

"I'm baffled," said Crook, still baffled. "Maybe it's that flamin'whiskey to blame."

"Not that Green Antler stuff ?" said Nancy, knowingly.

Part 1: A Bustle In The Hedgerow

"That's the one. Have you had something like this happen to you from it?" "Certainly haven't," giggled Nancy "I wouldn't touch that stuff with *your* barge pole but I know a few that it's, shall we say, 'affected'."

"So I'm not going mad? Just the effects of a dodgy drink? What a relief!"

"Probably," said Nancy. "Or you've upset someone you shouldn't have ..."

After Nancy Redfern, locksmith to the stars, had departed Russell Crook had a good think about who he might have upset. There were so many to choose from!

Then he thought about the possibility of insanity, again, altogether probable.

Then his mind wandered back to Demonia Cottage 2 ...

Pentagrams, broomsticks, owls, witches and that demonic black thing that was flying about.

"Has that Lane woman got something to do with this?" he pondered, "and those other two…and the cats…and the hats…"

He leapt into his car and drove for all his worth towards Jinny's house, screeching around tight bends and speedily passing the ladies (and cats) on the way without even noticing them.

Not only was he driving - he was driven! Like a man, oh wait… possessed.

At length, the car neared the cottage and skidded to a halt.

Crook dived out, ran up to the front door and hammered loudly on the black, bat shaped knocker.

No answer. "Is this woman *ever* in?!" he yelled to himself.

He sat on the wall and plotted his next course of action. He wasn't going the back way, that's for sure! "I'll climb up to the roof and go down the chimney … don't be ridiculous!" he scolded himself.
He was a very impatient man, so five minutes seemed like an hour.
He searched in his pockets, trying to find a scrap of paper. All he had was
Nancy Redfern's business card, so he pulled out his cheap ballpoint pen and wrote on the back "I know what you're up to" then added "and don't think I don't!".
He posted it through the letterbox, sweating profusely and made his way back to the car.
As it was en route, the thought came upon him that he may as well head down to Demmy's for a couple of pints in a bid to calm himself down, so off he shot, racing down the lanes like a crazed rally driver. *Vroooom*!

The exhaust smoke was still hanging in the air as Jinny, Lou, Riz, Jet, Spike and Stripes ambled up to the front gate.
"Blimey! What a whiff!" said Miss Riz wafting her hand under her nose. "Those fumes are highly toxic you know!" Riz continued, with a cigarette dangling from the corner of her mouth.
"Shouldn't those cats be on a leash?" said a nosey, horsey kind of woman as she looked up in passing.
"*You* should be, lady!" shouted Miss Lou whilst pulling a funny face.
The woman shook her head and walked on while Miss Riz gave her a strident 'V' sign behind her.

Jinny fanned her hand in the air, whispered something and the haughty woman went flying, flat on her face, as if she had tripped over an invisible rug.

"Ha, ha and thrice ha," rasped Lou. "El Snooto!"

PARCHMENT 12

Merry Meet Miss Redfern

Jinny magically unlocked the front door and they all piled inside, wiping their feet on the tattered porch mat on the way in.

“Bacardi please captain Jin. Two lumps.” squealed Lou.

“Got any Prosecco darling?” said Miss Riz, sounding for all the world like Patsy from Ab Fab.

“And water for us.” said Jet dejectedly.

Lou turned ‘round and lifted the shiny, black cat up into her arms, planting a big, red kiss, once again, on the top of his head.

“I *do* love your new collar Jet. It makes you look very dashing, see …” and she held him up to the mirror by the door.

“Oh!” she said, in mock surprise, “I can only see the collar Jet. You’ve disappeared!”

“You know as well as we all do Lou, that a witch’s cat’s reflection can’t be seen.” said Jinny.

“I didn’t know!” Jet said, a bit startled.

“Well you do now, so you’ll be better off avoiding mirrors and clear, still ponds and suchlike from now on,” winked Jinny “Unless you want to purposely freak people out.”

“So,” said Jet. “So far, I can walk through doors without opening them, hear distant sounds and not be seen in a mirror. Is that it?”

“For now. Magic is a continuous learning curve Jetty, you have to have patience and you must have experiences to draw upon. All will come to he who waits.” said Jinny mysteriously, whilst pouring the drinkie poos for Lou and Riz.

Part 1: A Bustle In The Hedgerow

"Fire on!" said Riz, pointing a long index finger towards the hearth. "This cold is making me want the toilet."

Lou and Jinny rolled their eyes upwards and laughed out loud as the flames appeared in the grate. There could only ever be one Miss Riz.

"Jinny," mewed Jet. "There's a card behind the door …"

Down in Windlestraws village, Mr Crook had miraculously reached his destination and was striding across the square to Old Demdike's Neck.

His head was in a tizzy and he really didn't feel himself.

He had just wasted almost two days which should have been spent on attending to the minutiae of his golf course proposals.

Tomorrow he would start in earnest, for now he needed to empty his head and relax.

So why was he going to a busy pub?

He veered round, headed for the off license store and purchased a bumper pack of classic mixed English real ales. And a large packet of cheese and onion crisps.

He got in his car and set off, back to the newly unlocked place he called

'home'.

Crook didn't drive as madly as he had earlier, he had calmed his brain and told it to behave a little less erratically.

As he passed Demonia Cottage 2, he could see the smoke rising from the chimney that he had earlier had the mind to climb down.

"She's in at last," he thought. "Well I'll just let her dwell on my message and see what happens next."

"What happens next?! It's almost threatening is that." said Lou pointing at the business card.

"I'm going to ring Nancy Redfern and see what all this is about." Jinny said defiantly. She picked up the receiver of her antique 50's style telephone and dialled the number …

"Hello, Nancy Redfern, locksmith to the …"

"You posted your card through my door missy, together with a rather cryptic message. What is it that you think I'm up to then?" growled Jinny.

"Who is this? I don't post cards through doors, though maybe I should. Not a bad idea actually." came the reply.

"This is Jinny Lane at Demonia Cottage (2) and I have your business card here with what seems to me like a threat written on the back of it!"

"I think you'll find that wasn't my doing Mrs Lane. The only cards I've ever posted have been through shops and none of them had 'threats' written on the back of them. They're not good for business!"

"I see … yes, makes sense. Are you busy?" asked Jinny, brightening up a little.

"I never know when I'm going to be busy. Everything's an emergency with this line of work. Why, are you locked out?"

"Of course I'm not locked out! I was wondering if you could find time to call round for a chat. I'll make you a brew."

"I could," said Nancy tentatively, "but if an emergency comes in I'll have to be off sharpish."

"Fair enough," said Jinny. "How about within the hour?"

"I'll set off now, just in case." said Nancy.

Part 1: A Bustle In The Hedgerow

"Thank you very much indeed and blessed be." smiled Jinny.

"Blessed be? That's … oh … nothing … see you in a wee while." and Nancy was gone.

All this time, the odious Mr Crook had got himself home, unlocked the front door (it worked!) and put his beer into the fridge to chill.

He turned his unromantic gas fire on and lay himself down on his beige, faux velvet couch, replete with those pointless little tassels.

Picking up the TV remote, he went through the dozens of channels available then decided there wasn't anything worth watching, not even an obscure football game or a brutal murder story.

He propped his head on an equally beige, velvet cushion and lay there, munching crisps, thinking all the time.

Nancy Redfern pulled up alongside the front wall of Demonia Cottage and walked up the stone steps to the front door.

"Ooh, I like that." she thought, admiring the bat shaped knocker and rapped it gently, just twice.

Jinny answered the door and bade the visitor inside.

"Jinny Lane - sorry if I came across badly on the phone."

"Nancy Redfern, locksmith to …"

"Yes, yes I know all that."

Nancy took in the ambience of Jinny's other worldly home. "What a place!" she thought, "I could live here."

"The harpy with the scarlet hair and lippy is Miss Lou and this blonde minx is Miss Riz," said Jinny. "And our cats, Jet, Spike and Stripes."

"Merry meet!" they all chanted.

"Merry meet!" said Nancy back, because, believe it or not, Nancy was no stranger to witchery!

"Are you? Are you …"

"A witch? Yes I am Miss Jinny, and so are you lot if I'm not mistaken!" Nancy giggled. "Blessed be!"

Back at the Crook abode the ale bottles had been removed from the fridge

(you can't have real ale *too* chilled you know) and Mr C had decided to listen to the radio.

He'd tuned in to one of those local, late night phone-in chat shows that they run in the early evening.

It was all his uncultured head could take to listen to a large quantity of music so this did the job just fine.

"Now, Kylie Higgins, tell me about this werewolf you claim to have seen on the hills…" said the announcer.

"Oooh, it were big and hairy and had them claws and things and roared and things. Then it ran off."

"Did you see any detail on this apparition." asked the Radio presenter.

"What's an appar … apperishern?" said Kylie

"A ghostly form, a shape, a shadow…"

"It were a werewolf I'm telling yer. I've seen 'em on films and that's what it were."

"Not a large dog, or a tramp or an escaped panther?"

"No, a werewolf, on the hills. It had tatty trousers just like they do on films."

"I see. Probably best to stay away from the hills in future then, eh Kylie? You might get filmed! Ha Ha"

"I'd like to be filmed. I sent a selfie to a model agency in Barnley you know. That's what I want to be - a model."

"Well, make sure you don't get near any more werewolves then, eh? You don't want your looks spoiling." said the announcer condescendingly.

"My Dad was a model."

"Was he indeed?"

"Yes, oven gloves. He used to model oven gloves."

"Thank you for your call Kylie ..."

PARCHMENT 13

Nutter

"What are your views on sparklers Nancy?" asked Riz.

"What? The fireworks sparklers?" said Nancy.

"Yes, what are your views on them?"

"I'd have to be perfectly honest with you Riz and say I have absolutely no opinion on sparklers whatsoever. Never have had." said Nancy.

"Oh. Fair dos." said Riz while everyone stared at her quizzically.

"Erm, well, that's that out of the way," laughed Jinny nervily. "Now then, here's the card that came through my door, oh, would you like a drink Nancy?"

"Thank you, just a black coffee please, no sugar."

"Easy." said Jinny. "Lou, would you be so kind as to rustle up a brew for

Miss Nancy please?"

And Lou clicked her fingers and the brew was there, on a saucer with one of those tiny, nondescript biscuits.

"Wow! Thanks Lou." said Nancy, awestruck.

"Mon pleasure captain." said Lou

"That's French, isn't it Lou?" chimed young Jet.

"Mais oui." purred Lou with a saucy smile.

"I like that." said Jet.

"Gomez." said Jinny, rolling her eyes.

"What beautiful cats you have. Have they cut their heads?" asked Nancy, concernedly. "It's a Lou thing!" smiled Riz.

"As I was saying, this card that came through my letterbox … a bit of a silly question but have you any idea who it might have come from?" enquired Jinny.

Part 1: A Bustle In The Hedgerow

"Let me have a gander," said Nancy. "It's from the ironmonger's shop, I know that because I mark each card with a different dayglo colour for each shop I send them to. That way, I know where customers get them from and I can send more back to whichever shop dealt it out, if that makes sense? This has an orange dot so it's the ironmonger's."

"Why would the ironmonger be threatening me? I've always got on with him and I've never done him any harm."

"It won't be him, it'll be someone he gave it to." reasoned Nancy.

"What time does he close today? About 5pm isn't it? Too late. I'll ring him tomorrow and see who he's been dishing cards out to. Thank you so very much for your help, Nancy. A very clever idea by the way."

"Not as clever as magicking a cup of coffee though, eh?" she replied.

"Can you not do that? I'll teach you if you like. You're welcome to come round anytime you like dear. Consider yourself one of us." said Jinny and gave Nancy a big hug and told her to take a seat.

"Redfern … that name rings a bell" said Riz, out of the blue. "You're not related to the Redfernes are you? You know, old Chattox's brood?"

"It seems I am Miss Riz. The 'e' at the end got lost over the years, for some reason."

"That's Wiccan royalty that is," Lou informed her. "Your ancestors were
hanged for witchcraft at Gallows Hill, Lancaster. 1612 it was."

"Woooh! Princess Nancy." teased Riz.

"I've never met a Princess before." said Jet and bowed his lipstick covered head.

“Steady on now,” laughed Nancy. “I’m a Locksmith you know!”

“To the stars!” sang Lou. “Which stars have you locksmithed for Nancy?”

“Oh, well, only one really … remember The Hollies, from the 60’s?”

“And beyond” said Riz.

“Aye, well, it was the drummer from them. It was the day that he unveiled that statue of Alice Nutter down in Toughlee. He’d rented a cottage out for the week and had lost the keys so that’s where I nicked in.”

“How fascinating,” said Jinny. “Was he rich beyond your wildest hopes?” “I - I never asked. He was very pleasant though,” replied Nancy, “and he gave me a tenner tip.”

“Loaded!” chanted Riz, Lou and Jinny together.

At that point Nancy’s phone rang to the theme tune of ‘Bewitched’.

“Heeey! We’ve all got that ringtone! Do you watch Bewitched Nance?” asked Jinny.

“I do, I download the episodes and watch them back on the TV from a memory stick. Every night. Excuse me a second … Hello, Redfern’s - Locksmiths to the stars.”

The caller’s husband, it turns out, had somehow managed to lock his mother-in-law in her Granny Annex and the keys had been mysteriously missing for over two hours!

The mother-in-law was of course frantic and it didn’t help that her dog was locked in with her and he desperately needed a poo.

“Where are you Mrs Wagstaff? Marley Lane. Yes, I’m only ‘round the corner, I’ll be with you within the next twenty minutes. Bye!”

Part 1: A Bustle In The Hedgerow

"I've got to dash ladies," said Nancy, "but I'll be back if you'll have me and don't forget to let me know how you get on with the threat thing, won't you?"
Nancy finished her brew, flew out of the door and zoomed off in her van. Was it mentioned that the sticker on the other back door of the van read
"Powered by a Wendle Witch"? What a synchronicity!

Mr Crook had, meanwhile, finished half of the box of classic English ales and was now comatose on the couch, halfway close to falling off the blessed thing.
He had spilled cheese and onion crisps all over the front of his shirt, complimented by the odd spattering of beer.
The radio was still playing away to itself. By now the programme had changed to one of those easy listening type of shows. Bland, boring and innocuous but then who was even listening?
He awoke abruptly to the sound of dinking and chinking at his window panes.
"What the blood ..." he grumbled sleepily and staggered boozily over to the window.
It was dark by now and due to the lack of street lights almost completely black outside.
Dink! Chink! went the noises on
the glass.
"What the hell's going on now?!"
he breathed angrily.
He couldn't see them, but a gang of pixies had taken it upon themselves to irritate Mr Crook by pogging stones at his windows. They were taking their aim at the 'O's of the 'BOO!' that Miss Riz had scrawled on the pane, seeing who could get nearest the middle. "What fun" they thought, collectively.
Crook strode woozily to the front door and called out "Who's there? What the bloody hell are yer playin' at?"

One more stone hit the window, bang on target and the pixies legged it off back to the faerie hedgerow, where everyone else was sleeping soundly. “It’s getting weirder by the minute this place.” Crook said under his breath, which was quite visible in the cold doorway.
It’s not like there were any neighbours or the kind of place you would pass by at night.
So what, indeed, *was* going on?
“I’ll have another bottle then get to bed,” he thought. “Work tomorrow.” The radio then decided to turn itself up to eleven and blast Crook with the sound of a thousand, soothing violins. Mantovani’s revenge!
“I despair!” Crook yelled, heard by nobody. “I bloody well despair.”

THE WITCH AND JET SPLINTERS

Part 1: A Bustle In The Hedgerow

PARCHMENT 14

Part 1

Bribery and Corruption

A new, miserable looking kind of day dawned and back at Demonia Cottage 2 the ensemble of Witches and cats made their dozy way downstairs to prepare for the day ahead.

"Anyone having any breakfast this morning?" Lou decided to ask as the six of them were lolling around on various chairs, couches, rugs and places.

"Fire on!" Riz said dopily. "… what was that screech?"

"I'll have some crunchy nut cornflakes if you're asking." said Jinny.

"Bacon, sausage, beans and mushrooms for me." said Riz helpfully.

"Are there any tins of Tuna in sunflower oil left?" asked Jet.

"Jimmy Jeez!" shrieked Lou. "I was only asking! Not volunteering!"

"Oh just magic it up Lou," said Jinny. "Surely that's no hardship?"

Lou closed her eyes, waved her hands in a circular motion and all of them had their breakfasts in front of them. On trays. With a tiny flower on each.

"Ta Lou," said Riz. "You're a star."

"Every man, every woman, is a star … allegedly." said Lou, sarcastically.

"I didn't know that." Riz said vacantly.

"Book of the Law. Aleister Crowley, 1904." Lou smugly replied.

Part 1: A Bustle In The Hedgerow

"You're a proper little font of knowledge, you are Lou." said her very good friend.

"And you do know that you're each capable of magicking your own breakfasts up, don't you?" Lou said, somewhat miffed. Lou wasn't a 'morning person'.

"Yeah, but it tastes better when someone else magics it up." smiled Riz, lighting up the first of many morning ciggies.

"Who lit the fire?!"
screamed Jinny.

"Twas me." said Riz.

"Well Stripes was still asleep in the grate, didn't you know?! She always kips there - warmest place in the house!"

"She's mental that cat," Lou lamented. "Is she alright?"

"Just a few singed whiskers, she'll live." said Jinny "I do wish you'd check things first Riz."

"Fire out!" waved Riz and out it went.

"It's a bit late now, isn't it? The damage is done!" said Jinny exasperatedly. "Fire on!" waved Riz without a blink and everyone continued, cosily, with their breakfasts.

Jinny leaned back in the old wooden chair at the dining table (sounds posh - it wasn't) still dressed in her favourite Chewbacca dressing gown and Zebra slippers.

"I'm going to ring the ironmonger and see if he can tell me anything." she said to no one in particular.

She got out her battered Yellow Pages directory and found the number. "Hello, I wonder if you could help me. Could you tell me please if you gave out one of the Locksmith's business cards to anyone yesterday?" Jinny politely asked.

"Yes, I did as a matter of fact, just the one. It was to a surly fellow, looked like he hadn't slept, a bit of a portly chap, breath smelt of stale booze. Very rude sort of demeanour. I wasn't too keen on him at all. Why? Has something untoward happened?"

"Crook!" Jinny said to herself "No, no, I was just checking, for a friend like, just checking if there had been any custom generated from the cards, you know?"

"Yes, yes. We're giving out two or three a week!" said the ironmonger enthusiastically.

"As many as that?!" said Jinny stifling a snigger. "That's good news indeed. Thank you so much for your assistance. Goodbye."

"He's for it! He's for it *tonight*!" said Jinny in a very aggravated voice "Girls, prepare your broomsticks … we're on a mission!"

"I'd better go and have a wee then." said Riz predictably and everyone in the room looked to the heavens and shook their heads, even Raph.

Jinny called Jet and took him aside "Jetty my love, today I'm going to teach you how to become invisible. How do you fancy that then?"

"Sounds fantastic! I'm up for that, definitely." the youngster replied.

"Right, let's go off into the back garden, away from the others and we'll get cracking. It's actually not as tricky as you might think …"

"Back in an hour or two girls. I'm just off to show Jet something." Jinny said as she made her way to the back door. "Won't be long! Help yourself to anything."

Then, on the way out, she stopped Jet in his tracks and said "Tomorrow

I'm going to get Spike to give you some lessons in scrapping."
"Scrapping what? Is that like rooting through bins?" wondered Jet aloud.
"Is it 'eckerslike, yer daft lad. Fighting. Proper martial arts cat fighting. Spike is the champion when it comes to that sort of thing. You wouldn't think it with his laid-back attitude, would you?" said Jinny. "Nobody picks on Spike!"
"Blimey!" said Jet. "It all happens at once 'round here, don't it?"
"Doesn't it?" snapped Jinny, ever so slightly school-ma'am-ishly.

Now might be a good point in the proceedings to give you all a reminder that not all witches are loveable, beautiful and kind.
And such was the woman that one Mr Russell Crook had an appointment with at the Council offices of the local Town Hall.
Isobel Mortem was the town planner and it was her job to,
quote:
'ensure that development was sustainable and that the right balance of development was achieved to preserve the countryside' unquote. Whatever that meant!
What it kind of meant was that someone would go to her with an idea, say, they wanted to build a piggery near a local 'A' road, on a green and fine patch of land, show her their plans, she would go over the plans, look for anything that might not be in keeping with the designated area and say
"No! you can't do that".

What it meant in reality, was, for example, Mr Crook would show her plans for a new golf course in a beautiful, unspoiled, rural area, she would say, "Definitely not!" and he would say, "Well, what if I gave you £10,000 pounds cash, just for you, in your back pocket, as it were, no questions asked?" and she would say, "Hmmm, let me think about it, I'm sure there will be a way around it".
And such is the way a lot of 'business' is conducted.

Isobel Mortem was very well aware that the area Mr Crook was interested in developing was home to faeries and pixies and all manner of woodland creatures.
She was a witch after all and local at that, and she wasn't a nice witch, put it that way.
To be fair to Mr Crook, odious as he was, he was not aware of such things, nor did he even believe in them.
He just liked the layout of the land and saw it as an excellent opportunity to make lots of money.

"Would you care to meet me at Old Demdike's Neck tonight, around 7.00pm and we could discuss this further, in private" said Crook.
"What is your phone number? I'll ring you back later in the afternoon and inform you of my availability." came the haughty reply.
Crook gave her his number, shook her hand and made his way out of the offices.
As he got out into the street, he rubbed his hands gleefully and smiled, thinking, "I've got this in the bag! No danger."

Back at Demonia Cottage 2 Jinny had taught Jet the simplest way to make himself invisible.

Part 1: A Bustle In The Hedgerow

I can't tell you how it's done, it's a secret, but take it from me, Jet was now fully conversant in the art of invisibility and he was feeling very empowered. "That was sooo easy Jinny, I can't believe it." he said proudly.

"Only easy when you know how, Jetty boy." said Jinny, sagely. "Let's get back and see what that lot are up to, eh?"

And off they toddled, all the way from the back of the back garden to the back door.

"Get the kettle on Riz!" Jinny said. "and lend us a cig will you please, I'm all out."

"Certainly madam. I'll just nip to the loo first. Two minutes - hang on."

"Can that woman do anything without the lavatory being involved?!" exclaimed Jinny as Jet laughed a catty laugh.

Finally, the six of them settled down together around the kitchen table. Jinny took it upon herself to be the spokeswoman.

"As you know, the message on the card came from Russell Crook …"

"Ooh! Did it?" Riz butted in. "I didn't know that. Nobody tells me anything."

"Actually, neither did I Jin." said Lou.

"I did!" said Jet.

Spike and Stripes had gone back to sleep.

"… well it did … and tonight we're going to launch a blitzkrieg on the Crook household. Broomsticks, spells, paranormal activity, the whole shebang! Are you up for it?"

"Aye captain!" said Lou holding her hand in the air.

"Count me in cap." Riz said, nonchalantly.

"I think so …" said Jet hesitantly as Lou picked him up and planted the day's first layer of lipstick on his head.

"Spike and Stripes - goes without saying. Now, here's the plan. Riz, listen carefully for once …" and Jinny went on to lay out the plot she had hatched. Over half an hour it took!

Back in town, in one of those lurid pound shops, Mr Crook's mobile phone buzzed in his pocket.

It was the Mortem woman agreeing to meet him at the pub at the proposed time of 7.00pm.

"Ha! It's a sealed deal. Fore!" he jabbered as he paid the requisite one pound for the 'Elite Back Scratcher' he had happened upon earlier.

"This is going to be a magical evening." he said to himself. Little did he
know …

"Right, so we're all au fait with what we're doing, are we?" checked Jinny. "French." said Jet dreamily.

"Gomez." said Jinny quietly.

"Right as rain captain." Lou assured her.

"Riz! Are you actually awake?" asked Jinny prodding the blonde one's nose.

"I am Miss Jinny, I am. Sorry, it's the weather …"

"*What's* the weather?!" gasped Jinny.

"Grey clouds … they affect me you know …" Riz said glazedly.

"What in the name of Pan's Labyrinth are you on about woman? There are no grey clouds! We're in the kitchen!" stated Jinny.

"*We're* in the kitchen but the grey clouds are outside …"

"I can't believe we're having this conversation. Right, so, the grey clouds, outside, are affecting you … in what way?" asked Jinny impatiently. "Remember when I was a little girl? I had a pet Tarantula called Cyril?" Riz went on, with tears welling up.

"Yes, we remember Cyril. How could we forget?" said Lou.

"The light of my life that lad was. I used to spend hours hunting crickets and mice for him. I even knitted him a jumper, remember? It had 'Cyril -
Beware!' written on it in big yellow letters …"

"Like we needed reminding Riz, yes." said Jinny with a concerned look.

"Well … didn't you ever wonder what happened to him?" said Riz sadly. "I presumed you grew up, got fed up of pampering him and let him out in the wilds or summat." said Lou.

"No, no I didn't" cried Riz. "I couldn't have done that, never."

The group drew in closer as Riz's voice began to go lower than usual, which was quite low.

"One day, I was on the loo, having a wee and reading a magazine when he jumped up on my leg. He fell off and went straight down the toilet. Sank without a trace. I've been m-mentally scarred from that day."

"Only since *that* day?" laughed Jinny trying to make light of the situation.

"So where do the grey clouds come into this?" asked Lou, intrigued. "Well, it was a grey, cloudy day when it happened" wept Riz.

Jinny and Lou looked at one another incredulously.

"And that's it? That's the tale of why grey clouds 'affect' you?" choked
Jinny. "In all my life I don't think I've ever heard the like …"

"Here," Lou said to Riz. "Have a cig and buck up!"
"That might explain why she's always running off to the loo." said Jet wisely.
"Maybe she goes in the blind hope that one day, Cyril will emerge from the toilet."
"Very philosophical, young Jet," said Lou. "Is that right Riz? Are you secretly hoping that one day a visit to the lavvy will bring your Cyril back?"
"No, I just go for a wee." Riz sobbed.

While these pearls of wisdom were being imparted, Mr Crook had driven home and had begun the process of preparing himself for his meeting with Isobel Mortem.
The lord only knows why he was making such an effort. Ms Mortem was, after all, a scabby old battle axe with a personality to match, but in Crook's mind, presentation was everything. If only he thought that way every day.
Out came his antique bottle of Paco Rabanne (pour homme) after shave, which he had bought in a charity shop in the eighties, then the turquoise silk kipper tie, again, purchased in a charity shop at some point in the seventies, a musty smelling blue pin striped suit and a pair of scuffed, ox blood loafers completed the, erm, picture.
Oh, and let us please not forget the off-white polyester shirt.
This was obtained only recently (otherwise it would never have fastened) from one of those ads in the colour supplements. You know, the ones where everything's polyester or crimpolene? Although new, it still had the appearance of a well-worn ten year old.
He laid the articles carefully out on his bed and skidded over to the running bath to add some bubble bath. 'Matey'! Remember that mums and dads? Grans? Class.

Part 1: A Bustle In The Hedgerow

In the meantime, Isobel Mortem was making no such preparations and was heading to the meeting straight from work, via a Witch Way Bus (Yes! They exist!) with her man bag over her shoulder.

It would have been wiser to bring her broomstick because the Witch Way

Bus doesn't journey into the wilds of the village of Windlestraws, which is where Old Demdike's pub is located. This, very sadly, meant poor old Miz Mortem had a long, cold country stroll in front of her.

"Hey guys!" Jinny shouted, still back at the homestead and making ready for the assault on the Crook dwelling "I've just realised, It's only twenty-nine days to Christmas! That's twenty-five days to Yule!"

"So what?" said Riz gloomily. "I hate Christmas." A short pause followed "I *do* like Christmas trees though. And Reindeer. Father Christmas, oh and Christmas pudding. Sprouts too."

"And presents?" asked Lou mischievously

"Oh yeah! Presents, that goes without saying," beamed Riz. "And snow. I love snow. Especially when I'm indoors. And parties, lots of parties. Chocolates and Brandy and all. Love 'em! Holly …" she added.

"So … what part of Christmas is it that you *don't* like?" asked Jinny, intrigued.

"Adverts." said Riz.

"You don't like Christmas because of adverts? That's it?!" Lou rolled her eyes habitually.

"They get right on my nerves they do. Buy this, buy that. You can't really love someone unless you buy them …*this*… you can't be a very nice person unless you buy …*that* … scandalous it is. Can't be doing with it." said Riz preachily.

"R*iiigh*t. Got ya. So, basically, the moral of this tale, which I now wish I hadn't even started, is, erm, if you don't like adverts … turn the TV off, isn't it?" Jinny said philosophically.

"Suppose it is, yeah." admitted Riz, blowing smoke rings.

"It's all immaterial anyway, we don't actually celebrate Christmas, do we?" Jinny reminded them.

"I must say, I *do* like Walpurgisnacht." said Lou, ignoring Jinny's statement.

"That's a Spring festival though, isn't it Lou?" said Jinny

"It is. But I love that song by Faun* - always makes me feel Christmassy."

*(Faun are a German Pagan Rock band that wrote a song by the title of "Walpurgisnacht", by the way).

"Even though it's a song celebrating a Spring festival?" quizzed Jinny.

"Yeaaah" said Lou, glazily.

And that was the end of the conversation with regards to Christmas. For now, anyway.

The man they call Crook was, meanwhile, languishing in his foamy tub, ponging of Matey bubble bath.

"The beginning of an era," he whispered to himself. "An Empire even! Dum de dum de dum …" he hummed ecstatically to no tune in particular, with not an inkling of what time it was.

Isobel Mortem was still winding her way through the wintry lanes on her journey to Windlestraws, shivering, muttering and going on with herself, as town planners do.

Part 1: A Bustle In The Hedgerow

“Blimey! It’s half past six!” shrieked Mr Crook, still bathing and going crinklier by the minute.

He hopped out of the bath tub, grabbed a towel and hurriedly rubbed himself down.

As luck would have it, he didn’t have much hair to dry so it was just a case of getting dressed and diving in the car, which he did with all speed. Down the lanes he darted and into the village, like a man still possessed.

He got to Old Demdike’s with about nine minutes to spare, and ordered a whiskey.

“Not that Green Antler stuff, thank you!” he shouted across the bar. “I’ll have a pint of bitter too.” he said bluntly as his whiskey arrived.

“Please?” said the Landlord. “Yes, PLEASE!” he barked.

“Meeting someone are we?” asked the Barman

“None of your bloody business!” came the harsh reply and off he swaggered, over towards the roaring log fire.

It was around 7.22pm when Miz Mortem walked through the door, trembling and still muttering.

By this time Crooky boy had downed 2 pints of bitter and three whiskies.

“Lost your way Mrs Mortem?” he enquired.

“Miss!” she replied. “Miss Mortem.”

“Sorry. Spinster then are you?”

“Nothing to do with you, what I am or what my persuasions are. We’re not here to make small talk. Let’s get this sorted, then I can be on my way.” said Miz Mortem sullenly.

“Want a drink then? Absinthe maybe? Hemlock on the rocks?” asked Crook.

“Do they do hot drinks here? I wouldn’t mind a hot chocolate …” she said, still feeling a tad nippy.

“I’ll go and see.” and off he went back to the bar.

"Hey pal … do you do hot chocolate?"
"Coffee and tea, a milk shake at a push. It's not a Bistro you know." came the answer.
Crook had a few seconds thought then said, "I'll have a chocolate milk shake and stick it in the microwave for a minute or two, eh? In a cup."
"If you insist." said the Bar chap, raising his eyebrows.
A minute and a half later he came back with the hot milk shake and placed it on the bar. "One pound seventy please"
"Bloody Hell! I could have bought nearly two bottles of milk for that!" he whinged.
"There's chocolate syrup, electricity and labour included in that." came the terse reply.
Crook humphed and carried the cup over to the miserable old bat by the fireplace.
"There you are *Miss*. One steaming hot chocolate."
"Thank you. Very kind. Much needed I must say." Mortem replied as she took a sip of the drink and immediately spat it into the fire.
"What in the world is that supposed to be?!" she cried.
"Hot chocolate." said Crook.
"It's hot something but it's not like any hot chocolate I've ever tasted. Take it back!"
"How about a nice coffee instead?" said Crook, realising he might have been rumbled.
"Anything but that!" demanded Mortem.
So off he trawled, back to the bar for a replacement.
"Hey up pal … apparently this is not like any hot chocolate she's ever tasted. Can we have a coffee instead?"
"I'm not surprised," said the barman. "Let's try it …" and he took a small sip of the beverage in question. "You're right, it isn't like any hot chocolate at all -

Part 1: A Bustle In The Hedgerow

Glenda! Did you actually put chocolate in this milk shake?"
"Chocolate? Yes, why?" shouted his wife, Glenda, from over the other side of the bar.
"Well you try this and tell me if it tastes like chocolate." said the barman angrily.
"Do I have to? I don't like drinking from other people's cups," moaned Glenda as she gingerly put the drink to her lips. "Ewww no! That's butterscotch I think."
"Look, can I just have a coffee? Do we have to go through all this rigmarole?" Crook said testily.
"Coffee milk shake or a straight coffee sir?" said the barman caustically.
"Just a normal, white coffee if it's not too much to ask?"
"Please?"
"F-f-f … PLEASE!!!" bawled Crook.
And so, after about ten minutes of haggling and bickering, Crook at last returned to Isobel Mortem with a coffee.
"Hope this is OK?" he said apologetically. "Apparently they'd given you a
butterscotch milk…, sorry, hot butterscotch, by mistake."
"Hot butterscotch? I've never heard the like." said Mortem as she finally settled down to discussing the business in hand.

By this time, Demonia Cottage 2 was a hive of activity and preparation.
"Now then, you've all got your wands, haven't you? Broomsticks? Hats?
Infra-red goggles?" asked Jinny.
"Infra-red goggles? I haven't got any of them!" said Riz, confused.

"I've got Infra-red lipstick!" came Lou's reply

"It was a joke, girls, calm down." said Jinny. "Now, battle commences at the witching hour, midnight, obviously, so while we're waiting, would you like to watch some TV or maybe have a little nap or something?"

"Stick 'Escape to the Country' on Jinno, but make sure it isn't an episode where they've got, like, nine hundred thousand quid to spend, will you?" said Lou. "It gets right up my nose how some people manage to get their hands on that kind of money. I mean, they're not film stars or Rock stars, are they?"

"Corruption." said Riz.

"What?" asked Jinny and Lou.

"They've acquired that kind of money by devious means, if you ask me." continued Riz, blowing cig smoke up the chimney. "Probably murdered a rich Aunt or blackmailed someone ..."

"Put an episode of Bewitched on Jinny, I've lost the will to watch 'Escape to the Country'." Lou said despondently.

"So, that's that, all done and dusted," said Crook with a smile on his face, for once. "We can start the building and excavation work from Monday the 9th of January."

"Yes, indeed. Now, please bear in mind what I told you about the folklore surrounding the area, will you? It could all get very nasty if you're not careful." said Mortem gravely, as she stuffed a large envelope into her man bag.

"That kind of thing doesn't bother me Miz Mortem. Do I look like the kind of man that believes in faeries and elves?" laughed Crook, the overpowering whiff of Paco

Rabanne aftershave suddenly hitting the back of Mortem's throat.
"Cough! You don't, not at all, maybe you should try reading up on the subject?" wheezed the old misery guts.
"I've got better things to do with my time than to trouble myself with that load of old wives' tales" said Crook confidently. "Fore!" he added and rose to leave his seat.
And with that, the odd couple shook hands in a not particularly friendly fashion and went their separate ways.
He didn't even ask if she wanted a lift! Pah! She didn't deserve one and anyway, she could afford a thousand taxi's now, if she so wished. Not that there were any available.

Crook, ten thousand pounds lighter, started the engine of his ancient Range Rover and screeched off towards the bland bungalow he called home.
Miz Mortem started her long, dark stroll back down the way she came, hoping the Witch Way buses were still running once she reached the town centre.

"Three hours to go!" announced Jinny dramatically. "Actually, better make it two and three quarters …"
Nobody was listening, as Lou, Riz, Jet, Spike, Stripes and Raph had all dozed off.
Log fires have a habit of affecting you that way.
Crook's car was just passing Jinny's house. She could *feel* he was in the vicinity, as the hairs on the back of her neck stood on end.
"Don't get too comfy, matey." she said in a very low voice.

Crook finally pulled up opposite his house, parked the car and swaggered up the driveway, full of a new-found confidence. There was no stopping him now.

Once inside, he poured himself a very large whiskey, turned on the radio and lay down on the couch.

It was another local phone-in chat show on the radio but Crook wasn't really paying much heed.

"Who do we have on the line now please?" asked the announcer, Bobby Razzler.

"It's Stanley, Stanley Higginbottom, hello there." replied the

Septuagenarian at the other end of the line.

"And what are your thoughts on tonight's chosen topic: Are there still witches operating in the Wendle area? …"

"There are indeed and I'll tell you that for *nowt* Bobby!" came the answer.

"I'm convinced my wife is one."

"Really? How's that?" the radio chappie, asked.

"She looks like one!" said the old man emphatically.

"Does she? How fascinating. And how, in your mind, does a witch look?" probed the announcer.

"Well, she's got one of those big noses with a kind of wart on it, she's got hardly any teeth, one of her eyes turns in and her hair's white and scraggy! And she's got a broom!"

"But isn't her appearance that way because she's an old lady?"

"She's only forty-seven!" said the old fellow.

"Surely she would have had to have had a rather hard life to look that way at forty-seven?"

"Hang on, I'll ask her. Elsie! … Elsie! How old are you?"

"Seventy-four!" said Elsie

"Oh, she's seventy-four. My mistake, sorry." said the confused old chap. "She makes broth and I once saw her talking to a frog." he added, quietly. "Hmmm. Does she do spells, or fly or anything like that?" asked the broadcaster.

"She's been out, at night time, when it's dark and she has something to do with that 'Save our English Bats' society."

"Who are you talking to Stanley?" shouted Elsie

"Bobby Razzler on the radio, wanting to know about witches"

A few seconds passed in silence then a sound, like the sound of a rolled-up newspaper hitting a head, was heard and the line went dead.

"Hello. Caller? Are you still there? Hello. It looks like we've lost Mr

Higginbottom, listeners. Who's on line four?"

Crook stared at the radio in disbelief, swilled down the last of his whiskey, grumbled a bit then turned it off and made for the main bedroom.

"I don't know why you didn't ask young Nance Redfern along tonight." Miss Lou said, yawning. "She seems just the type who'd be up for a bit of jiggery pokery."

"Three's a Coven and four's a crowd" Jinny smartly replied.

"And two's company!" Riz piped up.

"And…?" said Jinny.

"No idea" said Riz.

Lou threw a ciggie at each of them and the cats finally roused from their respective catnaps.

"Is it time, Jinny?" asked Jet, his eyes all slitty.

"Another hour and we're off. Then it gets *serious.*" Jinny said. "Serious? You mean like when you're really

hungry and you don't speak to anybody while you're eating? *That* serious?" said Jet naively.
"Yes, Jet - *that* serious."

"Have I got time for a wee?" said Miss Riz drowsily.
"Not if it's going to take more than an hour!" Lou cackled.
"I'll have one now then and sneak another one in before we set off."
"She's obsessed!" bemoaned Jinny as Riz made her way upstairs to the bathroom.
"We're a right weird bunch aren't we, really?" said Lou for no reason whatsoever.
"You speak for yourself Lou … oh, and Riz." laughed Jinny.
"Hey!" said Riz stumbling back down the spiral stairs. "What insect is green and eats children?"
"Eh?"
"It's a joke. What insect is green and eats children? Come on!"
"Haven't the faintest idea Riz, go on, do tell" said Lou.
"A Braterpillar! Ha Ha Haaaaaa!" Riz shrieked hysterically.
"Erm, but surely a Caterpillar, which I presume you're alluding to, is a member of the species Lepidoptera. I don't think it's classed as an insect." Lou said authoritatively.
"I just made it up while I was having a wee." said Riz proudly.
"We can tell!" Jinny and Lou rhymed.

"Miss Lou is very clever, isn't she Jinny." said Jet.

Part 1: A Bustle In The Hedgerow

"Ah, well she went to University you see. She actually attended the lectures and everything, instead of loping about in a haze." said Jinny nostalgically.

"What did she study?" asked Jet.

"Latin and Home Economics. Said it'd help her with her spells" smiled Jinny.

"So that's how she knows about leopard doctors and things…" said Jet knowingly.

"Pardon?!" …

PARCHMENT 14

Part 2

Assault and Battery

It was 11.40pm and the Witching Hour was nigh. Almost time to put Jinny's plans into action, though they were not so much 'plans', more like ordered chaos.

No one was quite sure what these actions were going to achieve but they were going for it anyway. Call it a Witch Workout.

Everyone marched from the kitchen, in line, through the garden and strode purposefully up the lane and out into the first field, where, under the dim light of a violet, crescent moon, they stood in a circle and Jinny, Riz and Lou laid their broomsticks on the ground in the shape of a 'Y'. Jinny raised her arms in the air and chanted:

"I am the blue-lidded daughter of Sunset; I am the naked brilliance of the voluptuous night-sky. To me! To me!"

And with that, the broomsticks floated upwards and made their way to their respective owners, hanging in mid-air, ready to be mounted.

"You didn't just make *that* one up, did you?" Jet said, almost terrified.

"On the back laddie," said Jinny determinedly. "It's time!"

Riz and Lou jumped astride their brooms (or jet packs as they liked to call them), with Spike and Stripes as pillion riders.

As if from nowhere, there emerged a large, black shadow in the sky. It was very high up but still appeared quite distinct, it's shape caught in the half light.

Part 1: A Bustle In The Hedgerow

With a loud swooping sound, the shape neared the gathering and showed itself it to be none other than the mighty Raph.

"He looks enormous!" Jet said in awe.

"That's what happens when he's let loose Jetty boy." Jinny smiled.

"Onwards!"

The seven of them swiftly flew into the night sky, through the fields, over the Spooky Wood and over the clearing where the faeries dwelt. There was no activity down there, just a small fire burning over by a cluster of gnarly trees.

Then, all at once, they were at their destination. The lights were still on in the front lounge so he was definitely home.

The little squadron hovered for a minute or two, as if deciding on how to actually begin the proceedings.

"Jetty - walk through the front door please, make sure Crook sees you, then back out again and walk through the back door, then back to me." ordered Jinny in a soft voice.

Jet jumped off Jinny's broom and ran up to the front door, going straight through it as if it wasn't there.

The front light was on but there was no one there. He must have gone to bed without turning it off. Maybe he was afraid of the dark. Maybe he had good reason to be!

Jet followed a light coming from a room towards the back and there was Crook, just getting into bed.

Jet let out a loud hiss and did that creepy thing that cats sometimes do, you know the one where they arch their back and hop sideways? That one.

It certainly did the trick as Crook screamed, leapt from the bed and proceeded to run on the spot, like you do in a nightmare but you can't get to where you want to go.

Jet then ran as fast as he could towards the back door, waited until Crook caught up with him then vanished through the door and dashed back to Jinny.
Mr Crook stood there flabbergasted. His gast was well and truly flabbered. “Maybe it’s whiskey in general that doesn’t agree with me.” he said, agog, as he unbolted the back door and stuck his head out gingerly.

All was still. He brought his head back in, bolted the door and went for the front of the house, unbolting the front entrance and, again, sticking his head out to see if he was imagining the whole thing.
As he raised his head, he was greeted by two huge red eyes that seemed to be floating directly on his eye level.
It was then that he became aware of two, gigantic black wings beating either side of the eyes and a beak big enough to tear a grown man’s head clean off!
Crook’s hair (what little there was - at the sides of his head and on his back) stood on end and he let out a high pitched shriek, which would have been a full powered scream had his voice not suddenly deserted him.
“I’ve seen that thing before.” he thought, in his panic.
Raphael darted back up into the air with great speed only to reveal three Witches, on broomsticks, hovering in front of Crook’s very face.
Their features weren’t all that clear but it was patently obvious what they were and that they hadn’t popped round for a nice cup of tea.

Crook’s whole head was numb, his mouth and eyes wouldn’t shut and he was rooted where he stood, kind of hopping on the spot.
Jinny, Riz and Lou then flew off like Red Arrows, each in a different direction.

Part 1: A Bustle In The Hedgerow

The cats, prior to this, had dismounted and were now striding towards the terrified fellow.

“What now?” Jet said to Spike “See what Stripes does, then make it up as you go along.” said Spike calmly.

Stripes, the quiet, timid looking Siamese, approached Crook and started a low growl. A growl that you would normally associate with the nastiest dog you can imagine.

The growl got louder and louder and, literally, petrified poor old Mr Crook, unable to move, as he was.

Jet and Spike tried to do the same but their growls didn’t have quite the same effect as Stripes’ so they settled for some sinister hissing instead.

Riz was currently occupied with sending the chimney pot flying from the roof, whilst Jinny had sent the guttering and drain pipes crashing to the ground.

Miss Lou was, can you believe it, hovering casually by the side of Crook, smoking a cigarette and posting spooky images on Twitter!

Raph then swooped down from out of the darkness and extended his talons to their full extent, gripping Mr Crook by the pyjama jacket and flying off with him as if he were a spring lamb.

Within two short minutes Raph was circling over the faerie clearing, which is where he unceremoniously dropped the stupefied Mr Crook, right in front of the faerie realm entrance. Bump!

By this time Crook was frantic, as you can imagine, but too scared to move a muscle.

A tiny head popped out of the hole in the hedgerow, checking on what was causing all the commotion, spotted the pyjama clad human and popped back in again to get help.

Back at the Crook residence, Jinny had put a spell on the doors again, this time, instead of permanently locking them they just opened and slammed shut non-stop, as if some deranged poltergeist had been let loose on them. Riz had finally managed to uproot the chimney stack and Lou was still checking her phone for tweets.

The cats had nipped inside the house to see if there was anything to eat or drink. There wasn't.

"Miss Lou!" Jinny cried in despair. "Did you actually participate in *any* of that?"

"Nah, not really captain, I just did a spot of hovering and looked a bit witchy. You lot seemed to have it all under control. I felt a bit left out actually ..." said Lou whilst simultaneously flicking her thumb over her phone. "Back home for a drink?"

Jinny couldn't believe her ears. Well, actually she could. She had known Lou since they were six years old so, really, nothing surprised her when it came to the deeds and misgivings of Miss Lou.

"Aye, I suppose so, we'll leave the rest to the faeries, eh?" said Jinny.

"Is that it?!" Miss Riz shouted down from the roof.

"No, before we go I'm just going to redecorate his lounge dayglo green and put a crack in the toilet bowl." Jinny replied cheekily.

"Oh, before you crack the toilet, can I just go for a wee? It's all the excitement, you see?" said Riz as she floated back down.

Jinny glanced at Lou and Lou let out an uproarious laugh "Beggars belief doesn't she? Don't forget to wash your hands Riz!"

"Boys! Girl! We're making our way back now, where *are* you?" shouted Jinny to the cats as she waved her wand and turned the whole of Crook's lounge into a disgusting vivid green colour.

"It's rubbish here," said Jet. "Can't even find a bowl of water, let alone a mouse!"

"No need to be killing innocent mice Jet, there's plenty of food at home, surely you can hang on a few minutes?" said Jinny, standing back to admire her handy work.

"Suppose so." sulked Jet as the other two mewed in begrudging agreement.

Mr Crook was lying on his back, on a patch of cold, damp turf, wearing only his pyjamas.

His mouth was agape and so were his eyes but he still couldn't move.

A tiny hand fanned across his vision but he didn't blink.

"Is it dead?" asked a very small voice.

"No, it's breathing like the clappers, feller!" answered another small voice. "Poke its eye and see what happens."

Crook received a tiny prod to the eye but
still didn't blink.

"It's bewitched that is." said the first voice.

"Petrified."

"I'll wake Miss Slinky up and see what she has to say. She'll not be best pleased ..."

And off he went, back down the hole in the hedgerow and down to the faerie realm where Slinky was fast asleep, dreaming about bees.

Were you an outsider, the faerie realm would appear, initially, to be a somewhat scary place, but as the senses focused in on the surroundings it gave the appearance of being inside, say, a giant Christmas tree.

One with thousands of tiny blue lights and no tinsel or baubles.

There were long, stone steps leading down, ever down to who knows where, with holes akin to caves dug into the rock faces on either side of the steps.

It was into one of these 'caves', about twenty-three feet down, that the second pixie went and knocked on, well, he knocked on the air! There were no doors.

A gentle, female voice asked "Who is there please?" This, of course, was Slinky's domain.

"Tis me mistress, Warren." replied the pixie respectfully.

"Why are you rousing me at this unearthly hour Mr Warren?" said Slinky in her usual, very proper tone.

"There's a human bein' on the grass outside - lay in our circle it is. It's not movin' an' it's not blinkin' an' it ain't sayin' owt. Just wondered if you might know who or what it might be or something?'" said Warren, not completely sure of what he was asking or even what he was doing.

"Very well, I will take a peak. Thank you Mr Warren." Slinky sleepily replied.

She donned her faerie slippers and, in yet another thousandth of a trice, winged her way up the steps to the hedgerow opening.

"How long has that been there Mr Cornelius?" asked Slinky.

"Just landed a couple o' minutes ago Miss Slinky. A huuuge black bird dropped it here, so it did. Made ever such a thud."

"A black bird you say? Very large? That can only be Mr Raphael ... Goodness me! It is the night of Miss Jinny's invasion. It had completely slipped my mind … I can only presume that this effigy is the brutal Mr Crook."

"What would you like us to do with it mistress?" asked Cornelius.

"Leave him be and let him come to his senses. When he can move, escort him back to his house. It is only down the lane there, to the right. Make sure you escort him invisibly please, would you?" ordered Slinky.

"Will do ma'am. Sorry to be wakin' you."

"Do not give it another thought Mr Cornelius, it is all in my job description." winked Slinky and off she scurried, back down the hole in the hedgerow.

On their way home the three mischievous witches and their faithful familiars had flown over the faerie clearing and spotted the unfortunate Crookster lying forlornly on the grass. They treated themselves to a loud guffaw and continued on their journey.

As they landed at Demonia Cottage (2) they spotted Raphael sitting on the wall patiently awaiting their return.

He bowed to the ladies and Jinny gave him a hug and stroked his head

"Tum samajhdar ho." she whispered and the extremely large eagle gave her a pat with one of his equally large wings.

Job done. Now for the repercussions!

PARCHMENT 15

Wizards in a Blizzard

And so it was that the bedraggled Mr Russell Crook found himself standing outside his bungalow, once again, wondering why he was outdoors, in his pyjamas and freezing cold.

The difference this time was that all the doors in the house were opening and shutting at a great rate, he had no chimney and the guttering and drain pipes were all lying on the floor.

Of course, he hadn't even stepped inside the place yet! What then?! Tentatively, he made his way to the front doorstep, avoiding the self-opening and closing door.

He snuck through an available gap in the swinging door's trajectory and tiptoed into the lounge.

One can only begin to imagine what this fellow's mind was going through as he took in his new surroundings, all of it a very, very bright green, even the furniture.

Crook sat down on what used to be the boring beige sofa and attempted to make sense of what was happening. But he couldn't because it didn't make any sense at all. Not to him anyway.

The banging doors were driving him to the brink of insanity and there was no escape. Who could he get in touch with? Who would believe him? The only thing was to get out of the house and hope that it would all have gone away upon his return.

He went to his bedroom, dodging the door and pulled some warm clothes from the wardrobe.

Next he went to the bathroom, where only hours ago he was luxuriating in his hot bath. Now, the floor was swimming in water from the crack in the toilet base.

Part 1: A Bustle In The Hedgerow

He hurriedly dressed, got his coat and keys (not that he needed his door keys!) and headed to his car.
Thankfully, the only thing broken on the car was a windscreen wiper and he could get that fixed in the village. He crossed his fingers and hoped it wouldn't rain or snow.
Crook started the car and then the truth suddenly hit him. It was 1.30 … AM!
There was nowhere to go!
He ran back inside, grabbed three blankets and a pillow and made his mind up to sleep in the car, for sanity's sake.

Turning the ignition, he switched the heater on, followed by the radio and lowered the seats back. "This is Bobby Razzler welcoming you to your local news and chat show. Tonight, our phone-in topic is Anxiety, depression and madness. In today's hectic society, do you ever feel like you *just* can't cope? Call us now on the usual number and let me know your thoughts. Here's a little bit of Michael Buble to help sooth you through the morning…" "Bugger! I didn't think today could get any worse." sighed Crook.

"You did well Jetty me boy. Not bad at all for a first night's harassment." praised Jinny.
"I added a touch of my own too," he said. "That bouncing sideways arched back thing."
"Wow! Thinking on the spot! You little darling." Jinny beamed.
"One day I'd like to learn how to growl like Stripes - that's quite terrifying." said Jet admiringly
"Aye, she's great at that, aren't you Stripes …?"

There then followed a miaow, the likes of which you've never heard and Jinny mock shrieked.
"Weirdo!" scolded Lou, aiming the taunt at Stripes as she sank back into her treasured white rum and coke with two pieces of ice.
"I think I'll have a lie in tomorrow." yawned Riz.
"I'll find you a potty." Jinny quipped.

It was 10.06 am when the dishevelled Mr Crook was disturbed by the dulcet tones of the local radio station's morning presenter, Alfie Wilcox.
"Good morning listeners!" he chirpily announced, in his broad Lancashire dialect "That was 'How Do You Sleep?' by the legendary John Lennon, and we're going to follow that swiftly with a trip back to 1974 with Queen and 'Stone Cold Crazy!'"
And as the not-soothing-at-all full-on metal riff of Brian May's homemade guitar rattled through Crook's brain he punched the car radio and hurt his hand.
"Please, please, please don't tell me that radio's been on all morning." he thought as he nursed his fingers and attempted to start the car.
Amazingly, considering he had had the radio, heater and phone charger on for hours, the wondermobile started first time!
It was then he noticed a note under his one working windscreen wiper. "Not a parking ticket, please?!" he said to himself in disbelief.
But it was worse than that. The note read: "CEASE YOUR PLANS OR LOSE EVERYTHING" in big, red capital letters. The note was finished off with some kind of symbol, marked in the bottom corner, but that didn't mean anything to him.

Part 1: A Bustle In The Hedgerow

“What is that all about then?” he muttered as he stared out of the window and noticed the still banging front door.

You would be forgiven for thinking that Mr Crook wasn’t the brightest coin in the mint, after all, how many ridiculously strange things had happened to him recently? Why had they happened? Who was behind it all?

Had he not sat and thought these things through? The simple truth is, he hadn’t had the time to think about any of it. He was too busy being harassed! He put the car into ‘drive’ and set off in the direction of the village. First things first.

In the rural idyll of Demonia Cottage 2, whilst awaiting some kind of comeback for the previous night’s shenanigans, the girls had decided to make plans for a Christmas party, only their celebrations were not like ‘normal’ people’s festivities. But you must have guessed that.

Their ‘Christmas’ was called Yuletide and was celebrated on the shortest day and longest night of the year - the Winter Solstice, on December 21st.

“How about going out to see a band on the Solstice? There’s one playing up at Spiderwood Farm. Supposed to be amazing!” Riz offered.

“That’s that new venue they opened not long ago, isn’t it?” asked Lou. “Yeah. I haven’t been there yet but I’m told it’s fantastic. Just the place for oddballs like us!” Jinny laughed.

“Will *we* be able to go?” asked Jet politely, pointing to Spike and Stripes. “Oooh, I don’t know. It’s not likely they’ll allow animals in coz they serve food. Look what happened at the pie shop.” Jinny answered “I’ll give them a ring and make some enquiries but don't hold out any hopes luv."

"Hey Jet, if you can't go we can still have a bit of a do here, can't we Jinny?" said Riz sympathetically.

"Aye, I was going to suggest that. The old burning of the Yule log, the oranges and apples with cloves, the candles, the mistletoe, the holly, the tree …" Jinny remembered wistfully.

"The spiced cider!" piped up Lou, typically.

"Eggnog, caraway cakes, ginger tea and wassail!" joined in Riz.

"Oh aye! The wassail!" cried Lou and Jinny in unison, doing a little jig. "Is there anything cats can eat and drink?" said Jet sadly, "and what's a wassail?"

"We could maybe spice a vole for you Jet." laughed Lou.

"Don't be cruel Lou!" scolded Riz .

"Look, we'll sort something out for all that later but first, should I ring for tickets for Wizards In A Blizzard?" urged Jinny.

"*What* are you ringing for tickets for?" Riz asked.

"Wizards In A Blizzard - top notch Rock band supposedly, surely you've heard of them?"

"Can't say I have Jinny. I've lost touch with the music scene … ever since Purson split up it's not the same … oh and since I left my violin on the bus that time." said Riz with the hint of a tear in her eye.

"Well look, trust me, I think you might be pleasantly surprised by Wizards In A Blizzard. Shall I order the tickets? They're only eight quid!" pleaded
Jinny.

"Oh go on then, if it makes you happy." said Lou.

"But I want it to make *all* of us happy Lou."

Part 1: A Bustle In The Hedgerow

"I'm happy if you're happy. How about you Riz? Happy with that?" said Lou.

"I'm happy if you're happy Lou. And Jinny and Jet and Spike and Stripes, if they're happy. That's when I'm happy." said Riz, happily.

"So, we're all happy then?" said Jinny through gritted teeth.

"As can be." purred Lou with a smile.

"What about Raph in all this? No one's mentioned him once!" Riz said indignantly.

"He doesn't celebrate Christmas *or* the Solstice. He celebrates Diwali and that's only just been and gone." said Raph's owner, erm, Jinny.

"How does an eagle actually celebrate *anything* Jinny?" asked Lou.

"He just goes off on one. Disappears for two or three days then he makes his way back and sleeps for another two or three days. What he gets up to, well, Heaven knows." explained Jinny.

"Sounds good. Sounds just like me!" roared Lou.

Down in the village, Mr Crook had gotten his wiper fixed and was now on his way to … er, he didn't actually *know* where he was on his way to.

Who *do* you go to to fix a door that magically opens and shuts, continually?

A Joiner? A Locksmith? A Mechanic? A Candlestick maker? Who? He headed back to his car and sat there thinking things through, for the first time since they started happening.

What do we have?

The lounge has been decorated bright green but anyone could have done that. A lot of trouble to get it done but still perfectly possible - they do it
on those house makeover TV programmes
all the time … The chimney off and the
guttering down. Sheer vandalism?
Leaking toilet? Wear and tear maybe?
Hermetically sealed windows and doors. Hmmm.
Doors that violently open and shut continuously? Well …
Three Witches hovering at eye level, on broomsticks? I, erm … Being kidnapped by a giant black eagle with big red eyes? Oh …

Crook had a sudden, inexplicable notion to reach for his phone and ring the Town Hall.

"Could I speak to Isobel Mortem?" he asked the receptionist.

"Who's speaking please?"

"It's Russell Crook. She'll know what it's about."

"I'll just put you through …"

"Good afternoon, Ms Mortem speaking. How can I help?"

"It's Mr Crook - I need to talk to you again. I'm in a spot of bother and I think you might just be the only one that can help me out of it. I can't really talk about it on the phone. Could I meet up with you in town, for lunch maybe?"

"It's past lunchtime Mr Crook, it would have to be after work - around 5.30pm?"

"That would be most acceptable Mrs Mortem, thank you so much." said Crook, creepingly.

Part 1: A Bustle In The Hedgerow

“Ms!” said Miz Mortem. “Outside the Town Hall entrance then, 5.30.” Crook switched his phone off, sat back in the car seat and let out a huge sigh.
He had a few hours to kill and he daren’t spend them in the pub.
He set the alarm on his phone for 5.00pm and decided to put the seats down and have a nap. Might as well put the pillow and blankets to good use while they’re here.

As all this occurred, Demonia Cottage 2 received two visitors - Miss
Slinky and her gormless young ‘chaperone’ Mr Sparrowhawk, via the letterbox.
“Greetings fair Jinny and everyone.” Slinky almost sang.
“Merry meet Miss Slinky and oh, I’ve forgotten your name …” Jinny sputtered.
“You’ve got a game?” misheard Spudsley Sparrowhawk.
“I’ve got a few games but that isn’t what I said …”
“You threw the games on your bed?” asked Spudsley. “Why are you tellin’ me all this?”
“I said … I. HAVE. FORGOTTEN. YOUR. NAME. …”
“Ill-gotten gains? What is she on about Miss Slinky?” asked Mr Sparrowhawk in a complete state of confusion.
“He is deaf as a post and twice as dense Miss Jinny, take no notice of him.” said Slinky.
“Why do you bother bringing him Slinky? He’s neither use nor ornament.” Miss Lou butted in.
“Appointment? I haven’t got an appointment.” Spudsley dimly uttered.
“He is … he is a sort of Minder,” spoke Slinky. “He is bulky you see. He could take a wasp sting or two for me,

very easily, with all that bulk. Even a squirrel bite. He would not feel a thing. Especially if they went for his head."

At that the three ladies began to titter loudly and Riz had to run upstairs for a wee.

"I noticed you had done that fellow over this morning." Slinky said, trying to keep on the proper straight and narrow with her P's & Q's.

"Yes, we saw him in your clearing as we flew over. We'd just scared the living bejeezus out of him. Left his house in a right state. Raphael flew off with him, you know?" said Jinny.

"Did he indeed? He is a big blighter that bird is he not? There was ever such a thud when he dropped him. Shook the whole faerie realm. Sleep desperation all around." said Slinky.

"You mean 'deprivation' don't you Slinky?" asked Lou.

"Who's medication's stinky?" asked Spudsley, deafly. "Don't touch it, it'll do you more harm than good."

"Spudsley my dear, would you mind waiting outside? You are beginning to vex me somewhat." Slinky implored.

"Text your Kumquats? I haven't even got a phone and I wouldn't want one. Anyways, they're too big for the likes of us and I didn't know you could get Kumquats 'round these parts."

Slinky pointed to the letterbox and mouthed the word, "GO!" and Spudsley understood, at last.

"Where were we up to? Ah yes, so, an almighty thud that woke the whole of Fairyland up at some unearthly hour and left me with a body to dispose of." Slinky moaned.

"You looked like you'd got it all under control Slinky, so we just flew over. Sorry about that." Jinny apologised.

Part 1: A Bustle In The Hedgerow

"We did have the situation under control, it was just a bit of a shock that is all. I was having a very pleasant reverie about bees …"

"How lovely for you." said Jinny. "I'm sorry Raph interrupted your dream." "No need for apologies Miss Jinny, you were only doing your job after all. Do you think, in your opinion, that it did the trick?"

"We're still waiting for the backlash Slinky and we haven't a clue what kind of state Crook's in. Quite severely mental I would imagine. Lord knows how he's ever going to stop those doors opening and shutting." Jinny informed Slinky.

"Only you can stop that Jin … or another witch" said Lou, delicately picking her nose.

"Well, you know I'm not stopping it, only if he came and begged on his hands and knees would I maybe consider it." said Jinny.

"I've been thinking …" said Riz.

"Get *out* of it!" shouted Lou.

"No, listen, I've been thinking … you said only Jinny or another witch can stop the spells?"

"That's the case Riz, yes." said Lou.

"Apart from in 'Bewitched' where only the witch that cast the spell can break it." said Jinny informatively.

"But that's a TV show and it's American …" Lou corrected.

"Stay with me." Riz continued. "… Mr Crook has been having meetings with someone at the Town Hall, has he not? And that would involve the Town Planning department, would it not? And the Town Planner is Isobel Mortem, is she not? And what is Isobel Mortem?"

"A fat git!" mumbled Jinny.

"Apart from that Jin, what is she?"

"A Lesbian." said Lou authoritatively.

"Come on! You know!" urged Riz.

"A vegetarian?" added Slinky.

"Know your enemy!" said Riz, pointing her finger at the group menacingly "She's a bloody Witch!"

"No way! That's not possible. Is it? I mean …" Jinny faltered.

"How do you know that to be true Riz?" asked Miss Lou, in a curious manner. "And why haven't you mentioned it until now?"

"I know it to be true because the other week I had to go to the Town Hall to pay the domestic rates on mum and dad's holiday cottage. There was a massive queue and I needed the loo …"

"You didn't?! No, no, no, surely not." teased Lou.

"I did, and the public loo was knackered so the next door down was the Town Planning department and I knocked and asked if I could use the toilet as the public one was broken …"

"And this Isobel woman flew over her desk and did one of those Wah Ha Ha Ha creepy voices like in the films?" further teased Lou.

"No, she said it was alright to use it, just be sure to flush it." said Riz, unfazed and pulling on a menthol ciggie.

"Did she not make you wash your hands afterwards Riz?" Jinny asked playfully.

"She didn't have to Jinny - don't be so childish"

"Wooohooowooo!" came the cry back.

"Are you taking this seriously or are you just going to keep taking the rip out of me?" Riz exploded. Well, sort of …

"Wooohooowooo!" came the cry again.

"I must say ladies, you are giving this young woman a very hard time," interjected Slinky, sagely "Is it really necessary?"

"No, of course it isn't," said Jinny, "but it's fun."

At this point, sensing that Riz was becoming slightly antagonised, Spike swaggered his way over and sat on her lap. Then stared unblinkingly at Lou and Jinny.

"Oh 'eck!" said Lou, "double trouble!"

"I'm not going to tell you now. You're doing my head in you two!" rasped Riz, stubbing her cig out aggressively.

"Chin up Riz - only having a bit of banter." smiled Lou.

"Yeah, come on Riz, what's got into you?" asked Jinny, concerned.

"I'm going for a wee and I'm going to try and calm myself down, then I'll see how I feel when I come back. Come on Spikey luv ..." and off they spiralled up the staircase.

"Never seen her react that way to our ribbing." said Lou. "There's something bothering her."

"And Spike, he was getting a bit narked, wasn't he?" Jinny said.

"She *is* his mother Jinny, what do you expect?" said Slinky. "She's not his biological mother Slinks, for goodness sake!" Jinny retorted.

"Now we're all getting a tad aerated, my chi's all over the shop." said Lou.

"Let's just shut up and listen to what she has to say, eh?"

Riz returned and slumped down in the armchair, Spike close behind.

"There isn't much else to tell anyway." she said grumpily.

"There is! How did you find out she's a witch?" implored Jinny.

"She looks like one!" shouted Riz.

"That's stereotyping, that is Riz" said Jinny, not believing what she had just heard.

"Only messing. When I went to say thank you, she was sat at her desk and she had a copy of Pagan Monthly magazine ..."

"Well that's no proof..." Jinny broke in.

"And a spell book on her desk. And I know a *real* Grimoire when I see one!" said Riz with authority.

"Still..." Jinny trailed off.

"Or maybe it was the framed picture of Alice Nutter and the pentagram ring that aroused my suspicions ..."

"Blimey! Was she wearing a wig too?" Lou asked, half seriously. "Like in

'The Witches' film?"

"No. They don't make wigs that bad." sniffed Riz.

"A wart?" asked Jinny, as if for final proof.

"Behave Jin!" Riz said scornfully.

Spike was still staring at Lou and Jinny, very unnervingly.

"I'll tell you what *is* happening in this house, right now." said Lou "A Goblin!"

"Whaaat?" said Riz, astonished.

"There's a Goblin in here and that's why everyone's so agitated. That's what they do - instigate quarrels. Stripes, locate the culprit please."

Stripes leapt up and held her nose in the air. "Sniff Sniff" she went, then stalked over to the corner near to what people of old called a 'vestibule'. The infamous Stripes growl was invoked and as it got louder the hidden Goblin knew it had been discovered, feared for its safety and jumped out from behind the umbrella stand, giving everyone a bit of a start.

"What do you think you're doing here, uninvited?" asked Jinny.

"Just having a nosey. I was bored." the Goblin replied.

"Well go and be nosey and bored elsewhere yer little stirrer!" shouted Lou angrily.

"I - I didn't mean no harm. Just my way of getting through the day … a wee bit of mischief." he smiled.

"Oooh, don't smile. Whatever you do, don't smile." warned Jinny.

"Why ever not?" asked the sprite impudently.

"Because you're likely to get one of those umbrellas wrapped 'round your head by Miss Lou, that's why!"

"I shall take care of this ladies." said Slinky in her best regal voice. "After all, this creature is a distant cousin of our kind and I think it only right that

I should deal with him."

Slinky produced her starry wand from who knows where and pointed it at the Rapscallion.

"You be on your way now Goblin, never to return here, or you will feel the wrath of my wand," Slinky said sternly, "and a faerie wand's wrath is not to be trifled with."

"I told you she was mustard when she got angry." whispered Jinny to Jet. The Goblin bowed to the faerie and turned to go

"Sorry about that." was his parting remark and as he closed the front door behind him the tension in the room lifted and a familiar, peaceful atmosphere returned.

"I hate Goblins!" said Lou.

"Hobgoblins are worse." said Riz.

"What's the difference?" asked Lou, intrigued.

"Haven't a clue." said Riz sloping blissfully into the comfy armchair and lighting yet another cigarette.

PARCHMENT 16

Bewitched, Bothered and Bewildered

The tortured Mr Crook woke to the sound of his phone alarm - it was 5.00pm.

"Have I just had the most terrible nightmare?" were the first thoughts that came into his head. "I hope so!"

As his sleepy head cleared he realised that, no, it wasn't a bad dream, all those things really happened and that is why he was going to start the car and head off to meet Isobel Mortem outside the Town Hall.

So that's what he did, arriving ten minutes early. He parked on the double yellow lines that you're not supposed to park on, and left his engine running, awaiting the arrival of the Mortem woman.

He turned the radio on to while away the time …

"You're listening to Drive Time on your local FM station with me, Billy Ainsworth as your guide. We've got lots of weather, travel news and lots of up-to-the-minute, dynamic tunes to keep you going on that dreary drive home. Forget the traffic queues, forget the engine overheating … here's the fantastic AQUA with 'Barbie Girl'." Crook decided there and then that the radio wasn't a good idea and swiftly turned it off. Even he had *some* standards!

As luck would have it, Ms Mortem appeared on the steps and made her way down. Crook gently pipped his horn and caught her attention.

"Want to talk in the car? It's a bit grim out there?" said Crook.

"Yes, alright, but I haven't got much time so could you make it brief?" said Mortem curtly.

Part 1: A Bustle In The Hedgerow

Crook began to tell the complicated tale of what had been happening to him, unbelievable as it sounded and Ms Mortem listened intently.

"You've been bewitched." she plainly stated.

"Bewitched? That's just fairy tale stuff, isn't it?" demanded Crook.

"What do *you* think? Can you explain what has happened any better?" gruffed Mortem.

"Well, I, I, I really can't actually …" stammered Crook.

"Have you vexed any local witches by any chance? Any Sprites? Come on man - you *must* know!"

"I, I've got a feeling that a woman who lives not too far away from me is involved in some kind of jiggery pokery but I can't think what I might have done to warrant all this malarkey." he said.

"What is her name?" asked Mortem.

"Do you know, I have no idea. Odd that, I thought I knew it. I know where she lives though." Crook's head was, understandably, in a bit of a scramble. "Ammoni, no, Demonia Cottage, that's it."

"I know the place well. Never actually been inside but I know the location." said Mortem, pondering.

"I can find out who the occupier is, no problem. What about all this rumpus that's going on at your house? What do you think *I* can do about it?"

"I, well, I think, I could be wrong mind, but … do you practice witchcraft, at all?" Crook said nervously.

"I would need another substantial payment to reveal that kind of information." Mortem sinisterly smiled.

"A thousand? A thousand quid to help me?" said Crook desperately.

"Not much in the grand scheme of things but I'm taking a liking to you. You're underhand, sly, devious, mean, unfashionable, grasping and ruthless. Why not?"

"Would you please come with me now and stop the banging doors and the leaks and … can you repair the damage and the distasteful decorating?" begged Crook.

"That's a lot of work by the sounds of it. Make it two grand and you're on." said Mortem.

"Do you take Visa?" enquired Crook.

"Yes, I do. There's a two pounds service charge - is that OK?"

"Crimes!" shouted Crook. "Yes, yes, that's fine."

Ms Mortem reached into her man bag and produced an electronic, mobile credit card thingy, took Crook's card and slid it into the payment slot. "Just type your number in would you please?" said Mortem efficiently.

A few seconds passed … "Right's that's excellent. Thank you for your custom," she smiled, handing him a receipt, "and don't put that through your accounts!"

Crook was starting to think that maybe he had shifted to some parallel universe as he drove off towards his unfortunate house.

Any cockiness that he once possessed was now completely unapparent. He was gradually becoming a broken man.

Was this golf course a good idea after all? Could he afford it? Are there really such things as faeries? Maybe a small crazy golf course would be a better idea …

Eventually his thoughts were interrupted as he drew near to his bungalow and spotted the still banging doors.

"Here we are Miz Mortem. Home Sweet Home"

"Well, well, what a kerfuffle." she said.

"Can you fix it?" implored Crook.

Part 1: A Bustle In The Hedgerow

“Yes I can!” stated Mortem, in a way that brought to mind that children’s TV programme. Bob something …

Mortem reached down into her bottomless man bag and produced a thin, black stick covered in thin, black feathers.

She muttered something in a foreign language, waved what was in fact her wand and aimed it at the troublesome door.

Silence. Apart from a distant banging sound which was coming from over the back of the house.

“Oh, I forgot, it’s *all* the doors, inside and out.” said Crook.

“Why didn’t you say so?” howled Mortem. “I’ll have to start afresh now!” She undid the first spell and the front door started to bang again then she uttered some different, unintelligible words and yes! All was still.

“What a relief!” cried Crook. “Thank you so much. That’s worth two thousand and two pounds of anybody’s money.”

“What’s next?” asked Mortem.

“Follow me please.” said Crook pointing to the displaced chimney and the broken guttering on the way.

“Want these putting back then?”

“If it’s no trouble. Thank you.” said Crook humbly.

Mortem raised both hands in the air, spoke more hocus pocus words, spun round on the spot and the chimney and guttering were back in place.

“Miraculous!” said Crook with undisguised admiration. “There’s just the bathroom and the sitting room now.”

As they walked down the short hallway Crook noticed that the floor was about half an inch deep with water … everywhere.

“This is going to cost a fortune in carpets.” he thought.

"Where's the leak coming from?" Mortem asked.

"I think it's just from the toilet Ms Mortem." Crook meekly replied. "Through here? Ah yes, that's it." she said twiddling her wand and instantly repairing the crack in the porcelain "I suppose you'll want the water removing from the carpets will you?" she asked.

"Can you *really* do that? That would be an enormous pressure off." said Crook very gratefully as the witchy town planner once more lifted her hands from the floor to the air and magically sucked every last drop of water out through the front door.

"Incredible. Incredible." was all Crook could say, apart from commenting on how much cleaner the carpets now looked.

"Here's the last bit." he then said showing Mortem through to the front lounge.

"Bit?!" she squeaked "Whoever did this to you is *very* sick indeed." she added as she surveyed the disgusting lime green décor.

"What colour do you want it?" she asked with a slant eyed glance.

"Well, it was pretty much all beige before. Rather bland looking really …" "Want me to put my 'stamp' on it? Trust me, do you?" she asked.

"I think I do Ms Mortem, yes. As long as it's not too overbearing, whatever you choose will be good with me." said Crook, seemingly a changed man.

"Please call me Isobel. It's pointless having a first name if it's not going to get used, don't you think?"

"I, I do Isobel." came the reply from the awestruck fellow.

"Now, if you would proceed to the kitchen, put the kettle on and oh, do you have any hot chocolate at all?"

“I’m not sure. I know I’ve definitely got some Ovaltine,” said Crook.

“I haven’t had that in such a long time - that’ll do. Thank you. Could you make it with milk please? By the time you get back your sitting room will be transformed.” she said with an unusually warm smile.

“You’re an angel.” said Crook.

“DO NOT call me that again. EVER!” said Isobel nastily.

“Sorry, sorry. Many apologies.” whimpered Crook as he toadied his way out of the door and into the kitchen.

“It seems very unusual that we’ve had no feedback from last night’s antics, don’t you think Lou?” Jinny said.

“It can only mean that he’s up to something. Odious as he is, he isn’t stupid. Mark my words lady, some form of comeuppance will be on its way, so don’t be letting your guard down just yet.” warned Lou.

“Why doesn’t one of us nip round to his place and see what’s happening?” Riz said sensibly, whilst painting her toenails turquoise.

“I’ll send the boys round.” said Jinny.

“Sounds like a gangster film Jin”. laughed Lou.

“Jet, Spike I need you to go on an errand. Raph - Raphael? Hellooo!” the

eagle from India was ‘relaxing’. It was a form of meditation that people (and eagles) from India had mastered. He raised his head and cocked it towards Jinny as if to say, “Who? Me?”

“Yes, Raph, you.” Jinny knew what his thoughts were. “I need you to cover the boys, from the air, and make sure nothing untoward happens to them. OK?” Raph nodded.

"Right. Off you go to Crook's place and let me know what's transpired please. Spike, look after young Jet will you? He's still learning."

Spike also nodded and off went the trio on what was becoming a very familiar route.

They had been travelling quite a few minutes when Jet noticed Raph soaring in the grey sky. "I wish I could fly. Do you think Jinny might teach me some day?" he asked Spike, who was older and wiser.

"Everybody always says that and the answer is 'no'. No, Jinny will never teach you how to fly because, 'A': she's got Raph and 'B': it's not in your job description. There's a possible 'C': it'd look ridiculous!" Spike answered.

"I Suppose you're right." Jet said morosely.

"Always!" said Spike as they pounced their way past the faerie clearing and through the side of the hedgerow that didn't house the faerie hole.

Three or four minutes later they were stood outside Crook's dwelling. There was a distinct lack of banging doors, the chimney pot had been reinstated and the guttering was all back in place. And the lights were on.

"Curious" said Spike, worriedly.

"There's summat amiss eh?" Jet said, obviously.

"Something amiss, yes, definitely. If only we knew *what.*" said Spike.

"If you keep very quiet and I move a bit closer to the house I can listen in and see if there are any voices going on." said young Jet.

"How are you going to do that? How are you going to hear anything through those thick walls?" asked Spike, incredulously.

"Jinny taught me how to do it. You'd be amazed at what I can hear these days."

Part 1: A Bustle In The Hedgerow

“I’ve never been taught that trick.” Spike said indignantly. “I’ll be having words with her highness when I get back.”

“I’m sure there’s a good reason Spike, but let me just sidle up and have a listen.”

Jet crept furtively to the underside of the window. All around was quiet apart from the two voices he could hear coming from the lounge, ever so scarcely muffled but still intelligible …

“That Ovaltine was marvellous Mr Crook.” said a female-ish voice.

“Russell, please.” said the only slightly deeper male voice.

“Russell, yes. That reminds me of an old joke.” said the female.

“Go on, what is it. Tell us!” said the man enthusiastically.

“No. No, it’s rubbish, really.”

“Oh please. I’d love to hear it.” he urged her.

“Oh alright. What do you call a man covered in brown paper?” she said.

“A Paperboy?” replied Crook.

“Ha Ha. Nooo. Russell! Rustle. Get it?” laughed the woman.

“Highly amusing that one Isobel. Highly humorous.” howled the man, affectedly.

So far, Jet had ascertained that what we had here was a man called Russell Crook and a woman called Isobel and they seemed to be very chummy.

Jet bravely stood on his back legs and peaked through the window pane.

The lounge was no longer vivid green, it was now done out like someone had just come back from an African safari, with all manner of stuffed animal heads on the walls, leopard skin rugs and throws, tiger skin wallpaper and the odd spear for good measure.

"I *Love* what you've done to my lounge Isobel," said the man. "I feel like an explorer! I must say, it's not a look I would have gone for when I was browsing through the decorating catalogues but it's, it's invigorating!" "Thank you Russell, I'm so glad you like it. Maybe you would like me to come around again and redo your other rooms?" the woman said.

"You know, I think I would." said Russell.

"How about tomorrow?" Isobel said.

"Yes, yes indeed. I'd like that very much."

"In the meantime, what about the floozy that caused you all this trouble? Demonia Cottage you say? Maybe I should pay her a visit." the woman said, drawing nearer to the window.

Jet slowly lowered himself down and hurried over to Spike.

"Come on Spike - leg it! We've got trouble!" he said and the two cats and the ever vigilant bird shot off as fast as their feline legs (and avian wings) would take them.

Spike, Jet and Raph reached Demonia Cottage (2) panting breathlessly, apart from Raph who was never, ever breathless.

They hobbled through the door (yes, literally *through* the door) and could barely get their words out fast enough.

Jet, inbetween gasps, related all that he had seen and heard to Jinny, and Jinny sat down by the fire and stared despondently into the flames.

"Told you she was a witch but would you have it? Oh nooo." said Riz triumphantly.

"There's no need to brag Riz, this isn't something to have a competition with you know." said Jinny.

"Don't look so worried, captain," Lou said to Jinny. "There's three of us, the three fammies (familiars = cats), Raph and all the pixies and faerie folk if we need 'em and there's ONE of her. No contest."

"I've just got the feeling that this is going to open up a horrible can of worms." said Jinny, deflatedly. "I mean, she must know what she's doing. She's just turned that bland bungalow into a safari park, undone all of my spells and by the sound of it she's making a new boyfriend out of the unlovable Mr Crook! That last one alone is some pretty hardcore bewitchment."

"She must have bewitched *herself* to want to end up with him!" snorted Lou.

"It's all down to money innit? She's sniffed that he's got a few bob, a property and a business, so who *cares* if he's ugly, smelly and rude?" said Riz.

"I'd care." said Jinny, brightening up a bit. "The man is scum!"

"Maybe she likes scum. Some witches are like that. A good thirty-five per cent of 'em I'd say." Lou reasoned.

"Whatever," Jinny said, "but there's going to be a knock at that door and she's going to be stood on the doorstep. What then? Do I just zap her without exchanging a word? Lame her? Blind her? I'm really at a loss as to what to do here..."

"Well you'd better get the first punch in Jin, coz she sounds like a right handful." Riz helpfully said.

"Maybe *you* should answer the door then Riz." said Jinny, sarcastically.

Back at the Crook dwelling Isobel and Russell (as they were now affectionately known to each other) were getting along famously.

Who would have known that a gnarly old ratbag like Isobel and an obnoxious, conniving fraudster like Russell could end up being such good friends?
Funny old world innit?

"It doesn't bother you that I'm a witch then Russell?" asked Isobel.

"It bothers me more that you're a town planner Isobel." Crook wisely replied with a smile.

"It shouldn't Russell, really it shouldn't." said Isobel breathily. "I may be of some use to you in that department in the future."

"May you? Would you? I'm not sure I could afford you Isobel."

"Don't talk of money Russell, it's so vulgar. Money disgusts me, did you know that?" Isobel said, not entirely convincingly.

"It disgusts *me* when I don't have it." said Crook* (*author's note: I can't get used to calling him Russell!).

"Anyway, that aside, I mean to call on the cottage tomorrow morning and have it out with the resident. Obviously I haven't had time to check out her name but no matter …" said Mortem* (*author's note: I can't get used to calling her Isobel!).

"She's tallish, slim, very attractive." said Crook. "She's got kind of very dark blue hair - it doesn't look dyed …"

"Indigo." said Mortem, as if she had just trod in a dog poo. "A rarity but highly favoured amongst the practitioners of the 'Dark Arts'…"

"Yes, well, she's got a black cat too, only a youngster by the look of it and two friends, one with blonde hair, very tall, very beautiful and one with bright red hair and lipstick, again, very attractive …" said Crook.

"A coven then eh? A very bewitching coven at that it seems." said Mortem, enviously.

Part 1: A Bustle In The Hedgerow

"So you think she's a witch? You think she's caused all this pandemonium?" said Crook.

"I think her middle name is 'Pandemonium' Russell. She seems to me to be a bit of a whirlwind. A hot head. Combine that with her 'friends' and you've got a very potent potion." said Mortem distractedly.

Now it was Isobel Mortem that was worrying. How could she approach this woman? Not as a fellow witch that's for certain. She'd have to be far more calculating than that. Then she thought back to her first Disney film. 'Snow White'. A poison apple! Come on! That was a bit old hat. It worked for her though.

"Let me think on this Russell, let's not be hasty. I'll go home tonight and have a good old ponder on it. I'll get going now and give you a ring tomorrow afternoon. Will that be alright?" said Mortem.

"Yes, that's great. How are you getting home? Flying? Or do you want a lift?" blabbered Crook.

"I have no broomstick Russell, as you can see, so it would be very gracious of you if you could give me a lift into the town centre."

"Bugger!" thought Crook. He was looking forward to a spot of TV with the fire on and no banging doors, reclining majestically in his new jungle lounge.

"No problem," he lied. "Come on let's get you back then eh?"

And off they went, into the darkness and over the road to Crook's trusty Range Rover.

At this point, it should be mentioned that they were almost, erm, on the verge of holding hands!

(you couldn't make this stuff up, could you?)

PARCHMENT 17

Day Tripper

Morning came and the whole of the occupants of Demonia Cottage (2) were sat around on tenterhooks and feeling fidgety.

Still no visitations, not even a knock on the door from a premature carol singer.

"Tell you what," said Riz. "Let's go down to the pub for something to eat." "And drink!" said Lou.

"I'm just going to book these Wizards In A Blizzard tickets first. You lot still up for going?" Jinny asked.

"Yeeeah!" chimed Lou and Riz.

"Don't forget to ask if cats are allowed please." reminded Jet.

"Ooh Jetty. I'd get that notion right out of your mind if I were you. Even if they did let you come along you'd have to sit outside on your own, you'd be dead miz." said Jinny, affectionately.

"Not if Spikes and Stripes come. We could explore …"

"No Jetty. You're to stay here and guard the house. We won't be gone that long anyway." Jinny said as she picked up the phone to dial the fabulous Spiderwood Farm. "A Rock concert isn't the place for cats, Jet luv." said Riz warmly. "Anyway lad, with your new extra sensory hearing the sound system would probably blow your head off!" said Lou.

"Hmmm, I suppose you're right." sighed Jet.

"Maybe if there's an acoustic night eh?" said Jinny as she was hanging on the line awaiting an answer. "Oh, hello, I wondered if I could book three tickets for Wizzards In A Blizzard on 21st December please?"

"Get Nancy one - she'd love it I bet." said Lou.

Part 1: A Bustle In The Hedgerow

"Sorry, could you make that four tickets please?" asked Jinny.

Jinny hung on while the person at the other end sorted the booking out … "It's Jinny Lane, Demonia Cottage (2), Windlestraws. Can I pay by card?

That's great, thank you …" and Jinny gave her card details and postcode and the deal was done.

"Sorted!" she whooped "All aboard for a jolly fine shindig!" and proceeded to sing Jethro Tull's "Ring out Solstice Bells" almost in its entirety.

"You'd better text Nancy and let her know what you've done Jin." said Riz, sensibly.

"Aye, good idea." said Jinny, and off she went to do just that.

"Are we going down to Demmy's then or not?" said Lou impatiently, after waiting another ten minutes.

"We are to be sure!" said Jinny beaming. "Walking or driving?"

"Let's walk. It's a nice, fresh day for it." said Riz. She quite enjoyed walking.

They all agreed and set off, leaving the cats and eagle behind

"Back in an hour or so boys and girl." said Riz.

"You know that's not true Riz," whispered Jinny. "More like three hours if you two have anything to do with it."

"Well … they have no concept of time, do they? I only have to go across the road to the shop and Spike thinks I've been on a two-week holiday!" Riz chuckled.

The trio had been strolling for about fifteen minutes when they noticed a woman, dressed in black and carrying a man bag, on the other side of the lane.

"Hey! That's that Town Hall woman." Riz said quietly.

"No way! Is it?" shouted Jinny … quietly.

The woman, who we now know to be Isobel Mortem, noticed the group looking over and immediately identified them "Indigo, bright red and blonde. I wonder who that lot could be …" she thought, knowingly. Anyway, she put her head down and carried on walking, ignoring the three glamorous witches.

"What's *she* up to then?" said Lou.

"No bloody good, I'll wager." said Jinny, worriedly.

"Should we follow her, do you think?" Lou asked.

"It's a bit obvious Lou, isn't it?"

"Trip her up!" said Riz, naughtily.

"Well that's not going to achieve much but a grazed knee, is it Riz?" Jinny said in exasperation.

"Let me have a think. No, let's *all* have a think, shall we?" and they sat down on a cold bit of banking and … thought.

"I need a wee, I'll tell you that for nothing." Miss Riz said, sharing her thoughts.

"How very helpful Riz. Thank you for your contribution." said Lou.

"It's just typical that we haven't even brought one broomstick between us, then I could have jetted back across the fields and warned the chaps." said Jinny.

"And girl." said Lou.

"Yes, yes." Jinny said pensively "Come on - think on girls - there must be *something* we can do."

And just at that moment, as luck would have it, Lou spotted Nancy Redfern's van coming up the lane.

"Yoo Hoo!" shouted Nancy rolling her window down.

"Shhhhhhh!" said Jinny loudly.

"What's up ladies? Trying to appear anonymous?" laughed Nancy. "You'll have a job on there!"

Part 1: A Bustle In The Hedgerow

"No, wait, can you give me a quick lift back to the cottage please Nancy?
It's urgent!" pleaded Jinny.
"Sure, hop in luv." said their affable new friend.
"OK Riz, trip her up! Now!" shouted Jinny as she jumped swiftly into the van "Be back in a bit!"
Nancy put her foot down hard on the accelerator and off they sped.
Riz mumbled something and waved her hands then watched as the spell took effect.
A proper head over heels trip it was. Miz Mortem was flat on her back on the pavement, higher up the lane, with the contents of her man bag strewn all over the road.
"Ha, ha and thrice ha!" snorted Lou. "Good show Rizzo!"
By this time, Nancy and Jinny had overtaken the unlucky woman (with Jinny telling Nancy to "Ignore her! Ignore her!") and were well on their way back to Demonia Cottage (2).
"A stroke of good fortune Nancy. You certainly solved our dilemma there, lass." said a relieved Jinny.
"Why? What's happening anyway Jinny?" asked Nancy, bewildered. "I'll tell you later. Just get me inside my house as quickly as poss please."
It didn't take long for the pair to reach the cottage.
"Do you want me to come in with you Jinny?" asked Nancy.
"You can if you wish." said Jinny dashing up to the front door. "Quick sticks though!"

Once inside, Jinny informed the cats and Raph as to what was occurring and told them to stand by.

"Want a quick brew Nancy?" she said to the locksmith to the stars.

"Go on then. Mine's easy - black coffee, no sugar. Ta." Nancy smiled.

"Have you got a job you're going to? I mean, are you in a hurry?" asked Jinny.

"Not at all. In fact, I was on my way up to you to thank you for getting me a ticket and to give you eight quid."

"Oh, don't bother about the money. It's payment enough to do me this favour luv." said Jinny gratefully. "I'm just waiting for the knock at the door then … wait a minute, she thinks we're all down the road. Maybe she's going to attempt a break in, or something."

It was then that Jinny heard a whirring sound at the back door. Raph jumped up and cocked his head to one side. The cats all arched their backs

and affected their best menacing looks. Nancy and Jinny couldn't move. A minute later there was another clicking, whirring sound at the front door, then silence.

It was *her*! Jinny knew immediately what had happened. She'd sealed the door locks. Revenge for the Crook incident! Then the sunlight through the windows disappeared, followed scarily by tons of soot falling down the chimney.

What a mess! Jinny switched a light on and ran upstairs to get her wand.

Nancy peered through the letterbox but there was no one in sight.

Jinny bombed back down the staircase armed with her faithful wand, Rosie, pointing it at the door lock. A wiggly blue light shot out and the lock was back to normal. She then went into the kitchen and repeated the process.

Part 1: A Bustle In The Hedgerow

"Right, that's the locks sorted, now what on earth has she done to the windows I wonder?" said Jinny hurrying out of the front door.

She could scarcely believe her eyes when she saw a full, overgrown ivy covering the whole of the front of the cottage, completely obscuring the windows.

"That looks quite pretty actually," she said laughing. "I'll just remove it from the windows and … voila!"

"Did you just speak French Jinny?" said Jet, as if from out of nowhere.

"I did Gomez, I did" she smiled lovingly and patted his little lipstick covered head.

"By the way Jinny, you forgot the soot." blinked Jet (because he couldn't wink).

Isobel Mortem had accomplished her underhanded act of vengeance and was now smugly limping off back to the village.

She was to meet Russell Crook in Demmy's for a lunchtime drink and sandwich.

They were becoming very pally, oh yes.

Lou and Riz had already ordered their drinks and settled in at the pub, nestled up by the fire, their new regular spot.

"I see they still haven't noticed that you turned that hanging witch picture to the wall Lou." observed Riz.

"Some people have no attention to detail." smirked Lou.

"I wonder how Jinny's getting on with old ratbag features?" Riz mused.

She was soon to find out …

Five or six minutes passed in genial conversation when Riz's eye was drawn to the entrance, and the appearance of none other than 'old ratbag features' herself - Isobel Mortem.

She limped pathetically to the bar, asked for a hot chocolate, was informed that they didn't do hot chocolate - would she like a chocolate milk shake, microwaved, like the one she'd had the last time she was in? Mortem shook her head in bewilderment and asked for a milky coffee instead, upon receipt of which she hobbled over to a vacant table by the door and put her leg up on the chair opposite.

A passing barmaid commented on this, informing Mortem that customers weren't supposed to put their feet up on the seats.

"But I've hurt my knee." Mortem whined.

"Tough! Go to A & E." came the reply.

"If *she's* here where the heck has Jinny got to?" said a concerned Lou. Her question was answered within the next two minutes as Jinny and Nancy breezed through the door.

"Ahoy captains!" shouted Lou, waving her hand.

Jinny and Nancy waved back and mouthed an obscure mime of 'just

getting a drink - won't be a min.'

Mortem turned round in her chair and smiled a self-satisfied smile, for as far as *she* knew she had just made a right mess of Jinny's house and Jinny had not an inkling.

"Hiya sweeties," said Jinny. "I've dragged Nance along for a bevy, see?" "Yes Jinny, we can see her, there, right next to you. Are you OK?" asked Lou.

"She came, she spelled, she came undone." was Jinny's cryptic reply.

"But she's over there Jin." pointed Lou.

"She may well be but she's got away with nothing!" smiled Jinny.

Part 1: A Bustle In The Hedgerow

So Jinny and Nancy filled Riz and Lou in on what had happened back at the cottage and how Jinny had overturned Mortem's spells … but Mortem didn't know about any of that. Yet.

"Nasty, deceitful cow." said Lou.

"I'll trip her up again when she next visits the toilet." Riz offered.

"You *do* that Rizzo!" urged Lou.

And they all laughed lustily.

"They'll be laughing on the other side of their faces (whatever *that* means) when they find out what I've done." smirked Mortem to herself.

Next to stroll in was the real villain of the piece, Mr Crook.

He spotted Isobel at the table by the door and gave her a cheesy wink, doing that thing where you shake your hand in the air, meaning "do you want a drink?"

Mortem declined, pointing to her still almost full cup, so Crook continued to the bar and ordered a pint of bitter.

"Tut tut." tutted Mortem to herself. "Alcohol at this hour indeed. I'll have to put a stop to *that.*"

Crook swaggered over, full of a kind of new lease of life and far from the downtrodden fellow of the last week or so.

"Alright Isobel? How's it going?" he said, as if talking to some random bloke at the bar.

"Fine, fine. Apart from a twisted knee." she replied.

"Oh dear. That's a nasty looking bruise too." said Crook, semi concernedly.

"Anyway," said Mortem. "The deed is done. They're all over there look and none of them the wiser."

"Just wait until they get home - they're in for a bit of a shock." said Crook

"What exactly did you do?"

Miz Mortem related the tale of what had happened with Crook listening on in glee.

"That's bloody marvellous!" he grinned. "A top notch bit of work there Isobel. I'm beginning to enjoy this witchcraft stuff."

"Keep your voice down Russell." hissed Mortem. "We don't want the whole pub knowing!"

She then took a small sip of her coffee and got up to limp to the ladies toilet.

"Hey Riz, she's on her way now," whispered Jinny. "Go on, give us a spectacular one!" said Lou, hoarsely.

Riz ducked down, as if she had just dropped something and had stooped to pick it up and uttered yet another magic incantation followed by a wave of her hands, then sat straight back up in her chair.

The very proud and snobby Miz Mortem proceeded to simply slip in mid-air, or so it appeared.

Very dramatic it was, like something from a Tom and Jerry cartoon, where they slip on a cartoon banana.

"Waaah! Ha Ha Ha!" rasped Miss Lou, but not too loudly. "Mine's a double!"

The remainder of the ladies put their hands to their mouths and stifled their amusement.

"No wonder you've twisted your knee carrying on like that." said the barmaid who was at an adjacent table collecting glasses. "Would you say you were accident prone maybe?" she continued.

"Glenda! Get the first aid box." ordered the landlord to his long suffering wife.

What a commotion. Strangers were offering their assistance and even Mr Crook had deigned to sidle over and see what the fuss was all about. Isobel Mortem never did make it to the loo.

Part 1: A Bustle In The Hedgerow

The Accident and Emergency department of the town's General Hospital was her next stop, aided by the reluctant, not to say embarrassed, Mr Crook.

"What an exceedingly jolly wizard wheeze," cackled Lou "What a, a … cataclysmic misadventure!" she howled.

Jinny, Lou, Riz and Nancy now had the pub to themselves, apart from a few stragglers at the bar, and were feeling contented, relaxed and mirthsome.

"The sad thing is, the old scarecrow thinks we don't know who she is." said Jinny. "It puts us at an enormous advantage."

"Sup up and let's get back, eh?" said Lou.

"Fancy a corned beef hash anyone?" asked Jinny.

"Yeeeah!" said the others as they put their coats on, ready to leave. And off they trailed, up the steepish lane back to Jinny's cottage, laughing all the way.

"Hey! I haven't noticed that ivy before …" said Lou, nearing the house. "Is that what *she* did?"

"Originally it covered the windows and everything but I decided it looked quite good so I just wanded the windows clear and left the rest." Jinny said "Like it then?"

"It looks fab that, Jin." said Riz.

"Very atmospheric." said Lou admiringly.

"I've already seen it," said Nancy, "*and* I've left my car in the village. I'm losing it, honestly. Better get back to it in case someone rings for a job. See you all soon!"

"See ya Nancy. Call round anytime luv and … thank you." Jinny waved her hand in farewell to Nancy, then waved it again across the door to let everyone in.

The cats and Raph were all dozing. Nothing new there.

“Fire on!” said Riz, after checking that Stripes wasn’t asleep in the grate. “Corned beef hash on!” said Jinny as portions of carrots, onions, potatoes, spices and of course, corned beef made their way into a medium sized black cauldron.

Jinny added a pint of water, two stock cubes and a few herbs then took the whole lot to the fireplace and hung the cauldron over the flames. “Give it an hour and we’ll be reet.” she said.

“An hour Jin? I could’ve died of malnutrition by then.” said Riz. “Why don’t you just wand it?”

“It’s not the same Riz. It’s a bit like microwaving - not very organic.” replied Jinny.

“You can’t get any more organic than witchcraft, Jin.” said Lou, unhelpfully.

“That Goblin’s not back is it?” said Jinny and they all burst out laughing. Again.

That loving, devoted couple, now known as Russell and Isobel, were making their way across the hospital car park. Isobel had her arm around Russell’s shoulder and was limping quite badly.

“Can’t you do anything magical to take the pain away?” asked Crook pathetically

“Not until I get home, no. I need my potions and spell books for that kind of thing.” she replied.

“It’s very unfortunate Isobel, falling over twice in one day, don’t you think?”

“Very.” she said coldly. “If I didn’t know any better I’d say it’s got

something to do with that rabble up at the cottage.”

“But they don’t know who you are …” said Crook.

“I don’t *think* they know who I am, but I’m telling you - stumbling like that is no accident.”

Part 1: A Bustle In The Hedgerow

"Let's go back to your place and I'll borrow a couple of painkillers from you. I want to go past Demonia Cottage and see what's happening." she added.
"Oh, OK. No probs." said Crook, staring emptily ahead.

Meanwhile, the much longed for corned beef hash was almost ready.
"Who wants red cabbage?" asked Jinny.
Lou and Riz put their hands in the air and so did the cats.
"Don't be ridiculous boys and girl. Cats don't eat red cabbage - you'll be sick." she said.
"I like nibbling on plants," Jet piped up. "Is it not the same kind of thing?"
"Is it 'eck Jet! It's soaked in vinegar and stuff …."
"Ewww, I won't bother then." said Jet.
"Nor us!" said the other two. Raph carried on kipping.
The girls were sat around the dining table waiting for their bowls to be filled when they heard a car pull up outside.
"Who's ordered a taxi so they can avoid Jinny's corned beef hash?" laughed Lou.
No one answered. Jinny put the cauldron down on the table and told the girls to help themselves as she walked over to the window.
It was an old Range Rover, sat there with its engine running. Two people were inside, both looking towards Jinny's beloved cottage.
"Ladies, we've got company!" said Jinny.
"Oh typical, I'm *starving*!" said Riz, slamming her fork down. Riz was known to become quite narky when it came to food, or the lack of it.

"The ivy's gone from the windows and they've obviously managed to get back in the house," said Isobel

Mortem. "So that was a waste of time. I'm going to have to come up with something more 'challenging'. Can we come back later Russell?"

"Aye, if you really think you must." said Crook.

"Of course I *must*!" snapped Mortem.

Crook put the car in 'drive' and set off towards his own newly safari themed abode.

"They're going now…" said Jinny.

"Good." said Lou. "Come on and get something down yer." "They're up to something, you know?" Jinny said tensely.

"Who are? Who was it?" asked Riz, spooning huge dollops of hash into her bowl.

"Those two! Crook and the Bride of Frankenstein." said Jinny.

"Oh, is *that* who it was? I thought you were getting a bit overly paranoid for a minute there." said Lou.

"I guarantee they'll be back later - *guarantee* it - just you wait and see …" Jinny said.

"Well, let's just not go to bed eh? We can have a nap after we've eaten and one of us can take it in turn to keep a look out. What do you reckon?" said Lou, ever sensible, sometimes.

"We've been asleep all day, why don't you let us do the look out and you lot get your heads down?" said Jet helpfully.

"Yes, great idea, sounds like a plan Jetty." said Jinny. "Hutch up and pass us the ladle please Riz."

Jet and Spike positioned themselves on the front window ledge and Stripes looked after the back window ledge. Raph continued to snooze …

THE WITCH AND JET SPLINTERS

Part 1: A Bustle In The Hedgerow

PARCHMENT 18

Pixie Patrol

Two pixies had been staking the Crook residence out, under the orders of their boss, Miss Slinky.

They watched Crook's car approach the house and saw both Crook and Mortem (sounds like a corrupt firm of solicitors, doesn't it?) get out and enter the insipid bungalow.

The pixies had been told to spy on them and to listen to any plans they might be hatching, so, with that in mind, they inched themselves closer to the house, scaled the front door, reached the letterbox and dropped themselves through it.

"You know it might have to wait until tomorrow for the next attack," said Mortem. "I'm not feeling too energetic after the falls and I need time to really consider what would be the most effective course of action with regards to that Demonia tribe."

"You could be right Isobel, no point in rushing things." said Crook, who, if the truth be known, couldn't be bothered to go back out again tonight. The pixies were hidden behind an African mask that hadn't made its way up on to the wall yet.

"No point at all. Revenge is a dish best served cold, or so they say." quoted Mortem.

"Do they? What, like a salad?" said Crook, disinterestedly.

"A salad? What *are* you on about man?"

"Fancy something to eat? All this talk of salads has given me a touch of the hunger." said Crook.

"Not really," said Mortem. "I'll have a Martini though, if you have any in. Extra dry."

"Naturally." said Crook and went off to the kitchen.
"Will you be staying over tonight, Isobel?" shouted Crook from the kitchen.
"*Staying over*?" she said, as if a dog had just cocked it's leg up on her. "With *you*?"
There was a short silence and after properly considering the invitation she replied "Yes, go on then. I'll stay on the couch. No! *You* stay on the couch and I'll have your bed!"
"Fair enough." agreed Crook. At least it meant he didn't have to drive her all the way home again.
The Martini was delivered, Extra Dry, just like Miz Mortem and Crook sank his teeth into a ham and cheese butty.
"I'm going to have to get my skates on if I'm to be ready for the excavation work y'know. January will be here before we know it." said Crook. "Time just seems to fly away these days. Maybe it's an age thing?"
"Speak for yourself, Russell. Time stays just the way it should … in my world." said Mortem mysteriously.
The pixies had all the information they needed, apart from an actual date, so they sneaked off back home via the letterbox.

"They're startin' work in January Miss Slinky," said the first pixie. "We didn't hear a date but that's when it's all goin' to start anyway. That man said."
"An' that woman. She's an witch an' not a nice one like Jinny an' she's going to attack her tomorrow. Jinny that is. Er, we didn't get a time though …" said the second pixie.
"Thank you very much for that information chaps," said Slinky, obviously pleased that her plan to put out pixie spies had borne fruit. "I shall go to

Jinny's immediately and forewarn her of the impending onslaught. Would you care to chaperone me please?"

"We'd be honoured to," said number 1 pixie, emphasising the 'H' in 'honoured' when he really shouldn't have.

"Come along then, there is no time to lose," she said as she hurriedly flapped her lovely wings, "ask those owls if you can have a piggy back, would you please?"

The owls looked at one another and, because it was for Jinny's welfare, they consented to giving the pixies a lift and off they flew, into the night sky and onward to Demonia Cottage (2).

Everyone in Jinny's cosy home had fallen asleep, even the cats who were supposed to be guarding the place.

A flap of the letterbox soon woke the cats (and Raph) and they all stood to attention, awaiting the worst, when in popped Miss Slinky with the two pixies.

"Awaken Miss Jinny if you please Mr Splinters," she said to Jet. "I have grave news."

"Oh dear." said Jet. "Hang on please." and he padded over to the dining table where Jinny's head was resting in her empty bowl.

"Miss Jinny," he meowed. "Wake up, quick - you've got a visitor!"

"Oh bloody hell! She's not here already, is she?" Jinny said sleepily

"Miss Slinky's here - not the one you were expecting …"

"Slinky? Blimey. An unexpected pleasure …"

Jinny got up from the table. She had tiny chunks of carrot, a smear of beef stock and the odd strip of onion in her hair but she didn't care because she didn't know.

Part 1: A Bustle In The Hedgerow

"What brings you out on such a chilly evening?" asked Jinny.

Slinky proceeded to tell her all about her pixie spies, Miz Mortem, the excavation work and the impending attack that was about to occur sometime tomorrow.

"At least we can all get ourselves to bed then." said Jinny, making light of the situation.

The others were soon stirred from their slumber and Jinny repeated to them what Slinky had just related.

"Miss Louise, you seem to have a piece of bread on your forehead." Slinky said helpfully.

"Have I? Again?"

Slinky smiled at the raggle taggle trio. Jinny was a true friend to her and her kin and it appeared she had now gained two new similar comrades in Riz and Lou. She had also developed a soft spot for young Jet, or 'Mr Splinters' as she called him.

It would pain her deeply were anything horrid to happen to them and she was determined to ensure that nothing did.

"Jinny - I will despatch a pixie patrol over to you in the morning, with the dawn. Do not concern yourself with providing refreshments for them - I will make sure they have provisions. I want you to concentrate on combating whatever that terrible woman has in store for you and the patrol will be right behind you." said Slinky.

"You're a real sweetheart Slinks, thank you." and Jinny kissed the end of her little finger, bent down and placed it on Slinky's cheek.

"Bless you." Slinky blushed and smiled a faerie smile.

"We had better be on our way now. I will return at some point through the day, all being well. Goodnight to you all and good luck. Chaps - home!" she commanded her chaperones and they disappeared in the blink of an eye through the letterbox.

The owls were still waiting patiently outside. The two pixies hopped on their backs as Slinky, looking for all the world like a firefly, led the way back to the clearing.

"Fancy a cocoa before bed?" Jinny asked her two best friends

"Cocoa? That's not very witchy Jin. Not very good for the ol' image, what. I'll have a sherry. A large one please." said Lou lighting her last cigarette of the day.

"Got any mulled wine in stock Jin?" asked Riz.

"Yeah, I've still got some left over from last Christmas. A pint?"

Riz was aghast. "Good lord nooo Jinny! Just half a pint and a bit more please."

"Orange slices and cinnamon stick?"

"Mais oui mon ami, s'il vous plait."

"French." Jet informed Spike.

Jinny rolled her eyes and headed for the kitchen. Would they *ever* get to bed tonight?

"I've devised the perfect plan." said Isobel Mortem, suddenly, to her half dozing partner in grime, Russell Crook. "I doubt they'll be expecting a return visit from me so this is going to be a splendid surprise. Ha Haaa. Drop me off at their confounded cottage at 8.00am would you?"

"Whatever you say Isobel." slurred Crook, already halfway towards a deep sleep.

"Goodnight! Don't let the couch bugs bite!" she shouted in his ear and took herself off to Crook's bedroom, humming an obscure medieval madrigal.

Morning seemed to arrive abruptly. Our loveable coven were still in their nightwear when they heard a loud grating, creaky sound emanating from the front of the house.

Jet leapt up to the window sill and spotted an old four-wheel drive on the lane.

He also spotted a huge iron gate covering the front door.

"Well, that wasn't there last night." he thought …

"What's going on out there Jet?" asked Jinny, yawning.

"You've acquired a new gate Jinny." he said.

"A what?!"

Jinny swept her hand across the door, and as it opened it appeared that there had indeed emerged the unwelcome addition of a large iron gate, erected right slap in front of her beautiful eighteenth century wooden door. Beyond the gate, her front garden was now covered in tomato frogstools (very similar to regular toadstools but bigger, deep red and, erm, called frogstools. They were also, supposedly, extremely dangerous to a witch). Further down the garden she could make out the sight of approximately a dozen pixies all bound in reeds, struggling to get free.

And was that really a stream running freely past her own front gate? "Lou! Riz! Boys! Girl! What on earth do you make of this?"

The faithful friends edged closer to the front door and took in the newly hampered view.

"She's gone the whole hog, Jin," said Lou. "She's had her old folklore books out and come up with, with … *this*!?"

"Call me naïve Lou, but what exactly is … *this*?!"

"What are witches supposed to fear?"

"The same things that anyone fears, I imagine." said Jinny, fearlessly.

"No Jin. Witches are reputedly afraid of iron, running water, salt and tomato frogstools. You really *should* have paid attention at uni you know."

"At uni?" Jinny said, nonplussed. "What did *I* study at uni that would have had anything in common with something like this?!"

"You're a witch Jinny, surely you've at least read *some* books on the subject?"

"Yes, well, yes, I've obviously read some books, but somehow all *this* seems to have bypassed me …"

"So you're not afraid of iron, running water, frogstools or salt?" Lou continued with her interrogation.

"Obviously not. We all had salt in our corned beef hash last night - did it scare you?"

"I don't think so luv, I ate it it all…how about you, Riz?"

"I'm scared of nowt. Iron? How can *anyone* be afraid of iron? Too much salt, well, that's not good for you but iron … and running water? Tosh!"

"I must say, I've never been afraid of all that either," admitted Lou. "Though those frogstools look a bit suspicious."

"She's calling our bluff then," said Jinny, "and I say if she thinks *we're* afraid of all this, then it's a good bet that *she's* afraid of it."

"Get rid of it all then, Jinny." said Riz.

Jinny ran upstairs to get Rosie, her wand, but her bedroom door was locked, and not in the usual way. It was locked with magic and the only way she could undo it was with her wand.

Jinny felt a sudden panic coming over her, then, just as suddenly, she let out a loud laugh and called downstairs "Jetty! Come here my sweet."

Part 1: A Bustle In The Hedgerow

In moments a familiar little black head, with traces of bright red lipstick on it, popped around the corner.

“Would you be so kind as to go through the bedroom door and fetch Rosie for me please, Jet?”

“It would be my pleasure.” he replied.

Through the door he magically passed, on to the bed and up on to the top of the wardrobe, using his paw to bring the treasured sprig out.

His teeth bit softly into the wood as he carried it from the wardrobe, jumped down onto the bed and back out through the door.

“Your wonderfulness.” he said presenting Jinny with her beloved wand. “Thank you very kindly, my darling.” she smiled and pointed it at the door, uttering the word “Simsim”, releasing it from its enchantment immediately.

“Next!” she then shouted and hurtled downstairs to rejoin her friends at the front door.

“TALASHAA!” she commanded and the feared iron gate disintegrated into the air.

The salt that was laid out on the floor behind the iron gate was a doddle.

“Woosh!” said Jinny and that too disappeared.

Now for the dreaded frogstools. Were they *really* hazardous to witches? Jinny boldly picked one from the ground and sniffed at it.

“Hmm, I’m not taking any chances with these.” she said and pointed Rosie at the Fungal crop. “AIQTILAE!” and they were gone.

“You’re quite impressive when you’re riled Jinny.” said Lou with an admiring smile on her bright red lips.

Next she stepped down the small slope of the garden, ignoring the pixies, for now.

She once again pointed her wand, this time towards the running stream of water outside her front gate.

“JAF! JAF!” she incanted and the water evaporated into nothing.

“Now then boys,” she addressed the pixie patrol. “You’re going to have to get yourself some walkie talkies aren’t you?”

“IITLAQ SARAH.” she said and the pixies binds came free.

“Oh thanking you, Miss Jinny.” said the pixie nearest to her. “That witch woman was truly ‘orrible. We didn’t stand a chance so we didn’t.”

“She said she was goin’ to come back and slit our throats.” added another. “The only way she’ll be making an appearance around here again will be in a hearse.” vowed Jinny. “Now you lot get back to Miss Slinky and let her know what happened. Tell her to saddle up the troops … This Is WAR!” Jinny made her way back up the garden steps and was greeted with a round of applause from her companions, apart from the cats and Raph because they couldn’t actually clap.

“That was a magnificent display, Jinny. World class! You scared the hell out of me, forget the iron and salt!” praised Lou.

“Remind me to never get in your bad books, Jin.” said Riz, timidly. “I’m reminding you *now*!” she laughed “Breakfast anyone?” and off they went to magic up a splendid feast to set them up for the rest of the day. And a very busy day it was to be …

THE WITCH AND JET SPLINTERS

Part 1: A Bustle In The Hedgerow

PARCHMENT 19

Pow Wow

"They won't be messing with us again Russell," said Isobel Mortem confidently. "They wouldn't dare!"

"No Isobel, I dare say they won't." said Crook, skimming through the morning paper.

Mr Crook was, at this stage, seriously beginning to think whether the golf course was really worth all the trouble. But what other plans did he have for his life? He needed to make his mark and this was the ideal opening for him. But *why* did he need to make his mark? Was he bullied and ignored as a child? Did he feel unworthy as a human being? A nobody. He *needed* respect. He craved it. But he didn't realise that this was the wrong way to go about getting it.

"Penny for your thoughts Russell." Miz Mortem butted in.

"They're not worth that much." he said grumpily.

"Please don't tell me that after all the commotion you've caused you're having doubts …"

"*I* haven't caused any commotion, it's you lot - the Witches of Windlestraws that've been doing all the hell raising." he said.

"I thought I was doing you a favour. Is that not now the case?" asked Mortem.

"I - I don't know. Really I don't. My head's all over the place."

"This is what they *want* you to feel like, don't you see? They're beating you if you continue to think negatively. Your dream was to own a golf course … why has that changed?" Isobel Mortem was beginning to get frustrated.

Part 1: A Bustle In The Hedgerow

"It hasn't changed, I'm just not sure if I'm going about it the right way. I mean, all this goblin/fairy/witch stuff. Why did I have to pick that particular plot of land? Surely there's another location that will do the job just as well?"

"If I didn't know better I would say that prile of harpies have somehow taken your mind over. You need to be strong Russell. Their fight is over. You're free to go ahead with your plans, unhindered." she said … rather prematurely.

"You're probably right," he sighed, "I just can't seem to get rid of these nagging doubts in my head."

"I'll make you a bacon butty and a brew, how does that sound? Then we'll go out for a walk. Clear the cobwebs, eh?" she reassured him.

"OK, thanks Isobel." he smiled for the first time that day.

"Brown or red sauce?"

"Brown of course! You shouldn't need to ask!" he laughed, unconvincingly.

Jinny, Lou, Riz and the cats finished their breakfasts and started to (playfully) argue who was going to have use of the bathroom first.

Well, the cats didn't - they could wash and groom wherever they liked.

"You go first Jinny," said Riz. "It's your house."

"You go first Jinny," said Lou. "You're the scariest!"

"You go last Jinny," said Jet. "You're the loveliest."

"Wooohoowooo!" teased Lou. "Hark at loverboy here!"

"Ma petite cherie." Jinny kissed Jet on his head as he gave off the loudest purr she'd ever heard. "Steady Gomez." she added.

The bathroom rota was finally sorted out and everyone had now, after about an hour, been fed, washed and dressed.

"I'm off for a pow wow with Slinky - anyone coming? Jet, you don't have a choice by the way." announced Jinny.

"Just you try and stop me matey!" There was a short pause. "Ermmm, I'll rephrase that: Yes, I'll come along if you'll have me." said Lou, remembering Jinny's earlier dervish-like exhibition in the garden.

"I'm in," said Riz. "Stripes? Spike? Coming?"

The cats stretched themselves, as they do, then stood in line as Lou planted her ritual lipsticky kiss on each of their heads.

"Ready!" they said.

"Quick sticks then!" said Jinny.

Lots of fake furs, scarves, witchy hats, twitchy tails and pointy wellies later they turned up at the faerie hole in the hedgerow.

Jinny collared a random pixie who was busying himself with some berries.

"Merry meet my good fellow, would you please tell Miss Slinky that Miss Jinny is here to see her?"

"Heeey! *You're* Miss Jinny? I've 'eard about you from the pixie patrol. You've got a fan club you know?"

"Have I now?" she blushed.

The pixie asked her to hold on a minute and went off down the faerie hole.

"Chaps! You'll never guess who's here! It's that Miss Jinny … she wants to see Miss Slinky. Would you pass the message on down please?"

Within a minute about two hundred different species of fairy folk appeared out of the hole: elves, pixies, faeries, gnomes … it was actually a bit tricky trying to make out who was what, apart from the faeries because they had wings and were all female.

They all crowded together in the clearing, near the faerie circle, looked up at Jinny and bowed in unison.

"Well! Is this the fan club then?" Jinny said, feeling quite pleased with herself.

"Form an orderly queue for autographs!" laughed Miss Lou.

Old Wilf, the gnome, was one of the folk at the front of the gathering and he was carrying something in his arms.

"This 'ere's for you Miss Jinny," he said reddening, "a token of our esteem for one so brave, noble and so … so … so … beautiful." and he passed the package to Jinny and quickly stepped back with the rest of the faerie folk.

"Thank you very much indeed. A thousand blessings on you all." said Jinny, as if she had just been awarded an Oscar.

"Open it when you get home please Miss Jinny." said Wilf.

"Princess Jinny." said Riz through her cigarette, baffled as to what all the fuss was about.

Jinny stooped down and kissed Wilf on the cheek and Wilf's face burned bright red.

"OOOOOOOooooh!" went a cry from the throng.

It was then that the leader of this assortment of strange but lovely little creatures emerged from the hedgerow. Enter Miss Slinky.

"A thousand greetings Miss Jinny. Miss Louise, Miss Riz …" she nodded. "We have much to discuss, do we not? Let us repair to Wilf's work den under yonder trees and we will ruminate over a cup of mead."

The trio, their familiars and Slinky then made towards a camouflaged little shelter which appeared much bigger inside than it did out.

Miniature lanterns gave light and a tiny fire warmed the place more than adequately.

They all sat on the twig covered floor,
circling the fire.

"This is cosy, Slinks." said Lou.

"It is Wilf's pride and joy, his palace if you will." she replied as Jet did a spray in one of the corners.

Wilf materialised through the entrance, on cue, still a tad red faced and laden with a tray of acorns filled with best honey mead.

"'ere you are ladies. Don't neck it all back at once." he wheezed, bowed and left.

"I'm going to start bringing my own cup to these meetings." said Riz quietly.

"You're *such* a lush!" whispered Lou.

Jinny was the first to address the conclave, "I presume you got my message from the pixie patrol Slinky?"

"I did indeed." Slinky nodded.

"Are you in agreement then that we wage a full-on assault on this woman, as soon as possible? We would need the help of every member of your faerie folk and more besides … even goblins! Can you arrange that?"

"I will have every gnome, pixie, faerie, elf, sprite, will o' the wisp, banshee and yes, even goblin, in the vicinity at your disposal as soon as you give the word. It will be a day not soon forgotten Jinny."

"Who knows what day it is today?" asked Jinny.

"Oh, I'm hopeless at this sort of thing but I'd guess it's now Saturday," said Riz, "and I only say that because old Mortem would've been at the town hall if it'd been a weekday and we all know she wasn't …"

"True!" said Jinny, "and I know it's not Sunday because there haven't been any church bells. How about next Wednesday night? Wednesday's child is full of woe and that's exactly what she's going to be when we've finished with her – woeful."

"Wednesday evening it is then. From about 9.00pm?" concurred Slinky. "Yes, an attack at the house from 9.00pm, but how about a modicum of mischief throughout working hours, at her office in the town hall? Just a few sinister pranks to set her on edge for the day?"

"That can be organised quite easily Jinny. Let us say from 10.30am? Just after she has had her morning break?"

"Perfect Slinky. Now listen, there is no plan as such, all we need to do on the night is create complete, unbridled chaos. Enough to make sure that the woman never sets foot in these parts again - ever! And if Crook follows her, all the better!"

"There will be an impish army awaiting your arrival on Wednesday. Ready to undertake your bidding, Miss Jinny. On that I solemnly promise." said Slinky, promisingly.

"So mote it be." Jinny said most earnestly, picking up her parcel, beckoning Jet and making her exit, with the others following close behind.

"Jin, I'm going to call in at the newsagents in the village. I'm desperate for something to read." said Lou as they neared Demonia Cottage (2).

"Righto Lou," said Jinny. "I'll get on with some housework while you're gone. I'm still finding bits of soot everywhere. Fancy donning a pinny, Riz?"

"I fancy no such thing!" came the reply. "I need a lie down."

So Lou ambled down the lane alone.

By the time she was halfway down she was already missing her fabulous friends, and a tear welled in her eye as she wondered how she would ever cope without them. Never were there friends so close, ever, she told herself.

"Mornin' ma'am," said the newsagent. "What can I get you?"

Lou picked up a copy of Village Life magazine and asked for three packs of her favourite cigarettes and a large packet of Jelly Babies.

"If you can't eat the real thing, these'll have to do!" she chortled dizzily, waving the bag of sweets at the newsagent.

He looked at her, mystified, and gave her the change. 26p.

"Good day to you sir." Lou said grandly.

"Call again." said the newsagent, and away she swept.

She set off back up the lane, whistling another tune from her vast repertoire of ABBA songs.

As she walked she flipped through the pages of the magazine and spotted a competition to win a three day Christmas holiday for four to Lapland. It wasn't like Lou to be interested in such things as competitions but she thought of Jinny and Riz and how much they would love to go on such a trip.

She sat on a low wall, lit a cig and carried on reading.

All she had to do to be in with a chance of winning was text the following answer to this question: 'Which feast day is celebrated in mainly Germany and Holland every year on the 30th April?' And it had to be the correct spelling.

"Bloody hell!" she cried. "That's easy!"

She immediately got out her phone and texted the answer:

"Walpurgisnacht" - her favourite!

To complete the entry, all she had to do was add her name and address, so she typed in:

Louise Dallion,
C/O Demonia Cottage (2),
Oldchurch,
Windlestraws,
Wendle, Lancs

seeing as she wasn't currently at her own home.

She got a text back thanking her for entering the Lapland Xmas Competition and should she be a winner she would be informed via post.

"Brilliant!" she said to herself. "That'll be a nice surprise if it comes off." and continued her walk back up the lane to Jinny's.

At this stage there should be a report on events at the home of Mr Crook and his new 'friend' Isobel Mortem, but there was nothing important or interesting happening there.

She was very pleased and self-satisfied and he was still in a bit of a flux. All was still and, on the surface, peaceful.

For now.

In the interim, Jinny, Riz and the cats were pottering about the cottage, dusting, sweeping, mopping and wiping.

Riz had been cajoled into helping Jinny even though what she really wanted was just a nice lie down.

And there she was, a picture, with a cigarette in one hand, mop in the other, staring blankly at the floor.

“Are you OK with this Riz?” asked Jinny. “You don’t look too happy.”

“I hate housework. I hate it more than flippin’ Christmas.” she moaned. “Don’t tell me … it’s the adverts for bleach, polish and scourers that ruin it for you?” Jinny had a bit of a sarcastic head on today.

“What adverts? I hardly watch television.”

“But you … oh nothing. Fancy a brew?”

Riz nodded dejectedly and fell into the armchair, putting her feet up on the coffee table.

“Hey Jinny! You haven’t opened this package that the old gnome gave you!” she shouted through to the kitchen.

“Blimey Charlie - I forgot all about that.” said Jinny as she came back armed with two cups of tea.

The package lay on the coffee table next to Riz’s feet. It was wrapped in plain, brown paper and string.

“Let’s have a look then, eh?” Jinny began untying the mystery gift.

“Just rip it open Jin! Stop fiddling with the knots!” Riz said impatiently.

“No. I like to keep brown paper. It’s always good to have some handy.” After about three minutes of ‘fannying around’ as Riz put it, Jinny finally revealed the contents of the much anticipated present.

It was a giant carrot. About two and a half feet long. Nothing more, nothing less.

“Oh” said Riz. “Well … that’ll do for at least ten corned beef hash suppers, eh?” said Jinny, bemused.

“Shame you haven’t got a herd of rabbits …”

Part 1: A Bustle In The Hedgerow

"Maybe it's got mystical properties. I'll give it a quick magical scan and see …"

Jinny swiped her hands across the carrot and muttered the word "Kushif", but nothing was revealed.

"Why not plant it Jin? Maybe it'll grow into a massive carrot tree and you could open your own greengrocer's shop!"

"Riz, carrots do not grow on trees and it'd be a pretty poor greengrocer's if all it sold was carrots!"

"Hmmm, true." said Riz, thinking of other possible uses for the large vegetable.

"Hey! You could sell it on eBay as the actual nose of a giant, melted snowman!" she said enthusiastically.

"How on earth does your mind work, Riz? Even Salvador Dali, God rest his soul, would've been hard pushed to come up with something that surreal!"

"I've got a Dali print at home. That one with all the weird stuff going on." "That narrows it down somewhat, doesn't it luv?" said Jinny, flabbergasted.

Jinny rewrapped the carrot and after several attempts to get it into her vegetable rack, gave up and lay it on the kitchen table.

"One last go" she said to herself as she swiped her hand again, this time with the words, "Madha taemal".

"Wow!" she blurted. "Riz! Come here! Quick sticks!"

"What's up now?"

"Guess what this carrot does … go on."

"I thought it did nothing …"

"No, go on, think about it logically."

"Gets put into a corned beef hash?"

"Riz, please, use your imagination, you usually do!"

"Erm … turns into some kind of spaceship?"

"I give up, really I do. What is supposed to happen to you if you eat your carrots?"

"You get orange bits between your teeth …"

"You can see in the dark! Dork!"

"Streuth! I thought that was an old wives' tale. So it's true then?"

"It's true with this particular carrot, Rizzo"

"I'm off for a wee to celebrate then." said Riz, inching up the staircase.

"To celebrate what?"

"Life!" said Riz enigmatically.

Jinny put her hands on her hips and doubled over with laughter. What *was* that girl on?

The front door opened and in walked Lou.

"Hiya captain! What ya laughing at?"

"Guess!"

"Riz?" said Lou. "Where is she?"

"Guess!"

"Toilet?" Lou said, without a moment's hesitation.

"She's celebrating life, apparently."

"She does a lot of that, doesn't she?"

Jet stirred for the first time in quite a while and looked up at Lou. "I wondered where you'd got to Miss Lou. I was getting worried."

"Ah diddums," she said planting yet another red kiss on his head. "It must be a tricky job worrying when you're fast asleep."

"Did you get what you wanted Lou?" asked Jinny.

"Oh aye. Cigs, mag and look …" and she held up the bumper bag of Jelly

Babies. "Dinner!"

"Jelly Baby stew? Jelly Babies on toast?" enquired Jinny.

THE WITCH AND JET SPLINTERS

Part 1: A Bustle In The Hedgerow

"Jelly Babies au natural!"

"French that is, Lou." said Jet, predictably.

"Calm down, Gomez." said Jinny.

"Hey up, Lou." said Riz, as she returned from her celebration of life. "What ya got?"

"These!" and re-presented the hallowed bag of sweeties.

"Yumzah! Come on then, get 'em opened." Riz said, with a half-burned cig hanging from the corner of her mouth.

"Patience woman. All good things come to her what waits." quoted Lou, badly.

"Fire on!" ordered Riz, and the room instantly began to warm up, at last.

"Oh, where's Stripes?" she added.

"Asleep in the fire grate, as always."

"Shi… Fire OFF!" she yelled, but Stripes wasn't there.

"I do hope you haven't incinerated my baby." said Lou, tongue-in-cheek.

"Oh Noooo! What have I done?" Riz screamed. "Nothing luv, Stripes is over there, sunbathing on the window sill. You should be a bit more attentive you know, Riz."

"Fire ON!" scowled Riz.

Jinny noticed an envelope by the door and went over to pick it up.

"Heeey, these might be our solstice tickets …"

She slit the envelope with one of her long nails and sure enough it was four tickets for the Wizards In A Blizzard gig at Spiderwood Farm. "Bonza!" she was quite thrilled. None of them had been out together properly for months and this was looking like it was going to be a very special night indeed.

The winter solstice and a top notch Rock band all in one go! Bonza! Bonza! and thrice Bonza!

The three of them settled down around the fire with a saucer of Jelly Babies each.

"I'll be glad when Wednesday's over and done with," said Jinny. "Although I'm quite looking forward to leading an army of fay folk, I must say." "Queen Jinny." said Riz through a mouthful of Jelly Babies.

"Oi you! Less cheek." spluttered Jinny.

"Only japing Jin. You'd make a great queen. Though you'd have to have your hair cut and permed and get one of those purpley grey rinses …" "Bloody hell Riz, you don't *have* to have your hair that way if you're a Queen!"

"You'd have to get a corgi dog too …" Riz rabbited on. "I can't see the cats liking *that* idea much …"

"Are you actually serious Riz? Is that what your idea of a queen really is?"

"… all that waving you'd have to do, changing guards, eating royal jelly

…"

"Royal Jelly? Do you know what Royal Jelly is Riz? Hang on …"

Jinny got her phone out and logged on to the internet typing in 'royal jelly'.

"Here we are - Wikipedia - royal jelly: 'Royal jelly is secreted from the glands in the heads of worker bees, and is fed to all bee larvae' etc etc." read Jinny.

"Good lord! That's disgusting! You'd think a queen could afford to eat something a wee bit nicer than that! Even *we* can afford *proper* jelly Babies!"

"Riz, I, I despair. Honestly I do. How do you manage to even *consider* some of these conversations?"

"You started it Jin." said Riz, eyes wide open.

"Did I? How's that then, Einstein?"

"Saying you wanted to lead an army and all that gubbins …"

"Goblin alert!" shouted Lou. "Break it up you two. Jet would you be so kind as to have a sniff around and find where the goblin's hiding please?"

"Aye aye captain," said Jet, who had been entranced by the various nonsensical outbursts.

"Miss Lou to you matey." corrected Lou.

"Soz."

Behind the curtain, completely unnoticed by the dozy Stripes, was none other than the same Goblin that had been evicted only a short while before. Jet grabbed him by the neck with his paws and dragged him over to the fireplace.

"What have you been told, mister?" Lou asked in her strictest voice.

"N-n-not to come back Miss?"

"Precisely. And yet here you are - back!"

"Beg yer pardon Miss but I just got wind of the battle that's about to 'appen on Wednesday. I was asked if I'd be prepared to take part, as it were. I told 'em Oooh no, that Miss wouldn't like that. She wouldn't want me there I said. And they said you would and I said you wouldn't, then they said 'Oh yes she would' and I sai …"

"Hell's teeth man - spit it out! Why are you here?" Lou butted in, for sanity's sake.

"Just, erm, just to ask if you would mind if I was to represent you all in erm your hour of need, like. I would be very 'onoured, really I would."

Miss Lou softened her aggressiveness.

"In that case sir, we would be equally 'onoured if you were to fight for our cause on this esteemed occasion."

"Maybe *Lou* should run for queen." said Riz behind her hand.

"Would you care for a drink of something? *What's* your name?"

"George, Miss. Have you any berry juice please?"

Jinny got up and went to the kitchen, in search of something along those lines.

"Mr George … would you be so kind as to turn your argumentative switch off please? However you do it …" asked Lou, warming to the little fellow. "Oh, I'm not sure how to do that, Miss. Wherever I go there's usually a bit of argy bargy and that's the way it's always been."

"Not to worry," said Lou. "Ladies, just remember, when you start arguing again, *why* it's happening and try to keep it down, eh? Would you care to partake in a Jelly Baby, George?"

"Don't mind if I do Miss, thanking you."

Lou offered him a green one to match his outfit and Jinny gave him a

small glass of berry juice. Well, it was Ribena Light actually …

THE WITCH AND JET SPLINTERS

Part 1: A Bustle In The Hedgerow

PARCHMENT 20

Viking

"Pig Brain!" yelped Riz, to seemingly no one in particular, although it could have been aimed at either Lou or Jinny, or maybe even the cats or Raph (remember him? He prefers to keep in the shadows you know).

"That's not very nice, Riz." said Jinny, for some reason automatically thinking it was her that it was aimed at.

"Three and five letters … 'American delicacy popular in the Midwestern United States and believed to be a dish handed down from German settlers in the area'."

"Oi! Are you doing my crossword, Riz?" said Lou, bordering on tetchy.

"Yeah, it's been sat here nearly three days and you haven't been anywhere near it."

"I was saving that for best!"

"Best what?" asked Riz, incredulously.

"Best keep your bloody hands off it Missy, that's what!"

"Is that goblin back?" Jinny said scanning the room.

"You don't need a goblin to instigate an argument over someone nicking someone else's crossword." said Lou.

"Do you want it back then, Lou?" asked Riz innocently.

"Yes, yes I do actually, thank you very much."

Lou swiped her Village Life magazine from Riz's grip and checked just how much of her crossword had been completed.

"You've answered one clue, Riz. One bloody clue!"

"You should be happy …"

Part 1: A Bustle In The Hedgerow

"You've answered one across and the lord only knows how you managed to answer it without the help of some other letters. You never cease to amaze me, lady."

"You finish it off then, Lou" said Riz helpfully.

"Finish it off?! It's not even been started! You've been looking at it for an hour that *I* know of!"

"Hey, there's a competition in there to go to Lapland for Xmas. Why don't we enter it?" said Riz randomly.

"The closing date's been and gone Riz." mumbled Lou.

"That's a shame. I quite fancy Lapland. Where *is* it?"

"Somewhere north of Norway, I think." said Lou looking for a clue she could answer.

"It's in Finland, Riz." Jinny corrected.

"Brilliant! Where's that then? It sounds familiar." said Riz, twiddling the old, mysterious looking key she always had hanging around her neck.

"Scandinavia - round that way." muttered Lou.

"Riz, correct me if I'm wrong but aren't you the very same Riz that has travelled extensively throughout Europe and Russia and beyond?" asked Jinny.

"I have, yes Jinny. Exciting times." she said wistfully.

"Do you recall *any* of the countries that you've visited?"

"I remember Greece, Italy - I met a lovely bloke in Italy, China …"

"China?! You've never mentioned China before!"

"It just came back to me."

Lou leaned forward.

"Please, just for once, can we desist from having any more of these off-the-wall conversations? Riz, I'm going to do a past life regression on you. One, it might stop you smoking and two, it might help to spark off something you can actually remember from *this* life!"

"Oh! Would you Lou? That'd be thrilling!"

Lou stared back at her sardonically and went back to her crossword.

While this stimulating war of words was in motion the cats had decided to play 'stick your nose up another's cat's bottom and see what reaction you get'.
It was a complex game wherein cat number one would approach cat number two and the first cat would stick it's nose up the second cat's bottom.
Then the first cat had to gauge as to whether the second cat was going to turn round and give the first cat a damn good walloping or whether the second cat would just stand there enjoying it.
Hence, there was a pile of three cats throwing themselves at each other in the corner of the room, near the TV set, with much howling, screeking and pawing.
"Will you *please* behave!" bawled Jinny. "It's bad enough listening to these two without having to put up with a background soundtrack from you lot!"
The cats immediately ceased their game, stared at Jinny then went back into sulk/sleep mode.
"May I just remind everyone that tomorrow we are about to wage war?" Jinny declared gravely.
"Oooh, is that tomorrow?" asked Riz, clueless.
"My stars on high Riz, didn't you put it in your phone diary? You know what you're like…"
"No need Jin, I'm here. I'll know when it's happening because you'll tell me."
Jinny stared at the ceiling and counted to eleven.
"I didn't forget, Jin," said Lou reassuringly. "I'll be ready with me armour and me trusty steed."
"Your what?"
"My wand and broomstick."

Part 1: A Bustle In The Hedgerow

"When this is all over, I think we should have a bit of a break somewhere, lay our heads low, so to speak." said Jinny, in hope.

"Brainy idea, Jin." said Riz, waving yet another cigarette in the air.

"Hmmm, maybe …" said Lou.

"Will I be able to come on one of these breaks?" asked Jet.

"Depends luv," said Jinny. "You might have to stay in a cattery for a few days but that shouldn't worry you, you'd be able to come and go as you please, unlike normal cats."

"But I want to be with you Jinny." Jet sadly replied.

"Now don't you go getting all soft on me, young feller. It's not as if I'll be leaving you forever, is it?"

"What if the plane crashes?" asked Jet.

"Plane? A plane to Scotland?"

"Is that where you're thinking of going?" he asked, still a bit sad.

"I've no idea but I know we can't afford to go abroad, so it'll be somewhere not too far away."

"If it's not too far away I'll be able to come then, won't I?"

"We'll see, let me think on it. Let me get tomorrow out of the way eh? Take a leaf out of Spike and Stripes book - they couldn't care less!"

"Hey! That's not true." said Riz "That lad's devoted to me. Who would he suckle?"

"He'd have to put up with the withdrawal symptoms, Riz. For goodness sake I'm only talking about a very short break! Anyway, forget I mentioned it. We need to focus on tomorrow."

"No focus necessary, Jin." said Lou. "You yourself said there was no plan so we're just making it up as we go along, aren't we?"

"Well, yeah, I suppose we are…"

"Great! Then let's go down the pub. I fancy a big pint of lager for a change. It's all this Scandinavian talk."

"It's made me want a wee." said Riz uncharacteristically.

"Surely not!" said Jinny and Lou on the count of three.

"I would like a pint of whatever Scandinavian lager you've got on please." said Lou, propping up the bar at Old Demmy's.

"We've only got John Willy's Pee, my love. We're a tied house, y'see?"

"A tied house? What the … have you no bottles of anything?"

"We've got 'Viking' in bottles, madam. Best Scandinavian lager brewed in Blackpool."

"Bugger. Well I'll have two bottles of that please. And a pint glass and a straw."

"Six quid please - the straw's free." smiled the landlord.

"Remind me to bring my horse next time." said Lou, cryptically.

Unsurprisingly, Riz ordered a large Pinot and Jinny opted for a big glass of advocaat with extra brandy.

"Hold the straw." she said.

"Are we staying at the bar ladies, or sitting by the fire?" asked Lou.

"Let's stay here for a change." said Jinny.

"Okey dokey, captain." said Lou and parked herself on one of the high barstools.

Part 1: A Bustle In The Hedgerow

"You've been very quiet, Riz. What's on your mind, dare I ask?" asked Jinny, daringly.

"Nothing really …"

"Now't new there then." shot back Lou.

"I was just thinking back to when I was in Egypt …"

"Egypt eh? Another one you kept quiet about." said Jinny.

"They'd love you there, Jetty," Riz said to our heroic feline who happened to be sitting near their feet. (By the way, if you were wondering why the other two cats weren't out, well, they just couldn't abide pubs). "They worship cats, especially black cats. They even have a black cat goddess

…"

"Bastet." said Lou.

"Yeah, Bastet," said Riz. "Did you know there were over three hundred thousand mummified cats buried with her in her temple?"

"It's a wonder they didn't become extinct." said Jinny.

"Anyway, I digress …"

"Ooooh! That's a big word, Riz." laughed Lou.

"I was just thinking about the time I sailed down the Nile at sunset on a

Falucca."

"What's one of them, Riz?" asked Jet. "Those." said Jinny.

"It's an ancient Egyptian boat, Jet…"

"Excuse me," an elderly gentleman had wandered over from a nearby table. "I hope you don't mind me interrupting but I couldn't help but notice … you seem to be having a conversation with your cat …"

"It's not my cat squire, it's her's." said Riz, pointing at Jinny.

"That doesn't alter the fact that you were having a conversation with it though, does it?" said the old man.

"Why? Is it illegal?" asked Lou.

"It's very peculiar madam, I must say."

"Familiar is what it is." said Lou caustically.

"You should get it on the adverts if it can talk. It'd make you quite a few bob I would imagine …"

"I can't stand adverts." said Riz.

"No, she can't." added Jinny, once again rolling her eyes towards the heavens.

"I definitely saw its lips move." said the interfering fellow.

"He doesn't have lips. None to speak of anyway. Wooha ha ha." Lou howled.

"The poor thing's cut his head look, you should get him to a vet …"

"Tell you what mister, I'll get him to the vet after I've taken him over to Granada TV studios for an audition. How's that?" said Riz.

"Yes, yes. Jolly good idea. Anyway, nice to have spoken to you … what's your name?"

"Riz."

"No, the cat."

"Jet." said Jet but as the man wasn't a witch, bird, cat or faerie he hadn't a clue what he'd said. It sounded like "Breee".

"Breee eh? That's a nice name. Lovely to have made your acquaintance Mr Breee." said the senile old chap as he doddered his way back to his table.

Part 1: A Bustle In The Hedgerow

"Couldn't make it up, could you?" said Lou staring over to the other side of the pub to check the hanging witch picture was still turned to the wall. "So … you were sailing down the Nile, Riz …" prompted Jet.
"Was I? Oh yes. That was it really. I was sailing down the Nile at sunset on a Felucca."
Jinny, Lou and Jet looked at one and other with slight despair on their faces. They should've been more than accustomed to this kind of tale by now though.

"Now let's not have too much to sup tonight, my darlings" said Jinny in her best authoritarian manner. "We've already had five rounds and we've only been here an hour and a half!"
"I'm off for a wee," said Riz, informatively. "Coming?"
"Why Riz? Why would we need the toilet at exactly the same time as you?" asked Lou perplexed, then, after a moment's consideration … "Oh go on then. I don't think I've ever been to the loo here."
Jinny stayed put. The advocaat was sneaking up on her and she didn't want to wobble.
"Eeee Jetty lad, just be thankful you don't drink alcohol. Hic!" she said as she put her head down to his level.
"I've never been given a choice, Jinny."
"No choices. No cat of mine is *ever* going to be allowed (Hic!) anywhere near this, this demonic brew. You're very well behaved you know Jet. I do Love you. I LOVE YOU JETTY!" she sang loudly for all the pub to hear "OH YES I DOOOO!"
"Who's that being loud?" Lou said to Riz, on their way back from the toilet.
"It's Jinny advocaat, she can't take her ale y'know …"
"She's only had Jelly Babies to eat since breakfast, to be fair." They passed the old gentleman's table.
"Can the cat sing as well?" he asked them.

"No, that's his owner singing, the cat's better behaved." said Lou, shaking her head.

"Still, a talking, singing cat, eh? Can he dance?"

"Haven't seen him dance. Yet." said Riz.

"Take care of him. He's a bloomin' marvel that cat."

"Isn't he just," smiled Lou. "I'll give him your regards."

Th0e pair reached the bar only to find Jinny slumped over her barstool and Jet trying to resuscitate her by licking her nose.

"Come on Jinny Lane, I think you've had your quota for the evening." said Lou, taking command.

Riz and Lou got on either side of the inebriated Jinny and carried her to the exit. Jet jumped on Lou's shoulder. Why walk when there's a shoulder to lean on?

THE WITCH AND JET SPLINTERS

Part 1: A Bustle In The Hedgerow

PARCHMENT 21

A Rum Do

"Oh my giddy Aunt." were the first words Jinny uttered when she eventually came to on Wednesday morning. "What happened last night? Am I at home?" she put her legs out of the bed and couldn't feel her feet on the floor.

"I'm dead," she said. "I've gone to Heaven and they've sent me back in disgust."

"Morning Your Wonderfulness." said Jet cheerily.

"Are you dead too Jet? Was there an explosion?"

"Only in your head I think."

"Oh no. It's that bloody advocaat again. I should stay clear of the stuff. Sneaks up and mugs you it does."

"Lou and Riz are making some breakfast. It's three square meals for you today Miss - no scimping." said Jet in a paternal way.

"Square meals? We're not having breakfast on those stupid slate things, are we?"

"I don't know. Lou just said you were to have three square meals today. I've no idea what the difference is between a square and a round meal, I'm only a cat."

"Not *only* a cat, my love. A sweetheart. My little Angel, that's what you are." said Jinny obviously still suffering the effects of the demon Dutch courage.

A voice screeched from downstairs …

"Jinno! Are you awake yet? It's half past ten you know?!"

"Go and tell Lou I'm up, there's a love." said Jinny gently so as not to make her head hurt more than it already did.

Part 1: A Bustle In The Hedgerow

At that moment Lou appeared in the bedroom doorway with a tray. "Sausage, egg, bacon, tomatoes, fried bread, mushrooms and a cuppa black coffee." she announced.

"I'm going to puke, Lou." said Jinny, heaving.

"Go on then - get it out of the way." said Lou leading her to the bathroom.

"Have you not got a hangover spell Lou?"

"Yeah. That breakfast I've just slaved over for you." she said.

Lou searched through the bathroom cupboard for some liver salts, always a handy remedy. She found them, sprinkled some of the powder into

Jinny's toothbrush glass, filled it with water and stirred it with Jinny's toothbrush.

"Get that down yer neck." ordered Lou.

"Bleeuugh." belched Jinny. "That's positively repulsive."

"Well you bought it! Anyway, nothing that's good for you tastes pleasant," said Nurse Lou. "Otherwise we'd all be on rum and raisin ice cream every day!"

"Suppose so." groaned Jinny, wretching.

"Now look, you've got to pull yourself together. There's no time for maladies today. There's a war to be won!" said Lou sternly.

"Bugger! I'd forgotten all about that."

"You told Miss Riz off for forgetting about it yesterday." scolded Lou. "Let the liver salts settle in, then eat your breakfast. We'll have you right as rain within the hour, captain." Lou saluted.

"Queen!" laughed Jinny.

"Pain in the arse!" laughed Lou.

Jinny had taken a shower then spent most of the rest of the day on the sofa, gathering her strength for the night ahead, Jet asleep at her feet.

Riz and Lou had been busying themselves by preparing some proper, organic meals, made by hand with no jiggery pokery involved.

Lou had set herself an hour aside to do the Village Life magazine crossword (£500 top prize!), and even with her vast knowledge of most things, had only managed to fill nine answers in.

"I'm going to have to do some 'research' on some of these clues." she said to Riz, who was having a hot brew, a ciggie and a sit down.

"Why not eh? If at first you don't succeed … cheat!" said Riz, helpfully. "It's not cheating Riz, it's *research.* Just checking that what I think the answer might be concurs with, erm, what the actual answer really is."

"Where I come from they call that cheating."

"I *know* where you come from Riz and it's still called research, wherever you live!"

There was a few minutes silence as Lou bit into the end of her pen whilst sporting her best intelligent look.

"What are you wearing tonight Lou?" asked Riz.

"Pardon? What am I *wearing*? For a battle? Does it really matter? I could go out in a pully full of holes and some pit boots. Who's going to take any notice?"

"It's not really a *battle* though, is it Lou?"

"That depends … it could get nasty, who knows? What are *you* wearing anyway?"

"I was thinking of going down to the fancy dress shop and hiring something ferocious." said Riz.

"You *are* joking aren't you? Please tell me you're having a laugh because I'm beginning to have doubts about your sanity lady."

Part 1: A Bustle In The Hedgerow

"What's wrong with dressing the part? I could go as a Valkyrie or something …"

"A Valkyrie? It's not a bloody fancy dress party Riz - it's *serious*!"

"Just trying to take the edge off things Lou. A bit of levity."

"I hope Jinny can't hear you. She'd probably ring the nearest nuthouse and have you certified."

"Don't be so nasty Lou … is that goblin here again, by the way?" Riz asked.

"No, I don't think so. Maybe he's gone down to the fancy dress shop for a costume for tonight's soiree …"

"I do enjoy a soiree Lou. The music, the lights, the wine, the …"

"But there'll be none of that *tonight* will there?! Save it for the solstice eh?"

"I'm looking forward to that. It's going to be the highlight of the year I reckon."

"A bigger highlight than the ten thousand quid you won on the lottery back in March?" asked Lou.

"Oh yeah, I'd forgotten about that. I did a spell you know? I know you're not supposed to spell for financial gain but I thought I'd give it a bash anyway. Nothing ventured, nothing gained."

"You're a jammy little sod you are, Riz."

"I'm taller than you!"

"You're a jammy *big* sod then!" Lou said, slightly disgruntled or perhaps envious because she hadn't thought to put a spell on the lottery.

"You're starting to become very impatient, very offhand, did you know that Lou? These last few days … it's as if your character's completely changed from the devil-may-care, charming and kind person you usually are and turned you into a bitter, sarcastic git."

"I gave you some Jelly Babies the other day!" said an affronted Lou.

"You took the crossword off me too!"

"Look, can we draw a line under all this bickering and try and get some semblance of normality back?" Lou implored. "And anyway, why don't you go and buy your own flippin' crossword?!"

"See?" said Riz.

"What's going on?" asked Jinny through a blurry, just woke up mouth.

"Just Lou being narky, Jin. Again! Narky *and* aggressive"

"I AM NOT BEING AGGRESSIVE!!!" screamed Lou, aggressively.

"You sound a bit aggressive to me, Lou" said Jinny.

"Right! Scout the house for a goblin!" shouted Lou. "There's something obviously happening to me and it's obviously making me unpopular and it's obviously being caused by some unknown force! Spike! Would you do the honours please?"

Spike began to prowl around the house, his nose twitching all over the place.

"Why don't you all have a look 'round," Jinny said to the other two cats. "There's something not right here …"

"You don't think that Mortem woman's put some kind of evil enchantment on the house, do you Jin? Something we overlooked?" said Riz.

"Altogether possible, Riz." said Jinny. "I know Lou can be a proper swine at times, but this really isn't like her."

Lou had left the room and gone upstairs for a cry. What was happening to her? Surely it wasn't the after effects of the Viking Scandinavian lager? Could be. She'd heard tales of cheap lager being made from fish heads of all things!

Part 1: A Bustle In The Hedgerow

No. That couldn't be it. Too much sugar from eating Jelly Babies? Nah! A troll? Too big. It wasn't a goblin, that had been sorted. So … it's … a … it's a boggart! Of course!

"Jinny, Riz! It's a boggart! I'm telling you now there's a boggart in this house!" Lou shouted excitedly.

"Oh great. That's all we need. A flippin' boggart." said Riz. The cats had scoured the whole house and found nothing.

"Well it's in here somewhere, it's the only explanation. Full to the brim with mischief they are, the little beggars," said Lou. "When did I start to become 'narky', as you put it Riz?"

"On and off since about Saturday, I recollect."

"Aye! Saturday, I think so too. After that meeting with Slinky." said Jinny.

"…then you went off on your own. Retrace your steps Lou," said Riz.

"Down the lane. Walk walk. Newsagents. Buy buy. Back up the lane. Walk. Sit down on a wall for a few minutes. Sit sit. Cig cig. Competition …"

"Competition?"

"Nothing. Ignore that. Set off back up the lane. Walk walk. Walk through the front door. Enter enter. Never saw a soul going there or coming back." "Did you have your bag with you?" asked Jinny.

"Well, yeah, course I did, why?"

"Because there's a funny smell coming from it …"

Jinny reached over and lifted Lou's bag into the air. "Follow me." she said, tightening the draw string at the top.

They were led out into the back garden.
"Stand back!" Jinny ordered as she undid the string and tipped the bag upside down.
Lots of Lipstick, a mirror, cigarettes, lighter, wet wipes, nail file, purse, stray Jelly Babies covered in fluff, more fluff, small bottle of hemlock, passport, tissues, an old lottery ticket, receipts, a pair of stripey socks, mascara, eye liner, a screwed up t-shirt, a wand … the whole lot fell out onto the grass - but no boggart. Jinny poked her head inside.
"Cor! This smells like someone's been sick in a sweaty sock!" she said, and there, clinging to the bottom of the bag, was a boggart, no more than eight inches tall but bloated with naughtiness.
"You wouldn't have thought there'd be room for anything else in there," said Jinny. "This bag's like a Tardis! Out yer come matey."
Jinny lifted the boggart out by its left ear and clung on to it while she got an explanation.
"Boggarts like dark, cluttered places you know." said Riz helpfully.
"Lou's bag must've been like a flamin' palace to him then!" laughed Jinny.
"Now, what's your game Mr Boggart, and who sent you?" Jinny began her interrogation.
"Nobody haven't sent me," he said. "I was in them bushes, down that road and spotted summat warm for to hide in. That's all. I were just fed up of being cold. Brrrr! An' I just, just stayed there, warm."
Now, boggarts are notoriously difficult to remove from a house once they've been allowed in and can cause all kinds of chaos - frightening pets, running taps, souring milk, pooing in corners, that kind of thing, so Jinny had to play this carefully.

Part 1: A Bustle In The Hedgerow

"Would you be so kind as to hold this fellow by the ear for a second please, Miss Riz?"

She walked over to Lou and whispered "How much do you like this bag?" "It's not my best but I quite like it," said Lou. "Having said that, it's going to stink a bit now, isn't it? There'll be no getting rid of a boggart pong."

"Then let's let him stay in it. We'll take him up to the woods, find a nice sheltered spot, chuck a few tissues in there for bedding and Bob's yer monkey's uncle!"

"Give him the fluffy Jelly Babies too." said Lou.

Jinny nodded in agreement and strolled back to the boggart who was wriggling inbetween Riz's fingers, probably because she had been tickling him.

"Myself and the owner of this bag, Miss Louise, have had a bit of a conflab Mr B and we have decided to let you remain in it, as long as you agree to never come back to this house ever again. Do we have an accord?"

"Whatever you said then that's what I say and I promises I won't bother ye no more again ever." said the humble boggart.

"Boggart's honour?" said Jinny.

"Aye, that too an' all."

"Then we will personally escort you to your new place of residence and you may stay in this very prestigious bag, rent free."

"Why's she talking like that?" whispered Riz to Lou.

"Probably practising for when she becomes a queen." said Lou.

"I thank ye very gladly from my heart's bottom." said the boggart. And with that, the jolly band of witches and their three cats and one boggart ambled down the side lane and headed for the dark forest.

"Blimey it doesn't get much darker than this place," said Lou. "It's proper spooky. Love it!"

"Dark *and* cluttered, with trees and leaves - perfect!" smiled Jinny.

She placed Lou's bag at the foot of an old, spindly willow tree which had a ready-made hole at the bottom of it's trunk.

"What a delightful setting for a boggart to set up a new home." she said.

"Mr B … would you care to take a look around your new premises?" The boggart popped his head out of the top of Lou's bag and soaked in the ambience.

"This will be just the trick" he said, delighted.

"We must be on our way now. We will leave you with these tissues and these three fluffed up Jelly Babies as a 'moving in' gift," continued Jinny, "and blessed be all who sail in her."

"I'm sure she's been affected too," whispered Riz to Lou. "She thinks she's

Napoleon or something …"

"More likely Josephine." said Lou, correcting Riz's mistake.

"May the powers be with you, young cunning woman." said the boggart and off he popped, back into the bottom of the bag.

"Well … that's a new bag for me." smiled Lou. "Oh noooo! Did you leave all my belongings on the grass?"

"We *all* did." answered Jinny.

"Oh sod it! There'll be a thousand flippin' magpies picking at that lot now," Lou sulked. "Thieving little, twerping …"

"Let's get back, eh?" said Jinny, linking arms with Lou and Riz and beckoning the faithful cats who had just come along for the exercise.

Part 1: A Bustle In The Hedgerow

"Fancy watching a DVD, Isobel?" said Mr Crook (remember him?).

"Let's open a nice bottle of plonk and do just that" smiled (!!!) Miz Mortem. "Do you like war films?" he asked.

"I most certainly do not! I've had a hell of a day at work and the last thing I want is shouting, explosions and things getting broken, again. I can't remember a day like it. It's as if the whole office was possessed! Oh. How about Disney? Anything by Disney?" Mr Crook wasn't really listening.

"Have you got any of those pirate films with Johnny Depp in? They're by Disney aren't they?"

"I've got the first one … can't get me head 'round the others." admitted Crook pathetically.

"I like Johnny Depp. He's very underrated as a serious actor you know?

Very accomplished." she said putting on a posh voice.

"It's not just that you fancy him then?"

"I don't *fancy* people! Good grief man! *Fancy*? I'm not a schoolgirl … he

is quite attractive though, especially when he's a pirate."

"Arrrrrrr!" said Crook, in tragic imitation of a pirate.

"Have you hurt yourself?" asked the miz one.

"No. I was being a pirate. Aaaarrrrrr!"

"What's the matter with you? Why do you keep crying out in pain?" "Nothing." said Crook and went to the tiger skinned cupboard to get 'The Curse of the Black Pearl'.

"It's very peaceful, isn't it Russell? A perfect evening for lolling about. Turn the fire up would you?"

"I'll just get this DVD going first Isobel …"

It was all go back at Demonia Cottage (2) …

"Do you think we should set off earlier and make sure Slinky's organised everything according to plan?" said Jinny.

"What plan?!" said Lou.

"Well, make sure she's got … ooh, I don't know!" Jinny was getting a bit frustrated and more than a little edgy.

"Give me five minutes notice before we're setting off so I can have a wee, will you?" asked Riz.

The cats were just lying there, as cool as cucumber cats.

A flutter of wings could be heard as Raph the enigmatic one readied himself for action. He'd had over a week to meditate on it, for goodness sake!

"You managed to find your wand didn't you Lou?" asked Jinny.

"I did. A magpie had dragged it up that apple tree. Quite a tussle wresting it back from him. I had to do him a swap for a ring I won on the fair! Tinker!"

"You only had to ask and I would've got it back for you Miss Lou." offered Jet, yawning.

"I didn't want to disturb your beauty sleep, darling." she said planting a freshly applied lipsticky kiss in the usual place.

"I never asked you Riz, did you actually hire a Valkyrie costume for tonight?" asked Lou.

"Naah. I couldn't be fussed. All those wings and things …"

"So … not that it really matters but what *are* you wearing tonight?"

"I'm going as a witch! Easy. I'll be wearing my best dark blue hooded capey thing, stripey socks, pointy boots, red bodicey thing and a lovely, long, medieval red skirt." Riz smiled.

"Isn't that a bit ostentatious for a night of warfare and destruction?" asked Lou.

“Do you think so? I’m stuck with what else I could wear …”

“For crying out loud! Just make sure you’ve got a wand and a broomstick! That’s all you need to worry about. It’s not a Ball we’re off to.” Jinny despaired. Again.

There then followed a rare few seconds silence until Jinny broke it.

“What are *you* wearing, Lou?”

“Ha Ha Haaaaa! Haaaaa! You are soooo fickle, Jin.”

Jet turned around to Spike. “Are you wearing anything special?”

“Am I ‘eck!” was all he got out of him, that and a dainty clip round the ear.

PARCHMENT 22

A Witch in Time Staves Nine

Isobel Mortem's phone rang …

"Is that you Isobel?" said the voice at the other end.

"Obviously, this is *my* phone! Who is it? Your number hasn't come up."

"It's Mabel Grunch from the Clitheroe Coven. Do you remember we met at that council do last Christmas?"

"Oh yes, Merry Meet, what can I do for you?"

"It's more what *we* can do for *you* Isobel. We've been passed some rather chilling information on. Have you heard any rumours about a certain *something* happening over there tonight?"

"Over *where*? Come on woman, don't beat around the bush - spit it out!" Isobel was getting irritated - it didn't take much.

"Apparently, there's to be some kind of offensive this evening and allegedly *you* are the target."

"Offensive? An attack of some sort? On me? Nobody knows I'm here. Do you have any details?" panicked Mortem.

"We've heard tell that at around nine o'clock you will be visited by hordes of faerie folk and a certain trio of witches that may be of your acquaintance …" said Mabel.

"Oh nooo! I thought all that had been taken care of."

"That's not what we've heard. I was ringing to see if you needed any help. There's at least eight of us that are willing to assist. We can be over there in no time if you want us."

Part 1: A Bustle In The Hedgerow

"Well, yes, thank you." said Mortem, by now quite flustered and not a little speechless.

"That's all I needed to know ... see you shortly. We know the address.

Blessed be."

The phone went dead as Isobel Mortem stared into space in disbelief.

She was going to miss Pirates of the Caribbean! On Blu Ray!

No, Isobel, pull yourself together, this sounded quite serious and should be treated as such.

"Russell!" she shouted through to the kitchen, where Crook was preparing a snack for them both. "There's going to be trouble!"

"Whaaat? What kind of trouble? When?" he asked, taken aback.

"Tonight at nine. We've got just over an hour to prepare defences."

"Defences? What the hell is going on?!"

"Those three down at the cottage - that's what's going on - them and their little friends."

"I thought that was all sorted. You seemed quite confident ..."

"I hadn't planned on that Lane woman's inability to accept defeat." said Mortem, through her teeth.

"I don't know what you expect me to do," said Crook. "What use am I against a gang of witches?!"

"Coven Russell, it's a coven. Thankfully the person who's just informed me of this inconvenience is coming over with a few friends to make the numbers up, so you just stay in here and cower behind the couch. Have you seen my broomstick?"

"I don't think you brought it, Isobel."

"Damn! The one time I *really* need it …"

"Righto, just over an hour to go. Are you sure you've all got what you need?" asked Jinny.

"In retrospect, I would've liked the Valkyrie costume Jin, but apart from that, and needing a wee, I'm all set." said Riz.

"Ready to sail captain!" piped up Lou.

"Boys, girl … all prepared?"

"Yes, Miss Jinny." came the reply, in unison, apart from Raph who, well, just didn't respond, but then he never really did.

Our seven heroes and heroines sat quietly, collecting their thoughts.

Jinny broke the silence …

"I don't know why I'm so nervous about this. It's pretty much cut and dried. She doesn't stand a chance. I feel a bit sorry for her in a way."

"She needs to be taught who's boss around here Jin … and don't forget the stunts she's already pulled on you, not to mention the threat to the faeries.

It's got to be settled once and for all, then we can get on with the simple pleasures of enjoying ourselves." said Lou, sipping on a black coffee.

"That reminds me." said Jinny.

"What does?" said Lou.

"I don't know but it does … hang on." and Jinny ran over to the kitchen, returning with the giant carrot.

"I want you all to have a bite of this please. It'll help your night vision." "Are you *sure* about this Jin? I don't want to be eating raw vegetables unnecessarily." said Lou.

"Sure as eggs is eggs, or something like that."

Part 1: A Bustle In The Hedgerow

Everyone took a bite of the carrot then Riz turned all the house lights off to see if it had worked.

"Give it a minute to kick in, eh?" implored Jinny. "It's not infra-red!"

Forty minutes passed after the carrot testing. Jinny suddenly leapt from her chair.

"Come on! Let's go *now*. I don't want to turn up with two minutes to

battle stations, I want to see what Slinky's lined up."

"Ooh, I better nip to the loo." said Riz, typically.

Upon her return, everyone stood to attention, Jinny inspected them all and double checked they had what they needed then off they solemnly marched towards the door.

Waiting in the clearing, lit only by the moon and a couple of small fires were the results of Slinky's recruitment drive.

Over a hundred faeries, at least forty pixies, eleven gnomes, nine hobgoblins (larger and stronger than normal Goblins), several elves, four steamy snouted bulls and one goblin.

A banshee had agreed to turn up but there was a last-minute emergency to tend to, so, no show.

Slinky hovered in front of her army, dressed in a tiny fur coat that Wilf had fashioned for her from the pelt of a white rabbit that had been involved in a road accident, and awaited the arrival of the Demonia Cottage (2) inhabitants.

"How now brown cow." said Wilf to one of the bulls.

"I'm a bull," snorted the Bull, "and I'm black."

"Just making conversation." said Wilf, double checking that he didn't have any red clothing on him.

“Yes, the flaming condensation...” said Spudsley, nodding.

“Whaaat?” asked Wilf.

Then, from over the brow came a large black shape shooting like a bullet through the air, highlighted, in part, by the moon.

Not far behind there emerged the silhouettes of three figures with bent, pointy hats with three long tails visibly twitching near their feet.

“Ready for inspection troops!” yelped Slinky, like an Elfin Sergeant Major. The gathering all stood up straight, chests out, apart from the faeries who just fluttered on their particular spot of air.

“Merry meet!” chimed Jinny, Riz and Lou.

“Greetings to you ladies,” said Slinky. “Are you set?”

Raphael hovered nobly about a hundred feet in the night sky. He was to lead the attack.

“No time like the present Slinks” said Lou, stubbing out her cigarette.

“HAVA KEE TARAH UD!” shouted Jinny and Raph zoomed down, levelled out at about thirty feet and soared in the direction of the Crook residence.

“Follow!” shouted Slinky and the army surged forward behind the magnificent bird.

Jinny, Riz and Lou arranged their broomsticks on the ground in the usual fashion; Jinny, once again, raised her arms high and chanted “I am the blue-lidded daughter of Sunset; I am the naked brilliance of the voluptuous night-sky. To me! To me!”

“You’ve done this before, haven’t you?” said Lou playfully.

“Wow!” said Jet, still overcome by his mistress’ powers.

The broomsticks rose into the air and the ladies jumped astride them, beckoning their cats to sit behind.

Part 1: A Bustle In The Hedgerow

"BIKULL SUREA!" yelled Jinny, and the brooms shot off at a pace only rivalled by Raph's mighty black wings.
"Wands!" shouted Jinny as they sped nearer to their destination.

With only ten yards to go before they reached Crook's house the whole ground army stopped dead.
One hundred and one faeries paused stock still in mid-air, as did three witches, three cats and the indomitable Raphael.
The sight of nine hovering witches, not very nice at all hovering witches, held them dumbstruck. This was not what was supposed to happen.
"Return to whence you came NOW! Or suffer the consequences!" shouted the leader of the grim sisterhood.
Silence reigned for what seemed like an hour, but was only a minute. "AAKRAMAN!" shouted Jinny and Raphael dived at the most terrific speed imaginable, beak first into the face of the rival head witch, knocking her clean off her broom, at the same time relieving her of one of her ears. Uuugh!
Raphael's wings clipped an adjacent witch and sent her also plunging to the ground.
The ground troops rushed forward to engage the fallen witches whilst the airborne faeries whizzed at great speed into the thick of the floating harridans, pulling their ears, tugging their hair and generally making real nuisances of themselves.
The bulls were instructed to begin the destruction of the bungalow, taking a long run up to maximise the impact.
Down went the doors, in went the windows, leading the way for the hobgoblins to enter the building and cause

total devastation to the interior. One hobgoblin is bad news - nine are BIG trouble!

The rival witches that could function properly, of which there were now seven (Mortem being one of them), were screaming spells and incantations like there was no tomorrow.

Many pixies and faeries suffered from them and were forced to retire from the fray.

Lou steamed head on into the middle of them, attempting to locate Isobel Mortem, which she did, after incurring many cuts and bruises.

"Crone!" she yelled, pointing her trusty wand at the centre of Mortem's forehead. "Quatara!"

A pencil thin orange beam blasted from her wand and Mortem and her borrowed broom plummeted to the ground.

"We need more help! Riz, do some hexing on the house, would you?" cried Jinny, as she turned her broom back from where they came and hastened to the faerie clearing.

She was there in two minutes after driving her broom at full velocity.

"ZORRO!" she shouted. "ZORRO!"

After only a few seconds the familiar features of the fine fox she had rescued appeared from the shadows.

"How can I be of service fair Jinny?" he asked.

Jinny explained her plight and the fox immediately darted off, back into the shadows. While she was waiting she took out her phone and rang … "Redferns, locksmith to …"

"Nancy! Are you busy? No. Do you actually have a besom? You know, a broomstick? No. Bugger. Do you have access to any old iron chain? Of course, your dad has a scrap yard! Can you get some? Enough to bind nine witches? Not too thick, obviously. How quickly could you get to Mr Crook's place in the van? Fifteen minutes? It's cutting it a bit fine but if you could, please. Bring your wand! Thanks luv."

Zorro reappeared with a large throng of handy looking creatures - owls, badgers, other foxes, stags, hedgehogs, weasels, even wolves that were thought to be extinct and other varmints, too many to count or name.

"Thank you, my friend." gushed Jinny. "Follow me!"

They dashed off at an alarming rate, some faster than others, following Jinny's lead.

Back at the affray, Riz had all but ruined the entire roof and most of the front of the Crook dwelling, with help from the bulls and hobgoblins.

As she hovered she spotted Crook hiding behind a sofa, shaking maniacally.

"Pathetic excuse for a human." she muttered.

Miss Lou flew over from the epicentre of the battle.

"We need to get this lot out of the air!" she shouted above the racket.

"Let the cats loose on their heads" suggested Riz.

"Brainy idea, Rizzo!" shouted Lou. "Come on then!"

Lou picked one of two of the most dangerous looking witches and instructed Stripes to attack, Riz picked out the other one and did the same. Once a cat, especially a magical cat, properly locks on to you, your days are numbered.

And so it was for these two unfortunate hags.

"Still four to go Lou!" said Riz. "Wands?"

"Where's Jinny got to?" said Lou, scanning the area.

"She said she was getting help."

"She'd better get a wriggle on." Lou said, biting her bright red bottom lip. And just as she spoke, all manner of woodland animals appeared, stampeding down the lane towards them with Jinny and Jet leading them from the air.

"Take these low life scumbags over the hills and far away!" she shouted to the menagerie below and the assorted animals obeyed her bidding, nine, maybe ten woodland creatures per evil witch, dragging them away with their teeth, with about ten various gnomes and pixies doing all they could to assist.

Jinny let Jet loose on one of the still flying crones, instructing him to take her eyes out.

Jet didn't think she meant this literally so made do with launching himself belly to her face and claws stuck tight into the rest of her head. It was enough to topple her from her besom and send her downwards where the woodland animals, pixies and gnomes were clearing the lane as quickly as the witches dropped.

Two headlights shone from down the other side of the lane. Luckily it wasn't a police car but none other than Nancy Redfern.

"What the …." she said to herself, her mind bewildered as teams of animals and faerie folk scurried past, dragging witches along with them. She poked her head through the van window and shouted to a responsible looking gnome.

"There's iron chain here to tie them up. Put their arms behind their backs, strap some round their wrists and I'll cut it to length and weld it. And get someone to burn their broomsticks!"

"Still got three up here." said Riz.

"I can bloody count you know!" shouted Lou.

"That goblin's nearby - I bet you anything you like." wagered Riz, laughing.

Part 1: A Bustle In The Hedgerow

Sure enough, the goblin was below, mingling between the captured witches and getting them to argue amongst themselves as they were being dragged unceremoniously away.

"Could do with him up here." said Riz.

Getting the three remaining witches to the ground was becoming a very tiring prospect. They too had powers and were using them indiscriminately. Many faerie folk had been debilitated by their magick. Faeries were magical, mystical creatures but were, after all, quite fragile, as Slinky was to learn after leading her clan head on, incurring some quite nasty damage to her body and wings. And her white fur coat was ruined!

Quick catch up: The animals and most of the pixies and gnomes were very much occupied with their task of re-homing the felled witches, Nancy was sat in her van, terrified, the hobgoblins and bulls were still wreaking havoc on Crook's home and the faeries, their numbers depleted, were still attempting to create as much botheration as possible so as to befuddle the remaining airborne witches.

Jinny, Riz and Lou and their familiars were doing likewise and Raph was waiting for that opportune moment …

After several failed attempts, Jinny sent witch number three hurtling to the grass below with a particularly well aimed hex to the forehead.

Two to go.

Make that three. One of the fallen witches had managed to make her way back into the air by sheer stealth and extreme nastiness.

Riz decided on a tricky manoeuvre to send her back, wherein she flew underneath her, somersaulted as she passed, then drove the shaft of her broom directly into the witch's spine, immobilising her immediately and permanently. Spike sat behind her licking her hair.

Lou lit a cigarette, took three drags on it and threw it down, all the time eyeing witch two unnervingly with her best manic glare.

Witch two raised her wand to strike but Lou was focused like a ninja and bulleted towards the hag with Stripes in her outstretched hand.

She placed Stripes calmly on the witch's neck and hovered back, waiting for the inevitable result, which wasn't pretty.

Witch two hit the ground screaming with the cat on top of her.

Stripes then let go of her throat and casually strolled off saying "Hi" to no one in particular, leaving the witch to be dragged down the lane to who knows where.

Was the one remaining witch brave enough to tackle these three formidable foes and their familiars? Perhaps 'brave' wasn't the right word.

Foolhardy, that's better.

Raphael wasn't taking any chances. He presumed that this one, solitary she-devil must have some kind of horrific trick up her flared sleeve or she wouldn't be still hanging there so fearlessly.

He swooped down from where he was gliding and raced towards the witch, who he met, eye to eye, revealing himself as the terrifying opponent that he most surely was.

The witch magicked her wand, as if from nowhere, and as Raph ferociously held her gaze she plunged it fully into his mighty chest, sending him spinning down.

"NO!!!" screamed Jinny "NOOOOOO!!!!"

Part 1: A Bustle In The Hedgerow

She flew blindly but with great speed at the witch but her head had gone so numb with what had just happened she didn't know what to do with herself.

As she reached the smugly smiling hag, Jet swiftly jumped from the broomstick, landed on the witch's head and angrily tore her eyes out. Just like that.

Even the smallest of felines are capable of enormous damage when angry and Jet was hyper angry.

The witch had no power other than her wand and that was embedded in poor Raphael, and now she was blind.

As she began her descent to join her unfortunate companions below, Jinny swiftly pursued.

One part of her wanted to rip the crone to pieces, slowly. The other part wanted to rush to Raph to see if she could save him.

She opted for the latter and knelt down beside her dying hero … her love. Raph was only just breathing but Jinny knew he could hear her.

She whispered softly to him. It translated as: "My darling, promise to come back to me one day. Return in another form. Whatever it takes ... Dhannyavaad, Mera Pyaar."

She removed the vile wand, blessed him and held him to her, weeping inconsolably.

Jet stood by her side, numbed. This was the saddest he had ever felt in his entire, young life.

Riz and Lou landed next to the terrible scene, scarcely believing what had just transpired.

Spike looked at Stripes - no words.

Lou bent down and kissed Raph's motionless head, leaving her trademark lipstick trace as a reminder.

Riz was frantically distraught. *Frantically.*

They had won the battle but lost their mysterious friend, their Wing Commander.

Nothing would be quite the same again.

PARCHMENT 23

Mourning Has Broken

The weeks had flown by since that terrible battle and the insurmountable loss of the beloved Raphael.

Crook's house, what was left of it, had to be totally demolished, so he moved elsewhere, a long way away, with the help of the insurance money (it took *some* story to convince the insurance brokers as to why his house was no more).

On the plus side, he had given up all intentions of opening the dratted golf course with adjoining club house.

He had sold the land that Miss Slinky and her fellow faeries occupied and a preservation order was made on it, making it an Area of Outstanding Natural Beauty, ensuring it would never, ever be disturbed or changed in any way.

Isobel Mortem was scarred for life but still working for the council, as many do.

Her new position was in the Bin Collections Department, which didn't offer many opportunities for bribery or corruption.

She still had Crook's money in her account but they never saw each other again and witchcraft was now, apparently, a thing of the past for her. You could say she had learned her lesson. Or had she?

You may also be wondering what became of the witch that brutally murdered Raphael …

She used to work in the Job Centre in the main town of Singeley but having recently lost her eyes it was thought that maybe her appearance wasn't quite the image the government were looking for and it was suggested that maybe she would be more suited to Madame Tussaud's Chamber of Horrors, or perhaps an extra in one of those gory zombie films.

But for Jinny, Lou, Riz, Jet, Spike and Stripes, life carried on as normal, or as normal as life can be when you're a witch and still grieving over the loss of a much cherished family member.

It was only three days until the winter solstice. They were due to attend the concert by the Rock band Wizards In A Blizzard, at Spiderwood Farm on December 21st .

The tickets were booked, paid for and in their possession but Jinny, especially, wasn't looking forward to going out on the razz anytime soon. The loss of Raphael had wounded her deeply and only the thought that he might return one day, albeit in another guise, was keeping her going.

Riz and Lou originally only came to stay for a week, but decided that it would be for the best to remain with Jinny and help her through this sad time.

Jet had not left Jinny's side since that fateful day, not once, and the bond between them was now superglue tight.

She lay on the settee, listless, Jet nestled on her feet.

Riz was doing a bit of cleaning with a feather duster.

"Jinny … I think the solstice gig will do you a lot of good, you know. You need to get yourself out and about *now*. Being miz is not going to solve anything and it's not going to bring Raph back …"

"I know Riz, I know … but it's as if I don't know how to begin to get my old self back again."

Lou walked in from the kitchen brandishing a bacon butty.

"Let's go for a drink tonight. A rehearsal for the 21st eh? Get yourself back in the swing of things?"

"Oh Lou, I don't even know if I can be bothered to get to the front door

…"

Jet woke up and stretched, then paddy pawed up to Jinny's face.

"I'll come to the pub with you and we can all drink a toast to Raph. It's what he would have wanted, I think."

"Go and have a nice hot shower Jin and I'll iron some of your best togs. What d'ya say?" offered Lou.

"Before you have a shower Jin, do you mind if I just go up to the bathroom for a quick wee?" asked, well, guess who!

Jinny smiled for the first time in ages.

"Some things will never change, eh Riz? Go on then, quick sticks, before I change my mind!"

Eventually Jinny went off for her shower whilst Lou ironed her best Jinny glad rags and Riz cleaned her Jinny boots for her. The letterbox opened and snapped shut.

"Faeries I'll wager!" shouted Lou.

But it was a red envelope that had landed on the mat, addressed to Miss Louise Dallion.

Riz picked it up.

"Hey! This is addressed to you Lou!" (told you).

"Well sling it over here then." Lou said with an ever present ciggie dangling from the corner of her mouth and a red-hot iron in her hand.

Riz glided the envelope across the room and Lou caught it with her free hand.

Part 1: A Bustle In The Hedgerow

“It can’t be a bill, they don’t come in red envelopes and anyway, one of my bills wouldn’t come to this address.” she said.

“Well why don’t you just open it and then you’ll *know* what it is?!” said Riz, exasperated.

“Alright, alright, hold yer horses.”

Lou put the iron down and applied two hands to the job of opening the envelope.

“It’s from Village Life Magazine!” she said excitedly.

“I bet it’s a subscription form.” said Riz.

“Not on this occasion Riz, no … I’ve won something … for once in my life.”

“Wow! Hey Jinny! Are you dry? Come down - Lou’s won a prize!”

Jinny spiralled down the stairs, sporting her favourite Chewbacca dressing gown and a towel wrapped around her head.

“What you won Lou?” she asked.

“Guess.”

“An Xmas hamper?”

“Nope.”

“A year’s subscription to Village Life magazine?” said Riz.

“Nope.”

“Sunbed vouchers?”

“Whaaat?! No, no, no.”

“Tell us Lou, come on, quick sticks …” Jinny said impatiently. “I have won … first prize … in the Village Life magazine …”

“Oh come on Lou, stop draggin’ it out!” yelped Riz.

“A three day Xmas trip for four to … Lapland!!! All expenses paid!”

At that moment Jinny had an uncontrollable urge to look up to where Raph would normally be perched, the result of which was an instant downpour of tears which she just couldn't stem.
"Oh Jin, I thought you'd be pleased …" said Lou, also with tears in her eyes.
"I - I - I am, I *am* pleased. You're so clever Lou and you really deserve it." sobbed Jinny, Jet now immediately at her side.
Riz went over and put her arm comfortingly around her shoulder.
"Don't Jin - you'll have us all at it. Come on, don't even think about it.
Get your hair dry, get dressed and let's get out of here."
"Yes, I will … I will" Jinny hurried off upstairs in search of the hairdryer.

"That's on a par with my lottery win Lou." said Riz, wiping a tear away.
"And no hocus pocus either!" said Lou proudly.
"Who's going with you then?"
"*You* are! You dozy bat! And Jinny!"
"Is there room for me?" asked Jet hopefully.
"We can't take you without the other two cats Jetty and you'd probably have to do quarantine even if you did come along. For three days it's not going to be worth the hassle, is it?" Lou said sympathetically.
Riz added her thoughts.
"Spike can open packets of cat food you know, so you won't starve and there's well water outside. All you'd have to do is sleep and eat. Not *that* bad, eh? We'll be back before you know it. You've no concept of time anyway!"
"I'd worry about Jinny." Jet said forlornly.

Part 1: A Bustle In The Hedgerow

"She'll be fine. It'll take her mind off everything and she'll come back a new witch!" smiled Lou, planting the first bright red kiss of the day on Jet's little noggin.

"We can visit my old mate while we're there. Lovely bloke he is … what are the dates Lou?" asked Riz.

"23rd of December, 5.00 a.m. flight and return on the morning of the 26th." "We'd have to call in on him on the 23rd then or we won't get chance after that …"

"Call in on *who*?" Lou was getting distracted.

"My old mate, I *told* you. You'll get on like a log cabin on fire!"

"I don't want to spend this holiday looking up old mates Riz, I want to get out and enjoy myself, see the sights, soak up the festive spirit."

"Bacardi?" asked Riz.

"No! Not Bacardi! Well, yes, maybe the odd one but that's not what I meant!"

"Suit yourself then," said Riz indignantly. "I'll go and see him on my own." "Do you know Lapland well, Riz? I'm presuming you've been there before?"

"Of course I have, I've been to most places, I just can't always remember *where* exactly sometimes."

"But you remember one old mate in one of the least densely populated areas in the whole of Scandinavia?"

"He's pretty hard to forget, Lou!"

"Really? Is he a film star or summat? What's his name?"

"Sinter Klaas."

"Well, I've never heard of him."

"You have Lou, trust me, you have …"

Jinny came downstairs, her hair dried, picked up her newly ironed clothes and newly polished boots and headed back up to get dressed, Jet in tow. "Jet's really looking after her, isn't he? Bless him."

Riz watched as Jinny and Jet trooped upstairs together.

"He was *made* for her that cat. You wouldn't get Stripes or even Spike showing us that much devotion, I'm telling ya." said Lou.

"Get a wriggle on Jin!" she then felt the need to shout. "The quicker we get away from these four walls the better!"

"Coming! Keep yer drawers on!" came the reply.

Five minutes later the entourage were strolling down the lane in a pub direction.

Riz had had another bite of the giant carrot to make sure it hadn't lost any of its night vision properties.

Lou was gently swaying along, smiling and dreaming of a white Christmas.

Jinny was feeling slightly agoraphobic but a few drinks would sort that out and Jet was still sad and a touch concerned about the forthcoming few days.

He wouldn't see his hallowed mistress after the 22nd, not that he had the faintest idea of when that was.

But he knew it was soon and he was feeling quite miz about it.

The 21st of December soon arrived, the winter solstice and a bitterly cold arctic kind of day to boot.

"There'll be no dancing around naked tonight girls, eh?" Lou stated the obvious. "Has anyone been in touch with Nancy? We haven't seen her for weeks." asked Riz.

"I'll ring her now." said Jinny.

Burr Burr. Burr Burr. Burr Bu…

"Season's greetings. Redfern's, locksmiths to the stars, Nancy speaki…"

Part 1: A Bustle In The Hedgerow

"Hiya Nance, Merry meet, it's Jin. How are you?"

"I'm good. Still a bit shaken by the other week's events like, but I'm OK."

"You haven't forgotten about tonight have you?"

"I *have* you know," said Nance forgetfully. "What's happening tonight? Not another war, is it?"

"It's the solstice gig up at Spiderwood Farm. You haven't lost your ticket have you?"

"Ahhh! I haven't lost my ticket because I was never given it … that's why I forgot."

"Oh, sorry Nance, it's my fault, I'm a bit absent minded myself at times.

Still playing out then?"

"Yeah, course, I've nowt else on, where are we meeting?"

"Want to make your way to the cottage? About 8.00pm? Drive up and you can kip over if you like. It'll have to be a couch job though so bring a sleeping bag."

"Yeah great! Thanks Jinny." enthused Nancy. "OK, see you later. Dress Goth! Bye!"

"Is she still coming then?" Riz asked.

"Oh aye, she's meeting us here at eight. Better get our wardrobes sorted

…"

The girls spent the rest of the day mixing and matching skirts, socks, tops, boots, bags, scarves, you know the kind of thing. It takes forever.

By eight o'clock they were ready and done
up to the nines. No, make that *elevens*!

Jinny wore *all* black: Brocade bodice, long medieval style skirt, pointy New Rock boots with dragons up the side, a velvet bolero and a velvet tie in the back of her indigo hair. A modest amount of turquoise jewellery finished the look off.

Should she wear her witchy hat? She'd take it with her, just in case. Riz was mostly in dark green: Long gypsy style skirt, a white, off the shoulder hippy top, thigh length suede boots and a military tunic similar to those worn by the British in the Napoleonic wars. Just like the one Sharpe wears on the TV.
Her long, blonde hair in a loose pony tail with wispy bits coming down by her ears.
"Do you think I should have my ears surgically pointed?" she asked no one in particular.
Lou was in varying shades of red and black (probably to compliment her lipstick): Black, off the shoulder top, black leather trousers, red (faux) leopard skin boots and a deep red suede jacket with tassels on the arms. All crowned by her vivid red hair and of course matching lipstick.

What a band they would have made! They outdid any rock star you can imagine!
The cats stared at them admiringly. These cats knew *style* when they saw it!
Nancy screeched to a halt at the front of the house and ran up the stone steps to knock on the door.
"Merry meet Nance!" said Lou. "Come in luv."
"Cool Yule," said Nancy, being younger and marginally hipper. "You lot look *amazing*!"
Nancy, of course, couldn't entirely match the three stunning figures before her, not many could, but she had done a pretty fair job of it and had taken
Jinny's advice and 'Dressed Goth' ish.
Nancy being a natural redhead it was a tad tricky doing Goth but she had made a tremendous effort with a black vest, black leather biker jacket with a very arty skull painted on the back of it, black and lilac hooped

leggings and a pair of big, purple, docking leather biker boots with huge soles.

All topped off with a black, suede witch's hat with one of those twirling points and lots of silver jewellery.

"Shall we form a group?" asked Riz.

"Not now Riz, too much like hard work luv." said Jinny.

"Got the tickets Jin?" Lou asked.

"Errr, no. Hang about …"

Jinny went off to search through her old welsh dresser as, what with one thing and another, she didn't actually know where she'd stashed them.

"No rush luv," said Riz. "I'll nip off for a wee."

"And has anybody ordered a taxi?" enquired Lou once more.

"It'll cost a fortune in a taxi, Lou. They have to come all the way from town." said Nancy.

"Well I'm not walking all that way and then back again."

"Broomsticks!" said Jinny from across the room.

"Easily done Jin, but not easily disguised once we get there." Lou said.

"We can all squeeze in my van if you like. I'm not bothered about having a drink." said Nancy helpfully.

As Riz was tip toeing down the stairs she decided to throw her two penn'orth in "How about if we *transport* ourselves?" The room went silent.

"You know, just wish ourselves there. Like Sam in 'Bewitched' does." "Have you done this before Riz?" asked Lou knowing exactly what the answer was going to be.

"Well, no … but …"

“Thought not. *I* can do it, leave it to me. Want to all join hands and I’ll see if I can get us all there? Found the tickets yet Jin?”

“Yep.” she said dashing back to the terrific trio.

“Boys and girl - good behaviour while we’re gone please. No bringing small rodents through the cat flap and no being sick in awkward places. OK?” ordered Jinny.

“Right, hands together.” said Lou as they made a small circle in the middle of the lounge.

Lou stared towards the ceiling and spoke the words, “Takhudhuna hunak … Spiderwood Farm” eight times after which the foursome vanished into thin air, materialising outside the venue just seconds later.

It was a good job there was no one about! Still, anything goes on the solstice.

A bit like Glastonbury without the mud.

THE WITCH AND JET SPLINTERS

Part 1: A Bustle In The Hedgerow

PARCHMENT 24

Spiderwood Farm

Spiderwood Farm! It wasn't a *real* farm. It was a Café by day and a music venue by night.

The locale was set high in the hills but with a good, wide, main road passing by it for easy access from the town.

Inside, there were creepy, twisted branches everywhere and everything was lit an electric blue, apart from the candles on the tables and the artificial flame lamps on the walls.

The old, stone floors were covered in Moroccan rugs and right in the centre of the main room was a free-standing stone chimney with a huge fire roaring away beneath it.

Over to the left was a compact but more than adequate stage area, complete with a substantial PA system and state-of-the-art lighting rig.

This was cool. And yet quite hot at the same time.

The girls made their way to the bar.

Every single person in the place was staring at them, mouths gaping wide. Who *were* these people? What band were they in? Or were they models? Film stars?

A tall, good looking, long haired, tattooed chappy 'accidentally' bumped into Lou.

"Oh, sorry luv," he said. "Want me to get you a drink as an apology?"

"You can if you like," she said graciously. "Bacardi, double please. Two ice cubes and a splash of Coke. Ta!"

"I was thinking more like half a lager…" said the chap, who was obviously waaay out of Lou's league.

"Then think again young man - over there in the corner." she pointed to the furthest corner of the room.

"Right luv," he said. "Will you be joining me?"

"Certainly not. Just go over there and stay there, out of my sight!" Lou scathingly replied.

The poor fellow was crestfallen and walked off with his head down low. "Bitch!" said Riz laughing.

"Witch!" said Lou.

"You all having the usual, ladies?" asked Jinny, knowing the reply.

"Aye!" said Lou and Riz.

"What about you Nancy? I don't know what your usual is …"

"I'll just have half a lager for now please." she said.

"Bloody Hell Nance! You could have copped off with that Neanderthal over there if that's all you wanted to drink!!" laughed Lou.

"Nah, not my type, him."

"What *is* your type Nancy? I'm intrigued." said Riz.

"You might not believe this but I'm partial to short haired guys, in suits or better still, in uniform! And I like specs."

"Well we all like *that*, don't we girls?" winked Riz.

"SPECS she said!" Jinny hollered over the background music.

"You need to call in at the Salvation Army hostel in the village, luv. There's plenty to choose from in there!" Lou cracked up.

More and more men continued to appear, strutting over to the glamorous quartet then sloping off with their tails between their legs, metaphorically speaking.

"They're getting on my nerves this lot now." said Lou accompanied by her very best evil glare. "Want to get a table over there?" said Jinny.
"Aye! Come on girls. Let's go and sit where no one will notice us." said Riz.
"Bit late for that Riz," said Lou. "I think we've overdone it in the dressing up department!"
"I could've come as a Valkyrie after all!" said Riz with hindsight.
"Indeed you could Riz, and you'd have been battling them off all night.
Like Ravens round a Valkyrie actually."
"Like flies round sh …"
"Sheep eyes." Jinny interjected.
"When's the band on?" asked Nancy.
"About another hour I reckon." said Riz, who honestly did not have a clue. There came an almighty CLANG! from the glowing guitar stacks, followed by the thunder of an over miked drum kit and the omnipresent too-high-in-the-mix rumble of the bass guitar.
Then the 'singer' appeared and everyone went outside for a cigarette, shot to the toilet or made for the bar.
Here was the support band. This was how you were *supposed* to react!
"What a bleedin' racket!" shouted Riz. "I'm going out for a fag. Coming?" As everyone smoked but Nancy, they all snuck out to the relative quiet of the smoking shelter.
"Shall we do one of those solstice dances?" said Riz.
"It's a bit cold for that kind of malarkey." said Lou.
"It'd warm us up." offered Riz.
"These'll do a better job." replied Lou pushing the switch for the patio heaters.

Part 1: A Bustle In The Hedgerow

“You’ve got an answer for everything, haven’t you Lou?”

“I seem to have, don’t I?” she said, blowing smoke rings.

The low thud of the support band was still audible outside but not enough to be a nuisance, whatever the neighbours said, the neighbours being sheep.

“I’ve been having a bit of a think,” Lou continued. “I’ve got a spare ticket for something rather special, haven’t I girls? It’s a bit short notice but what are you doing the day after tomorrow Nancy?”

“The day before Christmas Eve? Nothing really. Maybe wrapping a few presents…”

“What would you say if someone was to offer you a free, all expenses paid trip to Lapland?”

“What. Would. I. S-s-say?” Nancy was stunned. Speechless.

“You’d have to do all your prezzie wrapping tomorrow. Think you can manage that?” baited Lou.

Nancy had gone a bit paler than she usually was, which was quite pale, and sat with her mouth agape.

“I ……”

“What a lovely idea Lou. You’re nowhere near as bad as people say you are.” said Riz with a tear in her eye.

Lou was nonplussed, “Why? Who’s been saying I’m bad?”

“Well you can be, can’t you? You can be thoroughly wicked at times … you only have to use that stare …”

“It’s hardly wicked Riz. I only use it to put folk in their place. So who *are* these *people* of which you speak?”

“Nobody in particular. Not Jinny or the cats …”

“So what you’re actually saying is that there isn’t anybody, that you know of, that thinks I’m bad after all?”

Lou was getting Riz all flustered. “Not really, I mean yes, that’s what I’m saying.”

“Good. That’s that cleared up then. Nance, any chance of an answer before one of us expires and we have to give another ticket away?”

“See?” said Riz.

“I would dearly love to go to Lapland Lou, I’m made up, *really* made up.” Nancy started to sob.

“Don’t ruin your makeup, darling.” said Lou in her odd attempt at consolation.

Everyone giggled, sniffed a bit then settled down to make the arrangements for their most excellent Christmas outing.

An hour of excited chat and banter had passed when a sound of a different kind could be heard emanating from the venue - it was the headliners - Wizards In A Blizzard!

“Quick sticks you lot, they’re on!” squealed Jinny.

“Are they?” said Riz. “I don’t even know what they sound like!”

“They sound like THIS!” said Jinny opening the door back into Spiderwood Farm.

“What a flippin’ racket!” shouted Riz, again.

“Excuse me madam,” said a kindly voice, raised higher than usual due to the rack.., sorry, volume of the music. “Would you mind leaving your cigarette outside please?”

“Leave my cig outside you say? I’m not doing that, someone’ll nick it!” Riz said, horrified.

"Well would you and your cigarette mind going outside until the cigarette has run its course? Please." The doorman was now sounding not quite as kindly.

"It's freezing out there!" wailed Riz.

"You've been out there over an hour. It didn't bother you then!" he replied, loudly.

At this point, Riz was considering using, what she liked to call, one of her 'Jedi mind tricks' but thought better of it as it would only be a matter of time before one of the other doormen would jump in and collar her, so she returned outdoors and finished the offending gasper off, which took all of about thirty seconds.

"There!" she said, as she re-entered, affronted. "Happy now?"

"I didn't put the smoking ban in place you know," said the doorman. "Blame the government!"

"I shall. I will be in contact with my local MP first thing tomorrow!" she said snootily.

"But the smoking ban's been in force for almost ten years!"

"Has it? First I've heard of it. What a ridiculous rule, smoking is a part of one's DNA, don't you know. Could you point me in the direction of the ladies' loos please?"

"Only if you don't light up …"

"How do you know about my lighting up? Those kind of things are supposed to be well guarded secrets within the magic circle."

"I haven't the foggiest what you're on about Miss … they're over there, past the quiz machine, on the left."

"Cheers!" said Riz, and glided off somewhere in the vicinity of the coveted public convenience.

"Where's Riz gone now?" asked Jinny, knotting her eyebrows.

"One guess." said Lou.

"Oh, yeah, of course, silly me."

"I'll go and check she's OK," said Nancy. "I need a wee anyway."

"Don't you start," said Lou. "I don't want to be spending this holiday in and out of public lavatories, thank you very much."

"They're great this band, don't you think Lou?" beamed Jinny.

"Not bad. I prefer something a bit more Siouxsie and the Banshees myself
…"

"Hmmmm, I know what you mean. Now you come to mention it I'm not that keen on them either."

"You just said they were great!"

"Coming outside for a cig? Let's get a bottle to take outside."

"We've only just come back in! What's the matter with you woman?"

"I don't know, I can't seem to settle tonight … maybe it's the excitement of the holiday."

"Well let's wait for Riz and Nance to get back then eh?"

Lou and Jinny waited for over half an hour but still no sign of their friends.

Lou was getting very tetchy.

"What the hell are they doing in there?! I'm going to go and check."

"I'll come with you Lou. I could do with a visit myself."

The pair pushed and pulled their way through the crowd until they spotted the sign for the ladies' toilet.

"I feel like I've been dragged through a hedge." said Lou.

Part 1: A Bustle In The Hedgerow

A tall blonde woman caught the corner of Lou's eye and sure enough, there were Riz and Nancy pushing buttons and piling fifty pences into the infernal quiz machine.

Lou was vexed. "Oi! We've been stood waiting for you two for half a bloody hour!"

"Soz Lou," said Riz. "We just discovered this thingy. Damn good fun it is.

You just choose a category and then answer the questions. Brilliant!"

Lou looked incredulously at Jinny and then at Nancy.

"Riz … where exactly have you been most of your life? And don't say 'with you'! It's a quiz machine - they're everywhere. They've been going donkey's years for goodness' sake! Please don't tell me you've never played one before."

"I haven't. First time, Lou. Bloody good craic it is too!"

"Whaaaat?!"

"Have you won anything?" asked Jinny.

"Nah Jin, it's too clever for the likes of us. I reckon I've put about twenty quid in it already."

"Twenty quid?!" exclaimed Lou. "Shift out!" and she waved her hands, as witches do, over the machine.

"Sayasraf." she said, and piles of pound coins suddenly gushed from an opening at the bottom.

"There you are. Go and change them for notes at the bar." smiled Lou.

The night proceeded without further event and closing time was soon upon them.

The ladies waited until the majority of the crowd had filtered out then made their way to the exit.

"It's a nice place this but I didn't think much of the bands." said Riz.

The others agreed. Maybe they should return when they've got something a little more chilled on?
The consensus was 'yes', they would organise a trip back early next year but for now they must concentrate on getting ready for their imminent trek to Scandinavia.
"You know we're going to have to nip home and get some clothes, passports and stuff together?" said Lou to Riz, acting all orderly.
"And suitcases to put them in." said Riz.
"Well, yes. A very high level thought process Riz." Lou said sarcastically.
"Are we walking back or going by magic?" laughed Jinny.
"I'm not walking any distance in these boots." said Lou, repeating her charm and whisking them all back to Demonia Cottage (2) in no time at all.

They soon settled back into their usual places, feeling the warm glow of the Yule log burning softly in the grate and sipping spiced cider.
All was dozy. Jet on Jinny's feet, Spike licking Riz's neck, Stripes curled into a ball on Lou's lap and Nancy, well, Nancy didn't have a 'usual place' yet …
"Do you not have a cat, Nancy?" asked Jinny.
"I don't. I keep promising myself I'll get one but I never seem to get
'round to it."
Jinny pointed to Jet. "This little fella just turned up one night out of the blue. A freebie! Ha Ha!"
"He loves you so much Jinny. I'm really envious."
"And I love him. He's a little darling so he is." Jinny stroked Jet's chin and he purred happily.
"Where did he come from? Has he ever said?" asked Nancy.

Part 1: A Bustle In The Hedgerow

"Come to think of it, no, he never did tell me what he was doing sat in the middle of the crossroads that night. He said it didn't matter and we just kind of left it at that."

Jet stretched and let out a long yawn. "I'll tell you tomorrow, Your Wonderfulness."

Jinny smiled and rubbed his lipsticky head. "If you can bring yourself to be bothered, that would be very kind of you."

Morning came. *Late* morning. Most of the night, after their return from Spiderwood Farm, had been spent downstairs napping in front of the fire.

"Is it my turn to do brekkie again?" Lou asked her comatose comrades.

"Yeeeeah, go on then." said Riz laconically.

"Shall I come round with a pad and take your orders?" Lou suggested in a mildly sarcastic manner.

"Make one of your buffet style concoctions Lou, and we'll steam in and help ourselves, eh?" Jinny said helpfully.

Lou went into the kitchen and within a minute was back with platters full of bacon, sausages, eggs, mushrooms, you know, the usual kind of thing. She placed them all on the dining table, handed out knives, forks and plates and magicked up a pot of tea and a pot of coffee.

"Will that do you?"

Lou got the thumbs up from her friends who immediately tucked in to the fabulous feast she had 'prepared'.

"What about us?" asked Spike, and without a moment's hesitation Lou swished her hands and produced three bowls of fresh salmon, with no bones to ruin things.

"Wow! Thank you, Miss Lou." said Jet. The other two simply tucked in without any acknowledgement. You know what some cats are like.

"Me and Riz are going to have to scoot off back home after we've eaten," said Lou. "We'll probably be back around nine o'clock ish."

"Why don't you magic us home Lou? It'd be quicker." asked Riz.

"I fancy a nice relaxing drive and taking in a bit of scenery." said Lou.

"But you don't drive. It's me that has to do all that and it's not what I'd call 'relaxing'."

"Stop wittering Riz, let's make the most of the day, eh?"

"You can leave the cats here, I'll look after them. Frees you up a bit …" said Jinny, "and don't forget, the flight's at 5.00am!"

"I'd better get going and get my packing done. I don't even *know* where my passport is." said Nancy.

So off they went on their merry ways, leaving Jinny and the three cats to a rare taste of peace and quiet.

"Now we're alone Jet, you can go ahead with what you were going to tell me …" said Jinny somewhat timorously.

"Where to start …" said Jet gazing at the floor.

"At the beginning. It's a very good place to start, according to Julie Andrews." smiled Jinny.

"Who?"

"She's an actress."

"Oh." said Jet, none the wiser. There was a short silence while Jet attempted to gather his thoughts, or rather attempted to put into words a tale that he knew Jinny really wouldn't want to hear.

Part 1: A Bustle In The Hedgerow

"Did you know … that if I were to bite someone they would be dead within three days?" Jet started off hesitantly but rushed the last few words.

"Whaaaat?!" Jinny was struck senseless.

"I'm not what you think Jinny, I mean, I *am* what you think, *now* … but it wasn't always that way."

"You're scaring me Jet, and that's not easy to do."

"You wanted to know why I was sat at the crossroads, in the sleet and cold for half an hour …"

"I presumed you were befuddled."

"I was sent there."

"By whom? For what?"

"I was sent to meet the Dark Lord himself but I was early …"

"By the Dark Lord you don't mean …"

"I do ... Jinny, Jinny … I was … sent to kill you …" Jet broke up and shook his head.

Jinny's blood ran cold. She couldn't speak, she couldn't move. Every hair on her body stood to attention.

"My master is a terrible man, a warlock, and a rancorous, evil one at that. His name is Zyler Shadowend. Do you know him?"

Jinny finally managed to utter, barely audibly, "I've heard him mentioned - none of it good. You say your master *is*. You mean he's *still* your master?" "*He* thinks he is. I never want to set eyes on him again. I've been in his service since I can remember. He found me in a carrier bag, newborn, tied up and left to die."

Tears streamed down Jinny's face as Jet's story unfolded.

"Mr Shadowend has been responsible for many inscrutable, unrepeatable atrocities Jinny, but I somehow managed to turn a blind eye to them. After all, it was all I knew. When he sent me up here I was confused and

questioning what I was doing. I didn't know you or anything about you. I was instructed to kill and I was told to wait at the crossroads in order to surrender my soul, for what it's worth, to the devil, binding me to him and
Shadowend for eternity … but I was early and I had time to think …"

Jinny looked as if she had aged twenty years in a matter of minutes. "W-w-why did he want me dead?" she struggled bravely to get the words out.

"Your house, Jinny. He wanted your house and he knew you would never
part with it."

"But why? What's so special about here?" she looked around swallowing hard.

"Your cottage is built on the site that once housed The Mocking Tower - the most evil cubbyhole in the north of England. It was where the blackest of witches and yes, even the devil himself assembled to do their malevolent bidding. A place that was feared and infamous far and wide, so much so that after the 1612 Lancaster Witch Trials the local governors went about destroying the monstrosity once and for all. This house was built on that site a hundred years later. It's a beautiful home Jinny but below it is hell on earth."

Jinny staggered over to the kitchen and got a bottle of brandy from the cupboard.

To say she was severely dismayed would be an understatement of some enormity.

She poured a large glass full of the spirit and knocked it back in one.

"Continue … please." she whispered.

"His plot was to have you out of the way and, as you have no next of kin to bequeath the house to, he would be ready to step in and put an offer on it. Here he could execute his wicked will to maximum effect."

"H-how does he know I have no next of kin?"

"He knows *everything* about *anything* he cares to know about. I don't know how he does it but trust me, he does!"

"I can't believe you would kill me Jet … would it have been the bite?"

"Yes. One bite, anywhere, would turn your blood black within a day, the next stage would be the terrible hallucinations - enough to send you utterly insane, then you would die convulsing horrifically …"

"My stars … I wondered how you could appear to be so calm and collected on that night."

"Tiredness and stress mostly Jinny, and I'm a good actor." Jet allowed himself a wry laugh then looked back at Jinny, with eyes filled to the brim with sadness.

"But I knew from the second I met you that I wouldn't be able to carry out such a horrible task. I felt something I'd never known before - Love. You are very special Jinny and I wasn't going to be the one to take that away from the world."

"So all the tricks, the magic - you knew it all already? You just played along?"

"I did and I will treasure every second of it. You are a wonderful teacher Jinny and an astonishing woman. Anyway, *that* was why I was waiting at the crossroads, and I'm very thankful that I didn't wait any longer."

By this time Jinny had occasion to think about the short relationship they had developed together and she smiled through her tears at the memories.

"Are you going to leave me, Jet?"

"Do you want me to?"

“I can’t imagine my life without you now … you little shit.” Jinny sobbed. “If you’ll still have me, after such a terrible tale, I would give my heart to stay.”
“Don’t be giving your heart to anyone but me.” she cried and tugged him to her side, squeezing him for all she was worth.

Part 1: A Bustle In The Hedgerow

PARCHMENT 25

Christmas Eve Eve

"Tell me about you, Jinny. Where did all this begin?" said Jet after lying blissfully in her arms for what seemed like hours.

"What time is it? I've got to be at the airport at five!" Jinny started, still asleep but with her eyes open.

"You've got ages yet. Tell me your story." urged Jet.

Jinny was feeling quite groggy and not a little overwhelmed by the day's disclosures but complied nevertheless.

"Me? I was born in Cornwall. My parents were a bit 'off-the-wall' to say the least, but anyway, they died in a boating accident and I think there were

Jellyfish involved. It's all very sketchy.

I ended up living with my Aunt. She was a weird old thing who, it later transpired, was in fact a witch. Who'd have thought it?

She wasn't a good witch like me or Riz or Lou, she was horrendous and I vowed that as soon as the opportunity arose I'd be out of there like a shot!" Jinny blew her nose into a paper hanky then continued.

"I was hanging around the Museum of Witchcraft and Magic in Boscastle when I first bumped into Lou and Riz. They were a bit older than me and already what you might call quite 'cosmopolitan'.

I was about eleven years old so, they'd be about fifteen. Lord knows what they were doing on their own down in Cornwall at that age but anyway… I ended up chatting to them, as we obviously had a common interest in

witchcraft and it turned out that they weren't too keen on the darker side of it all but had happily dabbled in some areas…"

Part 1: A Bustle In The Hedgerow

"Was Lou already wearing that bright red lipstick then?" asked Jet.

"No, no, not at all. She'd have looked a right Lolita, what?" laughed Jinny. "Soooo, Riz was telling me about her upbringing and how her family were originally from France and their ancestors were nobility and had to make their escape from Madame Guillotine, so they picked on Holland! Ha Ha. In time, her parents inexplicably made their way over to northern England and settled here. They live up near the Lake District in a very grand house. Mr and Mrs La Croix. Very posh you know."

"Has she gone all that way back for her stuff?"

"Yeah. She's mental but I wouldn't have her any other way … stop interrupting matey, anyway, they invited me up to Riz's mum and dad's place for a holiday, so I went back to my Aunt's, chucked some togs and things together, I didn't have much in the way of possessions, and ended up on the train up to the Lakes! Riz paid for it. She's never known what it's like to be skint y'know but she's completely unspoiled. To cut a long story short I never did return to Cornwall. It's a beautiful place and all that but my Aunt sent me scatty. I lived with Riz and her parents for about five years until they helped me to buy my own place - this! I think they were glad to get rid of me … well … maybe not, maybe they were just being kind. I'd like to think so. We've been the best of friends ever since."

"Where did Lou live then?"

"Ask Stripes, she's been with Lou forever! She's supernatural that cat. Must be about forty years old!"

"I hope I live that long." said Jet staring into space, as he did sometimes.

"Lou came from another well-to-do family but they didn't really get on. She's very misunderstood is Lou, and her sisters and parents excelled in misunderstanding her. She lived at Riz's house for a while, before she hopped off to university. It was a big house. Plenty of rooms. I loved it so much. We had the very best of times. It was Lou that instigated the witchcraft stuff, after she'd just finished a stint with the Circus as 'Madame Citronella - Reader of Souls'! Her and Riz had obviously been experimenting with it before but when I came along I made up the magic number of three … for a Coven. Things kind of escalated from there on …"

"That was a nicer story than mine." said Jet sadly.

"Very much nicer. What are we going to do about this Shadowend fellow then? He knows you're here and he's going to come looking for you."

"I don't want to see him or think about him."

"I can understand that …"

"We need to get rid of the evil surrounding this area. Below the house for starters, then those damned crossroads. It has to be that Shadowend loses all interest in this place altogether." said Jet pensively.

"Spells you mean? I'm not sure we've got anything powerful enough up our sleeves to get rid of Old Nick!"

"Anyway, it'll all have to wait until you get back from Lapland, won't it?" "After what I've heard today I'm not sure it's a good idea to leave you alone here for three days."

"Spike and Stripes are here …"

"Not much use against an arch practitioner of the black arts though. I wish

Raph was still around."

"Hmmm, let me have a think …" mused Jet.

The hours were getting on and it wasn't long before Lou and Riz returned from the Lake District.

"Blimey! Did you fly after all?" said Jinny.

"No need to, not with the way Riz drives, luv." said Lou. Riz was a bit put out. "Oi! That's derogatory that is, Lou. I'm a blindin' driver."

"You certainly nearly blinded me … with terror!" Lou laughed.

"Anyway, have you both got everything you need?" asked Jinny.

"Yeah, think so … here, have you been crying?" Lou was very perceptive, well, an ex-reader of souls has to be!

"Just watching something sad on TV." lied Jinny.

"Jinny, the only things you watch on TV are your DVDs and I guarantee that not one of them has anything in them to make you cry. The Munsters? The Addams Family? Penny Dreadful? Father Ted?"

"Look, I'll tell you about it while we're away eh?" said Jinny, not wanting to relive the conversation with Jet just yet.

"OK, if you're sure you're going to be alright. I won't forget to bring it up you know, while we're away."

"I'd be happier to give it a couple of days if you don't mind, Lou."

There was a tap on the door.

"That'll be Nancy, I bet." said Riz, striding across the room. "Yeah, it's OK, it's her."

"Who were you expecting Riz - the Anti-Christ?" laughed Lou again.

Jinny looked gravely at Jet, biting her lip.

"Hiya girls," said Nancy. "All set then?"

"Aye." said Lou. "By the way, how are we getting to the airport?"

"I think you should 'transport' us there Lou, save a lot of messing." said Riz.

"By 'messing' you mean 'putting some effort in'?"

"Aww, come on Lou. I've just driven about two hundred miles because you wanted to see some scenery." bemoaned Riz.

"The speed you were going, any scenery I did see was completely blurred

Riz! But yeah, if everyone's happy with it I'll zap us there. Ready?"

Jinny hugged Jet and gave him a great big kiss on his still lipsticky head and promised to bring him a present back. Lou and Riz each kissed Spike and Stripes, then Jet and Lou chanted the words, "Takhudhuna hunak" four times, as before.

And there they were, at Manchester Airport, ready to board. No security checks, no customs. Sometimes it really was great being a witch.

"Fancy a drink before we set off?" said Lou, hopefully.

"I'll wait until we get on the plane." said Jinny.

Nancy and Riz agreed.

"Miserable buggers." muttered Lou, who liked to have a few 'settlers' before boarding.

Riz checked the departure time and that everything was running on schedule and before they knew it they were seated on the plane with a glass of champagne each, courtesy of Village Life magazine. How sublime.

"How long does it take Riz?" asked Lou.

"I don't know Lou. It's ages since I've been there and I didn't go from Manchester."

"It's about three and a half hours, Lou. I checked when I was at home." said Nancy authoratively.

"Does it take the same amount of time to get back?" said Riz dizzily. Everyone just looked at her and groaned.

Part 1: A Bustle In The Hedgerow

"I'll tell you something Riz" said Lou "You haven't been to the toilet for at least five hours! That's a record! Riz! Put that ciggie out! You can't smoke on here!"

"You could last time I went on a plane."

"Have you even any idea what decade it is, Riz?" asked Jinny, gob smacked.

"Don't be cheeky Jin, it's the twenty first century, even I know that." Riz replied, still with a cigarette dangling from her mouth.

"Look, take it in the toilet Riz. Kill two birds with one stone." suggested Lou.

"Why would I want to kill two birds? I love birds!" "What *are* you on woman? I want some!" said Jinny. "Yes," agreed Lou. "She's even dizzier than usual." "Have you eaten anything weird luv?" asked Nancy.

"Only a bit of one of them frogstools, you know the ones that were in your garden Jin? I saw one in a field near me mum's house."

"They're supposed to be dangerous for witches, Riz!" yelled Lou.

"Sssshhhhh! Somebody'll hear." said Jinny.

"I can't help being inquisitive." said Riz dozily.

"Better not mix champers with it. Could be lethal."

"Too late!" tittered Riz as her eyes slowly closed and she drifted off to who-knows-where-land.

"Well, that's her out of the equation. No wonder she never remembers where she's been!" snorted Lou.

"Never mind, we'll be there soon. Let's watch a film eh?" said Jinny.

"Don't think they do them on these short haul flights, Jinny." said Nancy.

"You're very clued up on these things, aren't you Nance?"

"I'm a mind of useless information. You have to be, being a locksmith." she laughed.
"I was going to ask how on earth you got into that line of work, but life's too short to hear the answer." said Lou.
"It started out as safe breaking." said Nancy, unasked.
"What?! See? I told you it wouldn't be an easy answer!" Lou glanced at Jinny.
"It's not a complicated answer, far from it, I was just fed up of never having any money and I certainly didn't want to work in dad's scrap yard, so I started tampering with locks. Simple really …"
"Yes, I can see how that might be the obvious answer to being broke Nance. And the witchcraft?"
"I read some articles online and got interested, so I joined the library and borrowed a few books. There were some good ones about locks and robberies too! Ha Ha. Aleister Crowley's my favourite bedtime read though. Stirring stuff!"
"I never thought I'd hear the day when someone admitted that the 'Great Beast 666' was their desert island bedtime favourite!" giggled Lou "You're almost on a par with this one here." she said, pointing at the conked out Riz.
"Funny old world, innit?" was all Jinny could think of to say on the matter. The trio finished the rest of the bottle of complimentary champagne and inevitably dozed off.
Nancy was the first to wake, with a little help from the stewardess. They had landed in what could only be described as a winter wonderland, the snow stretching for miles into the distance.
"Wow!" she thought whilst rousing Lou, Jinny and with more difficulty, Riz.
"Where am I? A plane?" drawled Lou.

Part 1: A Bustle In The Hedgerow

“Have we set off yet?” Riz was still quite drowsy as she endeavoured to stand up.

Jinny felt like she’d just come out of an anaesthetic and her first thoughts were ‘Jet’. Was he OK? Had Spike sorted the eating arrangements? She hoped no one had been to visit …

Just to stop you worrying, back at Demonia Cottage (2) the cats were having a carefree, lazy old time of it.

Spike had indeed looked after the eating arrangements and everyone was as happy as that Larry that you hear so much about.

Nothing to report and nothing to be alarmed about. Snug. That’s the word.

As we magically whoosh back to Lapland with its mystery, snow, abundance of trees and the new addition of four witches, the ladies are busy settling into the four-star hotel that will be their home for the next three nights.

It was a ruggedly beautiful place made entirely from logs and the girls were enchanted by it.

“I could live and die here.” Jinny said to herself, admiring the stag’s antler ‘chandelier’ in her room, then moving over to the window to admire the snowy vista.

There was a log burner in the corner, gently heating the room, a rustic four poster bed and even a personal sauna! And everywhere was wood!

Glorious wood.

Surely nothing on earth could compare.

The rest of the entourage were having similar feelings and it seemed that none of them were entirely sure if they really wanted to leave these magnificent quarters.

Jinny’s room phone rang. It was Lou, ever the organiser.

"Fancy a bevvie, captain?" was the not entirely unexpected question. "Yeah, go on then. Are the other two going down? I bet we can't get them out of their rooms. They're amazing aren't they?"

"Who are amazing? Nancy and Riz?"

"No! Well, yes but I mean the rooms - it doesn't get any better than this …"

"Drag yourself away, woman. See you at the bar in five!" concluded Lou. Jinny finally got round to taking her coat off, did a quick change into something more becoming of a giant log cabin and reluctantly kissed a temporary goodbye to her new 'home'.

She was the last to arrive at the bar and the girls were already getting stuck into a warm jug of Glogg, a kind of mulled wine in which they'd decided to add, well, Riz decided to add a glug of Koskenkorva vodka to. Danger!

"Here Jin, get this down your neck!" said Riz, handing her a thick handled glass of the potent brew.

"What is it?" asked Jin, slightly dubious.

"Who cares? Get it supped and let's start the party!" laughed Riz.

To which they all clinked their glasses with a hearty "Cheers!"

"I'm off to see my friend tomorrow … anyone want to come along and make a day of it?" announced Riz, now fully recovered from her frogstool episode.

"Won't he mind four of us turning up unannounced?" asked Lou. "Nah, I don't think so. He's an easy-going sort of bloke."

"Is he an old boyfriend or something Riz?" asked Nancy.

"He's definitely old Nance but no, not a boyfriend, more a sort of father figure …" and Riz giggled to herself.

Part 1: A Bustle In The Hedgerow

"You're a proper enigma at times aren't you Riz? You love these little cliffhangers ..." said Lou with one eyebrow raised.

"Ah look girls, it's a surprise. I promise you won't be disappointed" Riz replied.

"Let's go and build a snowman!" suggested Jinny.

"Get out of it," said Lou. "People will think we're tourists!"

"We *are*!"

"I know but ... it's not etiquette, is it?"

The drinks had gone straight to their heads, especially as they hadn't eaten properly.

"I'll magic one up." Jinny said, adventurously and rather giggly.

"In full view of all these punters? You'll get us banned!" said Lou sensibly.

"I won't. How are they going to prove it's me? RIJAL AL-THILJ!" she waved her hand and there, outside, perfectly visible from the bar stood a snowman of at least twenty feet in height, complete with huge coal eyes and a carrot nose to rival the one that Wilf had presented her with before 'the battle'.

You could see people doing double-takes as if to say "That wasn't there before, was it?"

Soon, the whole of the bar were peering out of any available window to admire the giant snowman.

"See? That's made their day that has." said Jinny proudly.

"This bloke doesn't look too happy, who's just stormed in." noticed Lou. There was a red-faced man ranting at the head barman. Jinny focused in on her extra sensory hearing and eavesdropped.

"I've got a James Bond replica Aston Martin DB5 underneath that thing!" bawled the fellow, "four hundred and fifty thousand dollar's worth!" he continued. "Who's responsible for this outrage?"

The barman managed to convince the American chap, for that is what he was, that no one working for the hotel would do such a thing and anyway, they wouldn't have the time!

"I'll find the manager." muttered the man and strode off briskly towards the reception desk.

"Now you've blown it, Jin." said Riz.

"Nobody can pin that on me - I've been here all the time."

The ladies moved away from the window and made for a cosy corner in which to keep their heads down.

"You're a silly sod, Jin. What were you thinking of?" said a disgruntled Lou.

"It's this drink you've given me, it's loopy juice."

"Don't blame the drink. You're being deliberately mischievous because you're on holiday." said Riz.

"Showing off!" said Lou. Nancy didn't say anything, it wasn't her place and she still didn't know any of them well enough.

"Soz," said Jinny with her head bowed. "I just love snowmen."

And the whole group burst out laughing. They sounded like four cackling, well, witches!

THE WITCH AND JET SPLINTERS

Part 1: A Bustle In The Hedgerow

PARCHMENT 26

Christmas Eve

The morning came quickly. The remainder of the day before had been spent eating anything that was put in front of the ladies and drinking even more.

They were a sorry sight to behold but fifteen minutes in the sauna followed by ultra-high powered showers soon knocked them back into shape. They all met up at a table by reception, where Riz presented everyone with a Gakti - a warm, indigenous coat favoured by the native Sami people, along with a 'Four Winds Hat' each.

"I nipped out to the local clothing store earlier." she said.

Riz never ceased to baffle Lou. "*Earlier*? How on earth did you manage that?"

"I put an Amethyst stone under my pillow. Works every time!" Lou, Jinny and Nancy looked at each other, again baffled.

"How does that actually work then?" asked Lou.

"Well … you get an Amethyst stone and you kind of just pop it under your pillow … no hangover."

"And where, pray, are we supposed to come by an Amethyst out here in the middle of nowhere?"

"There's an Amethyst mine just five minute's walk from here …"

"You mean you've been out and mined for one?" Lou was intrigued.

"Yes. Well, no. I already had it from last time I was here."

Part 1: A Bustle In The Hedgerow

"I really underestimate you, Riz," said Lou. "You never cease to amaze me. Never. Remind me, in future, to take note of every pearl of wisdom you come out with. And thanks for the togs – lovely."

Riz walked backwards over to reception. "You're welcome. Now get your Gaktis on and let's be off. I've booked a sleigh." she said as she collected a huge hamper from the desk clerk.

"You think of everything, sometimes." laughed Jinny.

"I'll just go for a Jimmy Riddle, won't be a min." said Riz.

"She's a bloomin' marvel, that girl. How does she manage it all?" said Lou, shaking her head.

They finally stepped out of the hotel and there before them was the most magnificent sleigh, pulled by four reindeer.

"Wow!" uttered Nancy, open mouthed.

"Wow!" uttered Lou, even more open mouthed.

"Wow!" uttered Jinny, even more, more open mouthed.

"Good eh?" said Riz. "All aboard!" and she flinged the hamper onto the back of the sleigh and jumped in the driver's chair to take the reins.

"Are you sure you weren't born here, Riz?" asked Nancy.

"I feel like I was sometimes. It's like I instinctively know the place. Like I've never been away."

"Déjà vu?" asked Lou.

"You've said that before." laughed Riz as she tugged the reins and set the reindeer in motion.

"Der der der der der … laughing all the way …" sang Jinny. "This is bloody marvellous, really it is." she said, as they flew at great speed through the snow.

"Is it far?" asked Lou.

"Oh don't be such a child!" said Riz, teasing. "Take the views in. The journey will go quicker."

"The views?" said Lou. "All I can see are snow and trees."

"Did you know that trees cover seventy-five per cent of the country?" said Riz informatively.

"No. I. Did. Not. Know. That. Riz. How did you?"

"I just do, it's common knowledge round here. Twenty minutes and we'll be there."

"And how do you know *that* one? It's not as if you can go by landmarks, is it?"

"Trust me."

"Whatever you say Riz. From here on in I trust every word." said Lou emphatically.

Nancy and Jinny didn't get involved with the girls' banter. They just sat and relished every minute of this fantastic trip.

Eventually, Riz pulled on the reins and shouted, "Whoah!" bringing the sleigh to a halt.

She got down from her seat, patted the reindeer and gave them an apple each.

"Not poisoned are they?" laughed Lou.

"Look up there!" shouted Nancy.

"Oh my stars!" exclaimed Jinny "That's the Aurora Borealis!"

This most magical and awe inspiring of sights was now in clear view of the group and they watched agog, feeling humbled at the sheer majesty of one of nature's greatest hits.

The green, shimmering sky curtains had completely taken their mind off where they actually were …

"Where are we then, Riz?" asked Jinny eventually.

"The Grotto, Jin."

Part 1: A Bustle In The Hedgerow

"Is this where your mate lives?"

"Yep. Hang on I'll give him a shout … Sinterklaas! Sinter!" she yelled. Lou laughed "Ha Ha. Sounds like she's shouting Santa Claus, doesn't it?" "It does a bit." said Jinny, apprehensively.

A door that couldn't be seen opened, in, what for all the world looked like a fifteen-foot high snow drift. A very sturdily built fifteen-foot high snow drift.

"Hello Riz! What a very pleasant surprise." said the voice of a hooded man with a great white beard, from which an old briar pipe protruded.

He was dressed in dark green with white fur trims and had a rather prominent belly.

"No bloody way!!! No way Riz! It can't …" Lou stammered.

"It's Sinterklaas. You heathens will know him as Santa Claus or worse,

Father Christmas." said Riz loftily. "Merry meet old friend."

Nancy, Lou and Jinny felt like they were going to faint.

Well, imagine you'd just met the biggest celebrity in the whole wild world. Imagine.

As it happened, Nancy did faint and had to be helped up by Lou and Jinny. "Come in, come in all of you, come and warm yourselves." said the kindly gent.

Riz introduced her companions to her beloved friend: "This is Miss Jinny, that's Miss Lou and this is Nancy. She's not a 'Miss' yet." she said somewhat obliquely.

"A pleasure to meet you all." said Santa "Are you, erm, are you all witches by any chance?"

"Yes." they chanted.

"We're in good company then." he smiled, striding to the fireplace to give the massive log fire a poke.

"Sit down, wherever you like. On the floor if it's comfier - make yourselves at home."

A small Elven looking chap with pointy ears walked in and asked if anyone would like refreshments. The ladies all nodded, "Yes please."

"He was quite nice." said Nancy wistfully.

"A bit short Nance, for goodness sake." said Lou.

"I don't fancy him …
just saying …"

"So, what do you do?"
Santa asked the ladies.

"We're just witches, sir." said Jinny nervously.

"I'm a locksmith, sir." Nancy piped up.

"A locksmith indeed?" said Santa raising his eyebrows. "I might have a little job for you …"

"Really? I'd be honoured to sort it out for you, sir." Santa waved his hand as if to say, 'all in good time'.

Nancy began to imagine a future business card and answer phone message:

'Redfern's - locksmiths to Santa Claus'.

"And how are you keeping, young Riz? I haven't seen you here for, ooh, twelve years is it?" asked Santa.

"Ten years Sinter. It's gone pretty quickly, if you ask me."

"I see *you*, wherever you are, every Christmas Eve, but you don't see me."

"So is it really you that keeps leaving me a silver ring every year? I've run out of fingers!" she laughed holding her hands out.

"Yes, I do Riz. You're very precious to me, as you know, so I leave you something precious in kind. And … they're not silver … they're platinum."

"Good lord!" said Riz taken aback "My hands are worth a flippin' fortune!"

Lou was a bit put out, "You're a jammy bugger Riz! I'm lucky if I get an orange or a pair of stripey socks."

"Ah, well, I didn't know you, Miss Lou." said Santa. "Watch out this Christmas!"

Lou looked at the others and did a big "Wooooo!"

"You've been here a good ten minutes and you haven't asked for the toilet once." Santa addressed Riz. "…not like you."

"I'm chilled out, but now you've mentioned it …"

"Remember where it is?"

"Yeah, course I do."

"And so you should, I think you went thirteen times the first time you visited me."

Everyone laughed as Riz sidled off to the loo. What an unbelievable day this was turning out to be.

The company had been eating, drinking and laughing (all the way) all day.

Ho, ho and thrice ho.

Santa remembered the job he had for Nancy to sort out.

"Follow me Nancy." he said as he led her through a tunnel lit by ice blue fairy lights. Yes, these were literally made by faeries (not ice blue faeries, it must be noted) and had a glow like no human had ever seen, apart from Riz and that little boy from The Snowman cartoon, possibly.

The tunnel tapered off into a vast cave, again lit by fairy lights but this time there were millions of them. Amber ones.

Nancy looked around and couldn't believe what she was seeing.

There was every denomination of toy imaginable, every perfume, aftershave, every type of socks, ties, CDs, selection boxes, books, musical instruments, oven gloves, chocolates, pyjamas, scarves - you name it, it was there by the thousand.

Nancy's eyes were everywhere, "You must need a lot of staff to get through this lot Santa."

"Seven hundred elves to be precise." he said affectionately.

"Where do they all live?" she asked.

"They have their own quarters farther down, past this cave. It's too big for a human being to comprehend and they're not keen on strangers so perhaps best not to go there."

"What can you possibly want little old me to do in a place like this?"

"It's not a big task Nancy. It's over here." Santa beckoned her over to an old oak table on top of which was a large chest, like the kind you would find treasure in, if you happened to be a pirate or something.

On the chest was a heavy padlock that looked like it hadn't been opened in many years.

"I need this padlock opening Nancy. I know, I could smash it or prise it open but it's such a beautiful chest and a handsome lock that I don't want to ruin them if I can help it." he explained.

Nancy had a good look at the lock and asked Santa if he had a toolbox handy.

He had one somewhere, hadn't seen it for ages. Nevertheless, off he went in search of the blessed thing.

While he was gone, Nancy continued to stare at the thousands and thousands of Christmas presents on display. The sheer scale of this operation was overwhelming and Nancy couldn't quite believe that all of this was real.

Part 1: A Bustle In The Hedgerow

Had the Glogg altered her mind in some way? She had heard tales about what Absinthe could do to your brain. Maybe this stuff had the same effect?

Presently (Ha Ha) Santa returned with a toolbox. “I couldn’t find my own so I’ve had to borrow one of these from the Men’s Hardware Gift Section.” “Let’s see what we’ve got then …” said Nancy scanning the metal box’s interior. “That’ll do, and this.” she said pulling out a couple of strange looking contraptions. She beavered away for about fifteen minutes until ‘click’ she was in, with no damage done at all.

She expected to see hundreds of shining jewels and maybe gold doubloons but all that was inside was some deep red cloth.

Santa lifted the cloth out and revealed it to be his famous red outfit!

“Haven’t seen this for years,” he said smiling. “It makes a difference, you know. Imagine Batman wearing pink, for example.”

“Yes, I see …” said Nancy, not seeing at all really.

“I locked it away for safe keeping ten years ago and it’s been in here ever since. Couldn’t find the blasted key anywhere. Thank you so much for getting it back … I’ve been fearful of anyone seeing me out on Christmas Eve dressed in green. Not that I don’t like green, it’s just that people expect red, don’t they?”

At that moment, Riz sauntered into the cave and wandered over to the pair.

“Has she sorted it, Sinter?” she asked. “Oh yes, a wonderful job she’s done too.” “What needed doing then?” asked Riz.

“Just that padlock on the chest. I lost the key for it ages ago.”

“This one?” said Riz, innocently pointing to the old key she always had hanging on a chain around her neck.

"Oh my giddy aunt!" laughed Santa, "I don't believe it!"
"You gave it to me the last time I was here and told me to look after it. Trouble is, I got waylaid for ten years!"
"Ten years it has been." smiled Santa "You might as well keep the blooming thing, Riz, it's no use to me now."
"Aww, thanks Sinter. I'd feel lost without it."
"You're a proper caution Riz, make no mistake." said Nancy mirthfully.
"I've never met anyone so intelligent, yet so downright dizzy."
The three of them laughed loudly and made their way back to the warmth of the lounge.

"What would you like as repayment for retrieving my outfit, Nancy?" asked Santa gratefully.
"Oh nothing, really, it was an honour to help, sir." she said, blushing.
"When Riz said you weren't a 'Miss' yet, what exactly did she mean?"
"I think she meant I'm not a fully-fledged witch yet …"
"Do you want to be? If you use your powers for good I can arrange it for you."
"I would love to be a proper witch, like the others." Nancy gushed.
Santa waved his hands and spoke some words in a language that no one understood then said, "There, Nancy Redfern. You are now a fully paid up member of whatever union this lot are in." he smiled kindly.
"Oh wow! Thank you so much Santa. That's the best Christmas present I have ever had." she said leaning over and planting a big kiss on his cheek. Now it was Santa's turn to blush and mutter something unintelligible under his breath.

Part 1: A Bustle In The Hedgerow

"I'll remember this day for as long as I live." she announced, as if she could possibly ever forget it.

The day was getting on and the group would have to travel back to the hotel in darkness. There are only just over three hours of daylight in Finland. Very similar to British summertime.
"Will you be alright negotiating your way back in the dark, Riz?" asked Santa.
"Should be, yeah." she replied.
"Do you have any lighting at all?" he added.
"The one thing I didn't think of -… a bit stupid really as it was getting dark when we set off!"
"Here," said Santa, passing her an old lantern. "This will stay lit, no matter the weather, for over eight hours."
"You're a darling, Sinter." Riz smiled lovingly at him. "Come on girls, we'd better be making our way back."
"Do we have to?" moaned Lou. "I love it here."
"Yep, that's why we had to come today. Sinter's got a lot of preparation to do - remember what day it is?"
"Christmas Eve! Blimey It'd completely slipped my mind." said Jinny.
"It's no big thing really," said Santa, "the Elves take care of the gifts, I just deliver them."
"In one night, all over the world. That's some going." said Lou.
"It is Miss Lou, but it's not like I have to do it every day, is it? And you four will be the first I call on so make sure you're in bed early, and most of all make sure you've been good, for goodness sake!" he laughed.
"Thank you for a wonderful day." said Lou planting a huge red, lipsticky kiss on Santa's beard. "I hope we can come back again some day."

"So do I Miss Lou. Just make sure it doesn't take you ten years!"
"Thank you for everything." Jinny gave Santa a big hug, she was still a bit starstruck you know.
"I don't know how to thank you Santa." said Nancy with a tear in her eye.
"Just by being here … that's thanks enough." said Santa.
"See yer soon me old mucker." said Riz wrapping her arms round his neck and kissing him on the forehead. "Blessed be and good luck tonight." she winked.
They left the old man with a fond wave and moist eyes. He had loved their company and was sorry to see them part but needs must … there was a very busy night ahead.

It seemed to take forever to get back to the hotel but there were no incidents or accidents en route, apart from Riz needing the loo, tricky at minus six degrees.
As they approached their temporary home, they noticed a large crowd had assembled in the front grounds.
"What do you think that's all about?" said Jinny.
When they got nearer it became clear that the crowd were all gathered around a giant snowman.
There were lanterns and a bonfire (Not too close, they didn't want to melt the poor thing), and it seems the owners of the hotel had set a festive barbecue up and a makeshift bar.
"It looks like they're doing some kind of Pagan ritual." observed Lou. "They're worshipping my snowman!" Jinny said excitedly.
"Worshipping a snowman? Hmmm, I suppose it has got a look of Buddha about it." said Lou satirically.
"By the way, Riz" Jinny said. "Where are you going to put the reindeer and sleigh tonight?"

Part 1: A Bustle In The Hedgerow

"Back where they came from, Jin."

"Where's that then?"

"No idea luv … I just magicked them up."

Lou, Jinny and Nancy looked at each other as if to say, "Of course!" and Riz parked the sleigh up by the side of the hotel, took out the hamper

(which they hadn't even used), and everyone's various bits and bobs then simply waved her hands. "AIKHTAFAA!" and the sleigh and reindeer disappeared.

"Right, let's see what all the fuss is about …" she said, tramping through the snow towards the gathering.

There were maybe eighty odd residents and staff and they seemed to be having a jolly old time of it.

Someone had even set up a makeshift mobile disco under a tree and as the girls arrived, one of their (Jinny, Lou and Riz that is) favourite tunes parped through the inadequate speakers - "Eagle" by ABBA, which fair brought a tear to Jinny's eye.

"Raph would've loved it here." she said, wiping her eyes.

"No he wouldn't!" snapped Lou. "He was from India! You couldn't get a hotter climate."

"It's cold on the mountains though, Lou." Jinny said, philosophically.

Lou realised she had been a tad harsh "It is, yes. Fancy a bevvie, captain?" "I'll try some of that stuff we had last night please." Jinny was a glutton for punishment, it seemed.

"Are you sure? That mental tackle?"

"Aye, go on, it'll help me to sleep."

Nancy and Riz where already at the bar sipping hot mulled wine garnished with orange slices and cinnamon sticks.

"This has been like a dream, Riz," said Nancy. "I mean, what a fabulous place … then you add Santa to the equation and … just Wow!"

"He's a lovely old soul, isn't he? Bless his bits." said Riz staring off into the billions of stars in the night sky.

Lou and Jinny got their drinks and joined Nancy and Riz, then they all went off to stand near the bonfire.

"Bloody good idea that snowman, what?" beamed Jinny.

"I'm amazed you didn't get us chucked out Jin, but it seems to have captured everyone's imagination, doesn't it? I wonder if that American guy got his car out …" said Riz.

Then, from the skies being completely clear, emerged a massive cloud, followed by what can only be described as an instant torrential blizzard and the snow just appeared to empty itself in one huge dollop on the crowd.

Four inches fell in two minutes!

"This is what it's all about girls, eh?" smiled Lou, thankful for Riz's warm Gakti gift.

"What have you got me for Christmas, Lou?" Riz asked out of the blue, well, white actually.

"Hang on … you don't even like Christmas, Riz. Why would I get you anything? And anyway, what about this holiday, for starters?"

"There's been no adverts or telly to spoil it Lou, so I'm loving it!" Riz bounced up and down on the spot.

"What have you got me Riz?" Lou thought she'd enquire.

"A hat, a Gakti, a sleigh ride and a visit to Sinter's grotto! What more do you want?!"

Lou had a think and came to the conclusion that she had, in fact, been spoiled rotten. "Get me another drink and we'll call it straight."

Part 1: A Bustle In The Hedgerow

The party went on for quite a while until it was nearing midnight when everyone, as if telepathically linked, made their way back into the hotel to sing Merry Christmas and shake hands and hug each other.

"Wassails all round!" shouted Riz, then realising that she didn't want to have to pay for eighty odd peoples' drinks, snuck off into a corner with her hood pulled over her head.

Jinny followed her over. "You alright Riz?"

"How did you know it was me?"

Jinny looked at her incredulously. "What?"

"Soz, just hiding in case someone takes me up on my drinks offer."

The music continued to play in the bar. It was all the usual standards, nothing changes much at Christmas, wherever you are in the world: Slade, Wham! Bing Crosby, Nat King Cole, Paul McCartney, Wizzard, Mike Oldfield, The Pogues, Dean Martin … the list went on.

"I really like Christmas now Jin," confided Riz, "and I always will!"

"That's good news Riz, I'm glad for you. Coming outside for a fag?"

"Yeaaah, come on."

"Where have those two got to?" Lou said to no one in particular because Nancy had popped off to the toilet.

"If you are looking for your friends, zay haf gone outside for a cheeky cigarette I thinks." said a fellow party goer who happened to be German and seemed to have taken a bit of a shine to Lou.

"Oh, right, thank you, erm, I mean Danke …"

Lou shot off outside and soon caught up with Riz and Jinny sitting on the steps, enjoying a smoke.

“Crash the ash.” she said in the hope of bumming a ciggie from one of them.

Riz, ever the benevolent one, handed Lou her packet and Lou slipped one out.

“You know something, since we’ve been here I haven’t felt the need to smoke as much.”

“It’s the air, Lou,” said Riz. “There are so many trees and so little bacteria over here.”

“What’s that got to do with it?”

“I have absolutely no idea, but I haven’t had to go to the loo half as much!”

“And what’s *that* got to do with it?”

“Nothing” said Riz, admitting defeat.

Jinny laughed at the pair. They were a proper comic act but they didn’t even know it.

“I’m off to bed in a bit.” said Riz, after a minute or two’s silence.

“Yeah, me too,” said Lou. “Santa said we had to get off early and be good …”

“It’s hardly early.” noted Jinny.

“Early for us …” puffed Lou. “I’d better go and find Nancy.”

They all stubbed their cigarettes out in the snow and set off back into the hotel.

A man with one eye and a very dark aura was standing in the doorway. He reminded them of Doctor Strange, you know, from the Marvel comics?

“Excuse me,” said Jinny as she led the way.

The man didn’t move.

Jinny raised her voice. “EXCUSE ME PLEASE!”

“Are you, by any chance, Jinny Lane?” he asked in a very sinister voice.

“I am, yes, why?”

Part 1: A Bustle In The Hedgerow

“I think you have something of mine …”

“Do I? Mind telling me what exactly?”

“You have my cat …”

Jinny’s heart sank. It sank lower than a deep sea diver with extra lead in his boots.

“What’s going on?” demanded Lou.

“Stay out of it woman … if you know what’s good for you.” the stranger replied.

Lou’s heckles went up immediately. “If I know what’s good for me? I know exactly what’s good for me and being threatened isn’t good for me!”

“It’s a long story and I haven’t told anyone about it,” Jinny said to Lou. “I was going to bring it up after the holiday, so as not to spoil things.”

Lou was unusually speechless.

Riz didn’t look happy at all as she approached the fellow. “What do you want with Jinny?” she demanded.

“As I told your friend, stay out of it or there’ll be trouble.” the man said menacingly.

“Trouble?” Riz turned away and glowered. How dare he speak to her like that.

She picked her wand from her pocket and swiftly turned “TAEWIM!” she shouted and the man rose violently into the air, banging his head on the door frame on the way up.

“Now, Mr Cocky, what is this about?” Lou and Jinny had never seen Riz behave so threateningly.

“Get me down woman or you’ll regret it.”

“You’ll stay there as long as I want you to.” said Riz through bared teeth. She then proceeded to trace her wand through the air and float the dark fellow away from the hotel entrance.

“It’s a brave man who’ll take on a whole coven,” said Lou. “Or a very stupid one.”

"And I am not stupid …" uttered the man.

"I happen to think you are." said Riz, controlling her anger admirably. "Now, tell me who you are and what you want or I swear I'll send you spiralling to the heavens."

Jinny did a quick spell that locked his arms to his sides so he couldn't do any funny business, after all, she knew exactly who he was.

"You hopeless harridans. I'll have Hell itself come down on you for this!" he screamed.

"Will you really? Well, if you're not going to cooperate …" Riz twirled her wand and in a very eerie and determined voice yelled, "USQUE AD CAELUM!" to which the odious chap was indeed sent hurtling upwards into the night sky.

"And you'll stay there until your attitude changes!" Riz shouted after him. "Do you know him?" Lou asked Jinny.

"I don't know him but I know *of* him."

"Pray tell then oh mysterious one."

"Oh dear, this may take a while …"

Jinny went on to relate Jet's solemn tale to her two friends who, by the end, were completely astounded.

"That's the saddest thing I've ever heard, Jin" said Riz tearfully.

"It certainly is." added Lou quietly, also with tears in her eyes.

In the meantime, Nancy had joined the trio, after spending ages fruitlessly scouring the whole hotel for them.

"What on earth has happened?" she asked, to which Jinny had to repeat a somewhat abridged version of events.

Part 1: A Bustle In The Hedgerow

"He's put the mockers on our celebrations good and proper, hasn't he?" Riz looked up to the sky spitefully.

"That's why I didn't mention any of it to you." said Jinny sadly.

"It's pointless going to bed girls, whatever Santa says," said Lou logically. "We'll never get to sleep tonight."

"You're right Lou, let's go back inside - it's a 24 hour bar - we'll get drunk!" "I'm not sure that's the answer." said Jinny, now at her wits' end with worry.

"You get off to bed then luv and we'll keep guard down here." offered Riz. "Yes, yes that's probably a better idea." Jinny murmured, now feeling as if she was in some inescapable bad dream.

"Take this," Lou gave Jinny a potion bottle from her coat "It'll help you to sleep."

Jinny took the bottle and thanked everyone, wishing them all a Merry Christmas, then wandered off to the stairwell to find her room.

It must have been about three o'clock in the morning when Jinny woke bolt upright in her bed. There was someone in her room and it wasn't one of the girls, she could tell that by the shape.

"Who's there?" she whispered.

"Do not panic Jinny, it is I, Sinterklaas." came the welcome reply.

"Praise be for that." sighed Jinny.

"I know what occurred earlier," he said, "and my Christmas present to you is my help."

Jinny didn't know what to say. She turned a side light on and stared at Santa quizzically.

"This man, this Zyler Shadowend, I know of him well. He is evil and unscrupulous beyond measure but I know his weaknesses…"

"You do?" Jinny felt a sort of ecstasy wash over her.

"I do. I have known him since he was a child. Do not forget, I had to deliver presents to him …"

"Was he a horrible kid?"

"Not especially, but there was an underlying nastiness about him and he would ask for magic sets, candles, cloaks, Werewolf masks - that type of thing. Very weird."

"Sounds like *my* childhood." laughed Jinny nervously.

"No! This mortal was in league with the devil by his eleventh birthday, Jinny. Serious, deep, black magic. Things that would make your hair stand on end and fly off into the sky."

Jinny was getting the shivers and began to wonder what she had got herself involved in. And what about Jet? Was he still OK? And how on earth did Shadowend find her in Lapland? Her head was spinning.

"I know what you are thinking Jinny because I'm quite magical myself, you know. But as long as you have me as a friend you will be safe, trust me."

"I do trust you Santa. You say you know his weaknesses, can you tell me them please?"

"Two weaknesses. One: he detests buttons…"

"Buttons? That's downright odd." giggled Jinny.

"Two: Foxes."

"What about foxes, Santa?"

"They petrify him. Just being in the presence of a fox can turn his powers to nought. It began when he was seven years old. He had been caught, by a vixen, torturing her newborn fox cub…"

"The bastard!" Jinny exclaimed indignantly.

"Indeed. The vixen leapt at his face and took his right eye out. She left him with a terrible scar down his cheek too. Not only can a fox literally scare him to death, he is also more than aware that they are a thousand times more cunning than he could ever hope to be. The combination is deadly!"

"That is very, very good to know Santa, bless you."

"If all else fails you can always reach me with these words." Santa passed her a piece of paper with words she didn't understand: 'Tule luokseni' was all it said.

"Say the words four times and I will be there before you can blink. These are my gifts to you this Christmas, Jinny Lane. All the best to you." and with a wink of his eye and a touch of his nose he vanished.

Jinny began to feel much better after this surprise visitation. What a thing - to have Santa Claus as a friend. A *real* friend!

She rushed down to the bar, finding her friends still up and still making merry.

"You won't believe what just happened" she gushed excitedly.

"Oh yes we would!" the girls chimed in unison.

Yes, they would believe just about anything the way things were going.

"Is that rat still up there?" asked Jinny.

"I presume so," said Riz nonchalantly. "He should be there until I say otherwise."

"Keep him there until our stay is over, then, once we are safely back home … release him." said Jinny.

"Are you sure you want him back at large? It's an extremely dangerous game."

"No game, this." said Jinny gravely. "I want him to revisit us on home ground."

Lou couldn't believe her ears. "You *want* him to?"

"I do indeed. I'll let you in on the plan when we get back but … just trust me, will you?"

"Don't we always?" laughed Lou. "To our peril."

THE WITCH AND JET SPLINTERS

Part 1: A Bustle In The Hedgerow

PARCHMENT 27

Christmas Day and Beyond

The remainder of their holiday was spent enjoying themselves, doing the things that normal people get up to when they're trying to 'get away from it all'.

After all the excitement and worry of Christmas Eve, the girls had relished their splendid Christmas dinner and all the merriment that went with it. They even got involved in a spot of karaoke!

They had all the right moves but unfortunately their singing left a lot to be desired. Some things never change.

Snowballing, skiing and more snowballing and skiing also provided them with major entertainment value, what with none of them (apart from Riz) ever having skied before.

Zyler Shadowend was still up there, floating twenty-five miles above the earth's surface. Good effort Riz!

It was now Christmas night and the ladies were preparing themselves for the flight back to England the next morning, Boxing Day.

There was a certain sadness in the air. They thoroughly loved this country with it's almost ceaseless snow, its mad drinks and its strange customs and were beginning to miss it before they'd even left.

Jinny looked out of the window. There was her snowman, still larger than life, but it now had a cutaway at its base where, she presumed, the angry American chap had shovelled his car out.

She smiled and began to think of Jet and the other two cats. She wished they could have been here. They'd have loved the snow, if only for about five minutes.

Part 1: A Bustle In The Hedgerow

Her thoughts drifted back to Raphael. No, he wouldn't have enjoyed it much. It was all he could do to stand the English weather, never mind these temperatures.
But he was gone. She did a little wishcraft and wished that his spirit would return in another guise sometime soon.
Then she thought back to Jet … how could you love someone that intended to kill you? That's like loving a deadly virus, she told herself. But despite all of these nagging worries she knew that she loved Jet and nothing would ever change that, especially once she had rid the world of Zyler Shadowend.
"Half a Euro for your thoughts!" said Riz, popping her head around the door. "Sold!" laughed Jinny, holding her hand out.
"Our lives are never boring, uh Jin?"
"I'm sure yours weren't half as complicated until you came to stay at mine."
"True, but hey, you're our best mate! With hindsight, it's been bloody good fun, on the whole."
Jinny smiled broadly. Riz really was a one-off. Nothing seemed to get to her much and she mostly always kept a positive outlook.
"Where's Lou got to then?" asked Jinny.
"She's packing, I think."
"She hardly brought anything to pack!"
"Ah but she's been and bought a few prezzies to take back …"
"I'm all done here. are we off to the bar for a quick snifter? It'll help us to sleep and lord knows I could do with more than three hours tonight!"
"Yeah, come on then, I'll treat you." said Riz and away they went.

"I'm going to try some of that dark lager. It's terrifically popular, apparently." said Riz.

"Go on then, I'll give it a go too." said Jinny.

"Coming over to the dark side, are you ladies?" someone behind them said, in a very deep voice.

Jinny froze. She instinctively knew who the voice belonged to. Riz calmly turned round. She knew the voice too.

"Who gave you permission to come down then?"

"I do not need permission for anything, from anyone." said Zyler Shadowend, for it was he.

"I think you'll find that there's always someone you've got to answer to." Riz said fearlessly.

"I certainly do not need it from you lady, make no mistake."

"My only mistake was letting my guard down matey. Come with me a second would you?"

Shadowend was taken aback by the young woman's insolence and boldness. He was used to being the dominant one and what he said was the law … in his world.

He followed Riz as she confidently walked over to the hotel entrance, taking a cigarette from her packet and lighting it.

She purposely blew the smoke upwards in thick plumes.

Within seconds the fire alarms were activated. The sound was overwhelming, so much so that having took Shadowend by surprise he panicked and opened the hotel doors to get away from it.

"You really shouldn't have done that." smiled Riz, unleashing her wand.

"USQUE AD CAELUM!" she yelled and away to the stars went Shadowend once more.

"And this time you'll come back when I give permission!" she screamed after him, still waving her wand. "CUM LICENTIAM!"

Riz spat on the snow covered ground and the spell was sealed. No one or no thing could undo it, only her.

She strode back into the hotel like a catwalk model, confident and assured. There was chaos all around as the hotel guests had vacated their rooms in confusion, presuming the place was on fire.

Jinny was still sat at the bar with her mouth open wide.

"I - I don't believe what I've just seen," she said. "That was like something off Mission Impossible!"

"If it was, they nicked it from me." said Riz coolly "What's the lager like then?"

Lou and Nancy appeared, both with their bags.

"What's going on?" asked Lou.

"Ask Ethan Hunt here." said Jinny laughing.

"There's no fire, Lou. Sit down and have a bevvie. Come on Nance, you too." said Riz.

"There's no bloody barman either!" Lou shouted.

"I'll do it." said Riz and, as no one was watching, she levitated two glasses from the bar and wafted them over to the beer pumps, magically pouring Lou and Nancy a dark lager each. "I've got one on me tonight girls." Riz laughed "Back in a sec." she said, wandering off to the ladies' toilets.

"Go on Jin, do tell. What's happened now?" queried Lou.

Jinny recounted the episode while Nancy and Lou stared in disbelief.

"That woman's changed," gasped Lou. "She thinks she's a … well, I'm not sure what she thinks she is."

"She's amazing, is what she is." Jinny smiled affectionately. "Completely, utterly amazing!"

Riz returned from the loo, still looking brimful of confidence. Lou couldn't help but notice, because this is a gift that Witches have, that she had the brightest golden aura she had ever seen.

A gold aura meant that angels and other divine entities were protecting you, that you're being mentored and guided to reach beyond yourself and Riz's aura was way above that!

"What did Santa bring you for Christmas, Riz?" asked Lou, seemingly randomly.

"He, er, nothing 'material' Lou."

"Something 'spiritual'?"

"Yeah, you could say that …"

"Did he touch your throat?"

"That's a bit of a weirdo question, Lou" said Jinny.

"Bear with me …" said Lou. "Well? Did he?"

"A bit, yeah. I think he'd run out of ideas seeing as I didn't need any more rings." Riz giggled.

Lou picked her dark lager glass up and had a sip, "That's all I wanted to know."

The little group looked at one another but no one said a word for a good minute and a half.

"Three cheers for Riz!" shouted Lou suddenly. "Hip! Hip! …"

The others joined in, even Riz, "Hooray!"

"What does 'Hip! Hip!' mean, anybody?" asked the still slightly naïve Nancy.

Lou was the one who usually had all the answers …

"Hip Hip is a nonsensical word with no meaning. It's just a chant to attract attention. I believe 'Hooray' was once a battle cry used by Genghis Khan and his warriors, a call to arms, as it were."

Part 1: A Bustle In The Hedgerow

“Well! Who would’ve thought it,” said Nancy. “I’ve learnt more from you lot than I ever did at school.”

“You’ve learnt more from *me* …” corrected Lou, with a playful smile. “Geronimo!” shouted Riz for no reason at all, downing her pint of lager in one gulp.

“Please, Nancy,” said Lou. “Don’t ask!”

As the hotel reached some semblance of peace and order, the girls had reached full-on ‘relaxed’ mode. ‘Relaxed’, in this case, meaning bordering on legless.

There were loud laughs and snorting aplenty, but it was all in good humour and none of the other guests seemed offended by them.

“We’ve got a plane to catch in five hours and fifteen minutes!” Lou remembered.

“So much for getting more than three hours kip.” noted Jinny.

“Couldn’t you just ‘transport’ us all Lou?” asked Riz. “Then we could have a bit of a lie in.”

“Oooh, I don’t know about that. It’s over a thousand miles you know. I’ve never tried to go that far before.”

“I think it’s safer to get the plane. We’ll have plenty of time to catch up on sleep when we get back.” said Jinny sensibly.

“Yeah! Sod it,” said Riz. “Let’s just stay up all night! What you having?”

“No more drink for me,” said Jinny. “Unless it’s cocoa or something.” “Wuss!” said Riz ordering a bottle of Pinot Grigiot and a cup of cocoa.

“Hey Lou, what did you get from Santa? You never told us.” asked Jinny.

“You never told us what you got either, captain.” replied Lou.

"I'll tell you when we get back. I can't be arsed right now, I'm feeling drowsy."

"Drowsy? Wrecked more like!" laughed Lou.

And on it went until it was time to make tracks for the airport, which they did, with a little help from Lou's 'transporting' powers and lots of black coffee.

Riz was the only one who wasn't suffering. She had an Amethyst stone after all … and a golden aura.

The flight back took three hours and twenty-six minutes exactly. It was completely uneventful as our heroic quartet had spent the whole duration sleeping, again.

The landing woke them, and much yawning and eye rubbing ensued.

"Blimey Charlie, that was quick." said Riz hoarsely.

Jinny glanced across. "Sore throat luv?"

"A bit, yeah. Must've been the coffee." lied Riz.

Before they knew it they were standing outside Manchester Airport, acknowledging the grim weather and the grimmer surroundings.

"It's not much cop is it?" scowled Lou.

"I'd hate to have to live round here." added Nancy. "Let's get back home then, eh? Quick sticks!"

"Hey! That's my saying!" said Jinny indignantly.

Lou conveniently ignored Jinny's comment. "Anyone watching? No. Off we go then."

They looked around and there stood the beloved Demonia Cottage (2) surrounded by hills and lush countryside. Their haven. "Home" Jinny smiled.

"Why don't we sell our houses and all come and live here permanently?" piped up Riz.

"Because Riz, you don't actually own a house, remember? You live at your mum and dad's house!"

Part 1: A Bustle In The Hedgerow

"Oh yeah… Maybe I should look into getting my own place. Somewhere nearby. What do you reckon?"

"What about me? I live at your mum and dad's place too you know!" reminded Lou. "We'll get one together then Lou. Brainy idea, eh?" Riz reasoned.

"Shall we just get in and get the kettle on? I bet the cats are fretting like mad." urged Jinny.

So off they trundled, up the stone steps and into the lounge of the beautiful, ivy covered dwelling.

"Helloooo!" shouted Jinny.

No reply. She looked around to see where the cats were. Stripes asleep on the couch, Spike in the window, also asleep. Not much sign of fretfulness. Where was Jet? Jinny felt a panic coming over her.

"Jetty! Jet! Where are you?" she yelled.

She ran upstairs and found him sleeping at the bottom of her bed. Oh the relief!

She picked him up and hugged him lovingly, then presented him with a small, brass replica of Thor's hammer, Mjolnir, to hang round his collar. He had no idea what it was all about but he liked it, because Jinny had bought it for him.

Lou had followed her upstairs. "You'll never rest until that Shadowend is taken out of the picture. Do it quick!"

"Tomorrow. I've got a plan." said Jinny.

Tomorrow was upon them like a shot. Jet was so happy to see Jinny again and likewise Jinny.

The pair had spent the afternoon of the day before running through Jinny's scheme, which they later ran by Lou, Nancy and Riz.

Obviously it involved Jet and it definitely involved his loathsome 'master'. All Riz had to do was drop

Shadowend back to earth and make sure that he knew that they were home.

"OK we're off," announced Jinny. "Don't forget, stay here and don't leave the house, whatever the circumstances."

"Ahoy captain!" said Lou cheerfully. "Go and do what you do best!"

Jinny and Jet were heading for the faerie clearing where they were to spend the rest of the day.

Riz held her arms high and chanted, "Reversus est … Reversus est …

Reversus est … Domi sunt … Domi sunt … Domi sunt …"

The chant reached Shadowend in the icy skies above Lapland. He spiralled downwards and landed bang in front of the steps of the hotel where Riz had banished him from.

"They're home," he said to himself. "I know it!"

The dark magician gathered his wits and stepped back inside the hotel, ordering a black coffee with plenty of sugar.

"Would you care to order food, sir?" asked the barman.

"I would have ordered food if I had wanted it." snapped Shadowend. "I don't need a prompt."

As he sat at the bar nursing his hot cup, together with his wounded pride, he decided that there was no time like the present and that his revenge would be immediate.

He swilled the last of the coffee down and walked quickly to the door.

Lou wasn't the only one that could 'transport' and within minutes Shadowend was stood outside the front of Demonia Cottage.

Part 1: A Bustle In The Hedgerow

Jinny and Jet, meanwhile, were sat outside the opening to the faerie realm. Pixies and gnomes were in and out but as yet there was no sign of Miss

Slinky, who Jinny hadn't seen for what seemed like ages.

No matter, she thought. Time to play her ace card in the battle with Zyler Shadowend.

"Zorro! Zorro!" she called loudly. What if he didn't hear? What if he wasn't even about? These minor details hadn't quite crossed her mind when hatching her plan. "Oh Jetty, I hope he's here."

"I remember him saying that wherever he was, he would hear you." comforted Jet.

"Yes, yes he did say that."

There was no need to panic, as just as soon as the words left Jinny's mouth Zorro the fox was standing before them.

"How can I help you, Miss Jinny?"

"Oh I'm so pleased to see you." Jinny said, almost crying with relief. She told him the whole tale of Zyler Shadowend and his wicked deeds and he listened intently.

"To be on the safe side I will go and gather some friends Miss Jinny. I will be back in less than a minute." said Zorro, darting off into the thicket.

"Greetings Miss Jinny, and you Mister Splinters." it was her old friend Slinky. "What brings you to this neck of the, erm, field?" she asked.

"Merry meet, Slinky." waved Jinny, and went on to retell the tale of the evil magician.

"I know of this person," said Slinky, "the planet would be a far better place without him. He is responsible for some terrible disasters both in the world of humans and our world."

"I can imagine." said Jinny.

"I *know*!" said Jet.

Zorro returned with a skulk of foxes, about seven in total.

"Armed and ready Miss, at your service." he said.

"That used to be a favourite song of mine … Michael Schenker I think.

Remember him?"

Zorro looked at her blankly, as did Jet and Slinky.

"Oh well, not to worry, you lot need some Heavy Metal lessons!" she laughed.

THE WITCH AND JET SPLINTERS

Part 1: A Bustle In The Hedgerow

PARCHMENT 27 B

The Beginning of the End

Zyler Shadowend made his way slowly up the steps to Demonia Cottage
(2).
He peered through the window and spotted Lou and Riz sat by the fire watching TV.
"Where is she? And where is my cat?" he had passed through the front door and into the living room.
Lou and Riz were snapped out of their comfort zone and sat bolt upright.
"She's not here, obviously!" said Riz defiantly.
"You had better tell me where she is then, hadn't you, young harpy." "Harpy? That's quite a nice name, I like it." smiled Riz. "You're not coming on to me, are you?"
"Coming on to you? Whatever are you babbling about? Tell me where Jinny Lane is or suffer the consequences."
Lou thought she would join in the fun. "You're very dramatic, aren't you?
Have you been to acting school? RADA or something?"
"He is dramatic Lou, and very well spoken for such a … Git!"
"If you are playing for time don't bother … I am on to you!" Shadowend spoke angrily.
"On to us? Woooo Lou, he's on to us!" teased Riz.
"He's on to nobody. He just thinks he is." Lou spat scornfully. "Enough!" he shouted "I shall stand no more of this yannering!" "Yannering? Is that Shakespeare?" asked Riz.
"I could make your lives exceedingly unpleasant … either tell me where

Part 1: A Bustle In The Hedgerow

Jinny Lane is or live to regret it."

"Jinny Lane? Isn't that near Farley Road, Lou?"

Shadowend stamped his foot and the whole house shook as if it had been hit by a thunderbolt.

"YOU GO TOO FAR!!!" he bellowed.

"Oh." said Lou.

"If you're looking for that black cat he's gone over to the faerie clearing and if you don't know where that is, well I can't help you coz I'm useless at directions." said Riz, playing dumb.

Shadowend glared evilly at the two young witches and floated backwards through the front door.

"Arsehole!" shouted Lou.

Riz just let out an almighty laugh and fell back into the armchair.

Shadowend knew precisely the whereabouts of the faerie clearing and was there in seconds.

There sat Jinny and her beloved Jet. *His* Jet!

"Jet Jupiter Splinters, come to my side NOW!" he ordered. Jet stayed put.

"I shall ask you one more time …"

"You didn't 'ask' you demanded." said Jet coyly.

"I am your Master and you will obey me and me alone!"

"You don't scare us Shadowend, not anymore." Jinny bravely declared. "If there is one person on this Godforsaken planet that you should fear … it is I!" he stated, extremely arrogantly.

Shadowend raised his arms and Jinny sensed exactly what was coming. "ZORRO!" she shouted and within seconds the black magician was encircled by foxes.

He stood paralysed and mute, the sweat rolling down his face.

"We believe you've been giving our friends some trouble, Mr Shadowend …" said Zorro in a malevolent manner, "… and we don't like people that trouble our friends, do we lads?"

While all this was occurring Mister Jet Jupiter Splinters was casually sauntering over towards his ex-master.

He went entirely unnoticed, which was very bad news indeed for Shadowend as Jet leapt sprightly on to his shoulder and sank his fangs deep into the magician's neck.

"That's you … over and out. Master!" he smiled contentedly, as much as cats can smile.

"Don't bite him. boys!" shouted Jinny to the foxes. "You might contract some of Jet's poison!"

A splendid finishing flourish was when Jinny reached into her pocket and pulled out a big, fat button which she placed carefully into Shadowend's mouth.

"Abqaa huna" she whispered as she moved away from the dying warlock. That was his fate sealed, good and proper, for once and for all.

"Top notch work Jetty! You're free matey! FREE!"

She turned to the foxes, "And a million thank yous to you Zorro and friends. You have saved many lives and I am forever in your debt." she said as she went down on her knees and hugged each fox one by one. Jet rubbed up against Jinny's leg then jumped into her arms.

"What a fabulous feeling." he thought, as the weary weight of the world was lifted from his young, little shoulders.

Jinny looked to her handsome, regal, shiny black cat and kissed him on the top of his head.

"Home, Jetty?"

"*Our* home, Jinny!"

"You know, I've just had a thought … I never did make that birdhouse for Mr Robin…"

UNTIL THE NEXT TIME … BLESSED BE.

ABOUT THE AUTHOR

Born via a woman, in a cross-fire hurricane, the Lancastrian Elijah Barns was raised by a Border Collie and subsequently bequeathed the soul of a black, Native American Scotsman that loathed buttons and loved animals.

The book you see you before you has been tormenting and fermenting the already tormented and fermented mind of it's author for too many moons and could no longer be contained.

Therefore, blessings must go to Lisa from Green Cat Books for having the courage and fortitude to believe and let it run free.

If you would care to pry into the psyche of the author, as an exercise in somehow understanding his tickage, his thoughts and inspirations are steadfastly rooted in the following locations, objects and folk of lore, for which, he assures us, he is eternally grateful and would recommend highly.

Amen.

THE WITCH AND JET SPLINTERS

Part 1: A Bustle In The Hedgerow

The Hilary Howard. The sons. The Beatles. The wonderful world of animals. Lily Munster. Morticia Addams. The Fae. Besoms. Caledonia. Werewolves. Siouxsie Sioux. Universal Monsters. Autumn. UFOs. Samantha Stephens (& Endora). Jimi Hendrix. Chocolate. Rosalie Cunningham. Batman. Kate Bush. Comic book art. Catwoman. Hammer Horror. Dan Brereton. Chinese 5 spice. Lemmy. Halloween (the 31st Oct - not the movie). Egypt. Ingrid Pitt. Thor. Charlie Dickens. The Duchess. Yorkshire tea. Tony Warren. Robert Roy MacGregor. The X Files. Rik Mayall. Enid Blyton. India. Maleficent. Jack Sparrow. Pendle Hill. Joni Mitchell. Haunted woods & houses. J.R.R. Tolkien. Witches Galore (a shop in the parish of Newchurch in Pendle). Cymru. Fenella Fielding in Carry On Screaming. Thomas Hardy. Spiders. Keith Richards. Marlboro Reds. Robert McGinnis. Snow. The Blackheart Orchestra. Victoria Wood. Folklore Thursday. Patsy Stone. Sinterklaas. Worzel Gummidge. Aunt Sally. The Crowman. D.H. Lawrence. Open fires. Salvador Dali. James Bond. Cold beer. Kenneth Williams. Night scented stock. Merry meets. Captain Scarlet. Robert Nesta Marley. Chewbacca. Jonathan Pie. Tunnock's teacakes. Richard Sharpe. Outlander. Robin of Sherwood. Colman's English mustard. Moorhouse's White Witch ale and, naturally, witches by the coven load.

AUTHOR'S NOTE

Although a great admirer of JK Rowling and the Harry Potter works, it should be mentioned, due to a portion of the general public's preconceptions, that this book and it's sequels, bear no similarity, in any shape or form, to the afore mentioned series, apart from the involvement of a few witches and a touch of jiggery pokery.

The sooth is out there!

THE WITCH AND JET SPLINTERS

Part 1: A Bustle In The Hedgerow

Other Authors With Green Cat Books

Lisa J Rivers –

Why I have So Many Cats

Winding Down

Searching (Coming 2018)

Luna Felis –

Life Well Lived

Gabriel Eziorobo –

Words Of My Mouth

The Brain Behind Freelance Writing

Mike Herring –

Nature Boy

Glyn Roberts & David Smith –

Prince Porrig And The Calamitous Carbuncle

(other Prince Porrig books to follow)

Part 1: A Bustle In The Hedgerow

Peach Berry –

A Bag Of Souls

Michelle DuVal -

The Coach

Sean Gaughan –

And God For His Own

David Rollins –

Haiku From The Asylum

ARE YOU A WRITER?

We are looking for writers to send in their manuscripts.

If you would like to submit your work, please send a small sample to

books@green-cat.co

GREEN CAT BOOKS

www.green-cat.co/books

Made in the USA
Columbia, SC
20 October 2017